Praise for **LIKE LIGHT,** \

"This is a novel about the light of vision, and music in the blood. Emmeretta has the 'mountain gift' of synesthesia, and she sees with her ears as well as with memory and imagination. But *Like Light, Like Music* is also a mystery story about uncovering secrets of the past, of family bonds and family ghosts. It is about the pain at the heart of country music, and joy in the place the music comes from. It is a story of the complexity of family ties and romances, and of the way confronting painful truths can make us free. It is a ballad of a novel, both timely and timeless."

—Robert Morgan,
author of *Gap Creek* and *Chasing the North Star*

"Austin has written a highly original and captivating novel filled with the mountain music and lore she loves so much—haints, broonies, banshees, shades, and revenants share the stage with all the memorable real characters of Red River, Kentucky. Contemporary issues merge with a developing romance in this spellbinding story, truly a ballad itself."

—Lee Smith,
author of *The Last Girls* and *Guests on Earth*

"*Like Light, Like Music* captures the way the past haunts us and shapes our reality. With the help of their ancestors, the resilient McLean women are determined to prove the innocence of one of their own. The pulse of this lyrical novel beats: Believe women. Believe women. Believe women."

—Savannah Sipple,
author of *WWJD and Other Poems*

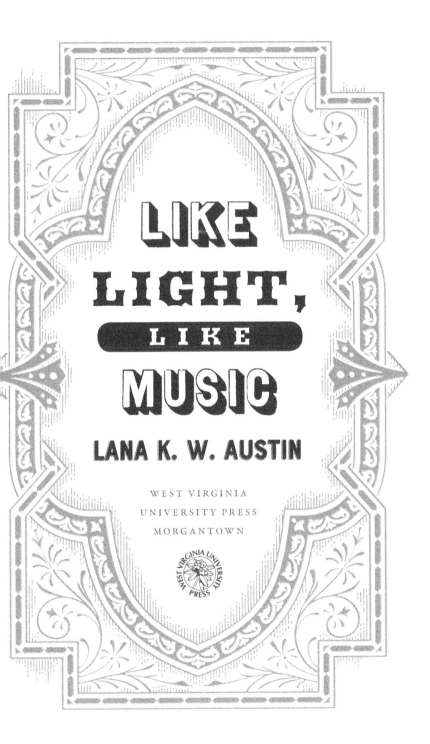

LIKE LIGHT, LIKE MUSIC

LANA K. W. AUSTIN

WEST VIRGINIA
UNIVERSITY PRESS
MORGANTOWN

ISBN
Paper 978-1-949199-57-4
Ebook 978-1-949199-58-1

Library of Congress Cataloging-in-Publication Data
Names: Austin, Lana, author.
Title: Like light, like music / Lana K. W. Austin.
Identifiers: LCCN 2020008806 | ISBN 9781949199574 (paperback) | ISBN
    9781949199581 (ebook)
Subjects: GSAFD: Suspense fiction.
Classification: LCC PS3601.U8628 L55 2020 | DDC 813/.6—dc23
LC record available at https://lccn.loc.gov/2020008806

Book and cover design by Than Saffel / WVU Press

For Ashley and Robin Sievers

Who so loves believes the impossible.

—Elizabeth Barrett Browning

CHAPTER 1

EMME MCLEAN hadn't sung in years. Not since her friend Evan died. But while she spoke to her editor, a song began to fly powerfully around in her chest, and she suddenly felt an urge to sing. The song slammed against her ribs like the trapped blackbird that had once thrashed against the walls in her old farmhouse until Emme had gently carried it outside.

"This is tough for me," she said. "How can you expect me to rat out my own family?"

Emme held onto the phone receiver with one hand and placed her other over her mouth while Richard, her editor, spoke. She didn't want to spontaneously start singing, but the blackbird in her chest was picking up speed, about to burst out of her mouth in the form of a Loretta Lynn tune.

"The article has to be your priority. This isn't about ratting out anyone. You can get the inside story."

Just as quickly as the overwhelming desire to make music had entered Emme, it left her. No longer needing to stifle herself from singing, Emme removed her hand from her mouth and poked around the pay-phone change slot.

"I don't want to betray anyone, especially not my people. I'm not in Kentucky yet, anyway. I'm still at the Nashville airport."

Emme knew Richard wanted murder details. And to hear what had made so many women in Red River, many of them Emme's kin, half-mad and ranting about ghosts. They all got sick just before Emme's cousin, Kelly, confessed to killing her husband. Though frustrated, Emme had been polite. She listened to Richard and tried to answer his questions, even as she felt the tiniest flutter of a song still deep in her chest.

"Think like the journalist you are. Pretend you're back in DC."

Emme hurled her next words into the phone.

"I can only tell you that things are linked. Not just what's happened to Kelly, but everything I've ever seen. So many murder tales end up being twisted love stories. And love stories, at their heart, are about us being haunted. We all see ghosts from the past. But do I believe my cousin killed her own husband? Or do I think actual ghosts are hanging around Red River now? No. But things are complicated."

Emme hung up the phone without giving Richard any more details about Kelly or Red River's women, some still in the psych ward. She then picked up her rental car faster than she thought humanly possible until she remembered how much smaller the Nashville airport was than the airport in DC.

When she started out from Nashville to Kentucky, Emme felt flummoxed from her call with Richard. She didn't turn on the radio so she could think about it, and about how to help her cousin Kelly. A few miles later, it came as a shock when Emme recognized that she herself was singing. It was the old Child Ballad, "Lord Lovel." As Emme found refuge in the song's lyrics, she forgot the call. When she reached the part where Lord Lovel's lover asks where he's going and he responds, Emme sang the same lyrics over and over, "strange countries to see." She thought of the strange country that was Kentucky and the stranger country where she lived inside her own head. Emme then repeated the lyrics one more time. She felt them buzz on her lips, then richochet throughout the car, and inside her, too.

Singing again. After so long. Emme relished it, even if it made her think of Evan. As her car made its way into Kentucky, Emme let the ballad lead her to the strange country of memory, which she thought the strangest country of all.

Not long after she crossed the state line, she turned onto Price's Mill Road and stopped at Cecil's Gas and Bait. She wanted to get a cup of coffee and take a few minutes to gather herself. In the ten years since she'd graduated from high school, Emme had only been home a handful of times.

Emme felt as if driving the rest of the way up to see her beloved aunts, Fiona and Deirdre, was going to be as difficult as driving to her parents' funerals. Those sweet aunts of hers, worried to death about Kelly. Emme needed a little more time before she faced them, and Cecil always made her smile with his duck calls, even though he'd never hunted ducks a day in his life.

Cecil's was the last gas station on Price's Mill before Emme would turn onto McLean Farm Lane, named after her family. Her aunts' house was just a few miles outside of Red River. Whenever Emme came home, as soon as she crossed over into Kentucky, she'd start going through her family tree in her head, trying to name everyone.

Emme's family's complicated history was intertwined with Red River's equally complicated one, a town that many thought was haunted by ghosts. Civil War ghosts. Ghosts of children drowned in the river when it flooded. And the ghosts of their ancestors stubbornly refusing to leave the very land that had, in many cases, killed them. Emme tried to recall every ancestor all the way back to before they came to Kentucky. An impossible task, but she tried. She knew she could at least name all her cousins who still lived in Red River or a county or two over.

Emme was still naming cousins as she walked into Cecil's. She realized her aunts were waiting for her and it would've been nice to let them know she was almost there. But she couldn't call Fi because her aunt no longer had a phone. Aunt Fi proudly had a phone for years, but recently had gotten rid of it, when Kelly's husband, Cy, had called there nonstop when Kelly had stayed there after the trouble started.

Emme couldn't believe that in 1999, even in rural Kentucky, her aunts were phoneless, despite all the ruckus Cy had caused. Emme had a tough time comprehending that he was dead. To Emme, someone as ornery as Cy surely would've outlived them all, his sheer meanness keeping him alive forever.

Emme's time at Cecil's was brief. She finished her coffee, laughed at Cecil's duck calls, and thanked him as she went outside. She was grateful he didn't say anything about Cy or Kelly. She quickly opened the door of her rental car, but then just stood there.

Emme needed to fortify herself, and focusing on the simple splendor of the trees around Cecil's helped. Emme imagined taking hold of the leaves she saw, the ones beginning to shimmy in the breeze. She loved the way they flirted with a tinge of changing hues. Emme wanted to rub her cheeks with the leaves, toss them into the air, and watch them meander back down. Emme wanted to watch all the leaves on all the trees in Kentucky drop, the chaos of thousands of them falling a cascade of distraction.

The undone allure of her home helped to pull Emme out of herself even though she was still grieved by Richard's questions. He wanted to cover only the sensational parts of Red River, like those who believed ghosts came down from the mountains to haunt the hollers.

What so many back in DC wanted was the cliché. Not everyone, but enough to hurt Emme so deeply that she felt the agony of it stuck in her throat, a sharp stone too new for time to have softened its edges. Emme would never give DC the cliché it sought. Not only because that would be turning against her people, but because it wasn't the whole story. Emme didn't know if any outsiders would ever want the full narrative of her home, but she wanted to tell the truth. The kick-you-in-the-gut truth of what was wrong. And the more nebulous truth that there were people and places of raw beauty in Kentucky, too. An impossible duality where the truths twirled inexplicably together, a DNA double helix of despair merging with a magnificence so pure it was daunting.

Emme got in the car and drove out of the store's lot, past the woods that surrounded Cecil's, until she came to her family's cornfields. They appeared desolate after being harvested. Jagged cornstalk pieces jutted out of the earth.

She turned onto her aunts' road, away from the acres of stripped fields and into the woods that sheltered Fiona's house. Off in the distance were strewn the hills that would, if you traveled east, grow into the mighty Appalachians.

And that's when Emme's mountain gift, as her family called it, started back up. Emme was spellbound by the color of the hills beyond Fiona's. They were equal parts gray and plum, with a hint of shimmer. And Emme heard actual music. It was as if the best upright bass player from the jazz clubs in DC was right there in Emme's tiny rental car. And Emme saw something, too. A boy. *The* boy. The one she met as a child at a wedding. The one she'd dreamed of and seen grow older in her dreams. And there he was, all grown up, in her car. If she squinted, she could see him. Not in the car with her exactly, but somewhere not too far away, a barely-there image superimposed on top of what was actually right around her. Aidan, with dark hair and gray eyes, the same gray as the mist that rolled down from the mountains and settled in the hollers. Aidan, who had a guitar and seemed to somehow be part of the same music that Emme heard. Aidan, who was trying to sing, or say something. Yes, he most definitely wanted to say something to Emme. His mouth moved rapidly, almost fiercely. Emme was about to ask, "What?" when the boy from her dreams left as quickly as he'd arrived.

But the bass music continued, and Emme was caught up in its rich sound that seemed to resound inside her very bones, even more so since she'd seen Aidan, however strange that'd been. She realized she must be completely exhausted if she'd imagined the boy from her childhood sitting there in the car with her, but she kept humming along as she pulled into the gravel driveway. As soon as she parked, the music stopped. Emme sat in the silence. She rested her forehead on the steering wheel for a few seconds before she opened the car door and walked towards her aunts' steps. She was prepared to ask hard questions about Kelly and Cy. And about all those women, women Emme knew and loved, who had gone crazy.

At least Emme knew she would see Great-Aunt Deirdre again. Older than time. That's how her aunt described herself. And she was a spitfire, with more stories from Scotland and Ireland than anyone else. And more songs and recipes. Aunt Deirdre was always more.

But first Emme had to talk to Deirdre's daughter, Fiona, and the idea of it made her sick to her stomach. Aunt Fi could put up corn, bake a casserole for a sick friend, and make a mental list of what was needed at the store, all while letting you cry on her shoulder when you were upset about something. And then she'd dance a jig right there in the kitchen to make you feel better. Still, Emme knew her aunt could never have imagined her daughter would be arrested for murder.

Emme looked up and saw Fi's home. She fell in love all over again with the small yellow farmhouse with its red metal roof and hurried up the stone steps to the porch that was remarkably straight for being so old.

Before Emme could knock on the door, or even look up at the blue paint she loved, her aunt flung the door open and grabbed Emme so tightly she felt as if her shoulder blades were going to break through the skin of her back. And Aunt Fi caterwauled. Emme kept trying to smooth the hair, still red with only the tiniest of tendrils gone gray right around her temples, back from Fi's face.

Before Fi could speak, her mother came barreling out.

Great-Aunt Deirdre had always been tall and hadn't shrunk a single bit. At five feet seven, Emme wasn't short. She was exactly the same height as her mother had been and that Fi still was. But Emme had to lift her head up to look as directly as she could into her great-aunt's eyes, eyes that were a mix of blue and greenish gray, the same as Emme's.

"Emmeretta, it's about damn time. You've been in that God-forsaken city too long, even before all of this, but surely you know they arrested Kelly and she had surgery two nights ago."

"Mama, leave Emme alone. She got here as soon as she could." Fi let go of Emme as she admonished her mother, then hugged her niece again.

"I'm sorry about that, sweetie, I really am, that no one could come and get you."

"Aunt Fi, I understand. Really, I do."

Aunt Deirdre startled so violently then that Emme and Fi jumped along with her. Fi said *shit* with a long *i* like they did back in Ireland. Then Aunt Deirdre leaped off the front porch and started screaming at something neither Emme nor Fi could see, "Go away I tell you. Go back to hell!"

Granted, the porch was only three steps off the ground, but Emme knew there weren't many eighty-one-year-old women who could jump like that. The thought would've comforted her, made her proud even, if she weren't scared to death that Deirdre had finally gone mad like the others.

"Mama, what are you doing? There's nothing there. Even if there was, it couldn't come close since we've kept the porch ceiling painted the haint shade you like."

Fi walked down the steps and wrapped her arms around her mother. But Deirdre pushed away and spoke frantically to Emme.

"Emme, I knew she was gonna come back like I knew you were. I dreamed that you came riding up the Red River in a birchbark canoe, white as snow. You had your camera around your neck and you were taking pictures of all the trees on either side of the riverbank."

To Emme, it seemed as if her great-aunt had truly lost her mind. Deirdre, gesticulating wildly, yelled out her next words.

"You were humming that ol' Jean Ritchie tune. The one your mama sang and played on her dulcimer, 'Shady Grove.' But that was after her. After . . . it. Oh my God, Emme, it came."

"Aunt Deirdre, what are you talking about?" Emme started walking across the porch, but stopped at the top of the steps when she heard Deirdre's next words.

"The bean-nighe. I seen her. Three nights in a row in dreams. With Kelly and that bastard Cy. But Kelly and Cy came the first night. Then the spirit was washing Cy's bloody shirt and Kelly was crying."

Deirdre took a gigantic gulp of air before she started yelling again.

"The second night she was howling until another came, the Bell Witch. They were laughing and running around the trees and speaking Druid-speak. They were poking their heads out from behind the trees, just long enough for their faces to turn gray."

Deirdre's voice grew wilder with every word.

"Their hair, it was moss-covered like the evilest tree come to life. Then the third night I saw her floating up the river in the boat."

Deirdre closed her eyes. A calmer look fell across her face. Then she opened her eyes again and looked up at Emme at the top of the porch steps.

"I shut my eyes in the dream and willed myself to open them again. I saw you, beautiful Emme, coming home in the canoe."

Emme went down the porch steps to stand with her aunts.

"I'm home. Not just in the dream."

"But the bean-nighe was just here, too. I saw her peek out from the tree right next to where your rental car is. I swear it true. But she seemed to have wings, like angel wings. I saw them fluttering behind her, but I've never heard of an angel like that. The wings I seen were brown."

Emme had seen her great-aunt cry just twice in her whole life. Only at funerals. Emme cradled Deirdre's hands in her own to try to calm her down.

"Aunt Deirdre, the banshees aren't real. Neither is the Bell Witch. I don't think that's what you saw. I don't even know if angels exist, either."

Fi tugged on Deirdre's arm. "Mama, listen to Emme now."

"I know your mother told you stories and her mother before her. You can trace them all back to Scotland and Ireland before our kin crossed the water to get here. But I promise you nothing's out there. You're just exhausted."

Emme thought for a bit. She didn't want to insult her aunt, but she felt she had to say it anyway.

"You're afraid. What you're really afraid of, though, is Kelly being arrested for killing Cy." The thought of Kelly and Cy made Emme stop talking. She squeezed Deirdre's hands tighter.

"I know you've seen so many things, you and Uncle Andrew getting out of the mountains, leaving the coal mines in Hollis Mill. I swear I can sometimes still smell it on you, the burning from the mines exploding. I know I'm imagining it, but it's there. You've told me a hundred times growing up that you could still smell it."

Deirdre said just one word. "Yes."

"So it's not the bean-nighe. The banshees were vanquished long ago if they ever were real. And the Bell Witch, well, if she's real, she's stuck down there in Tennessee."

"Tennessee's so close. You know she could hop on the river and be up here in no time. Here we are straddling the state line and that Red River comes sneaking on up into our property. The water is a-weaving in and out of two states."

"I'm not trying to sass you, but have you thought this through? If she's a ghost or witch, why would she need to ride on the water to get here?"

Deirdre looked down for a few seconds. But then she raised her head up so fiercely that Emme had no way of anticipating what she was going to say next.

"It's not just these two witches. If it's just them, they're so powerful they're taking over everyone. Over twenty women got visited, all of them good women who would never lie. It started a couple nights before Cy was killed. Just because they travel by the water in my dreams, don't mean they don't fly in another. They could materialize out of thin air to someone else. They're not just in dreams, either. They're here, and they're mad as hell."

"I know things got really weird here. Right before Cy died, we'd already heard about it all the way in DC."

Emme bit her lip as she remembered first learning about Red River in DC. It was only a few days ago, but Emme knew that so much had already changed.

"I was thinking about coming back even before Kelly was arrested."

Emme linked arms with both her aunts and walked them back up the stairs and into the house. The sun was going down and the sky was streaked in its moody watercolor way. Emme turned to look at the colors draping the tops of trees. What she saw made her hear music again, a funeral dirge. It was so mournful that Emme had to draw her hand to her chest. As she turned away from the door and followed her aunts into the kitchen, she pressed her hand down hard right above her heart, as if the force would somehow slow the quickening there.

"Mama, sit down and let me get you some water as I put on the This 'n That. Some soup will do us all good. Emme, you need to sit, too. I know you must be exhausted."

Fi moved with a rhythm that Emme admired. Her motions were machine-like in their precision as she rapidly seated her mother and motioned for Emme to sit, then quickly got two glasses of water, then moved to the refrigerator to take out a huge container of soup, brought it to the stove, and put it in a massive red pot that was already sitting out, turned the heat on, grabbed a ladle out of another drawer, and started stirring the soup with one hand. So many separate actions, deftly orchestrated.

Fi stirred for a good long while, adjusted the heat lower, and put a lid on, then she finally turned back around. She stepped into the middle of the room and, though she didn't look directly at them while she spoke, addressed both her mother and Emme.

"Mama, you know I would never disrespect you. I believe you. That's the problem. I know you haven't lost your mind. Something's going on around here and it's bad. Not just with our sweet Kelly, either. She still hasn't spoken anymore and I can hardly think of her lying in that hospital bed, with a bad fever. All the while she's cuffed to the bed and with Teddy, or one of them others, standing guard outside her room."

Emme knew that if Fi was a dog, her hackles would be up.

"As if she could get out of those cuffs, all beaten like that, just out of surgery. As if she needed to be cuffed in the first place. That tiny girl can barely pick up a cat, let alone toss Cy around."

Fi's anger abated and was replaced by weariness. "Seeing you like this, Mama, it grieves me maybe worse than seeing Kelly. But I can't take anymore this evening. Let's eat in peace, listen to some old songs, and then go to sleep."

Then Fi gestured slowly towards Emme, her fatigue becoming more evident. "I know Emme feels the same. She's had a long day today getting here and she'll have an even longer one tomorrow trying to see Kelly. I bet she'd just like to sleep."

Fi, fidgeting with her dishtowel, seemed tuckered out to Emme. More than that. She was bone weary.

"Mama, whatever you think, keep it to yourself. At least for tonight. I believe we're safe in this house and I just need for you to believe it, too."

Emme worried that Fi might keel over right in the middle of the kitchen until Deirdre did something that made Emme smile.

Deirdre snuck a peek at her great-niece and winked before she turned to her daughter.

"Oh honey, come sit down with us. You know I don't mean to cause you no trouble. I feel safe in this house, too. We'll be safe together tonight."

After supper, Emme tried to guess what all Fi had put in the This 'n That. Then they drank tea in the living room. Aunt Fi even brought out the 'shine. She said they all needed a "special touch of warmth" that night. Fi and Emme sat on opposite ends of the couch with their feet up and Deirdre settled into the recliner.

Fi started to sing "Down by the Riverside." She sang the first line, "I'm gonna lay down my burdens, down by the riverside," by herself. But by the time she got to the next line, where she repeated "down by the riverside," Deirdre had joined her. They sang in a close harmony, their vocal cords the same at their genetic core.

Then Emme started to sing three-part harmony with her aunts. Their bodies were vibrating along with their voice boxes, not only in their chests and faces, which were always such perfect resonators, but in their every cell.

Someone could have attached them to a lie detector and asked, "Do you swear that everything in this living room is vibrating with you while you sing, the couch, the recliner, the fireplace, every single thing?" They would've said, "Yes, I swear it." And they would have passed the test.

Everything was indeed vibrating while they sang, a magnificent hum of music, kin, and history, all of it folding over and into itself. That was the only thing that allowed them to finally go to sleep.

CHAPTER 2

WHEN EMME woke up the next morning, she was disoriented until Deirdre came in and said she had just enough time to shower before the coffee was ready. Emme wasn't surprised that her elderly great-aunt was up before her. That was just Deirdre.

Though at her core she was trembling at the thought of soon seeing Kelly badly injured, Emme let the banality of morning activity lull her into some semblance of normalcy. She sank into routine as she showered, put on jeans with a green blouse that made her blue-green eyes seem more green than blue, and a navy blazer that she normally wore when she went into the office at the *Washington Herald*.

Emme's hair was neither straight nor curly, and the color was not fully red or brown. She kept it midlength with long layers because she could easily put it in a loose French twist. The style felt casual enough that no one in town would think she was too citified, but professional enough that any doctors she encountered would take her seriously.

As she began to walk downstairs, the cognitive dissonance in her brain screeched painfully. Making decisions about what to wear and how to fix her hair like any other day when she was about to visit

Kelly, who was handcuffed to a hospital bed after being nearly beaten to death by her husband. A now dead husband whom Kelly had confessed to killing.

As she came into the kitchen, Emme heard Fi and Deirdre discussing whether they thought she would want buttermilk with her cornbread, her favorite food that had been cooked in the same cast-iron skillet she'd grown up loving. Emme was shocked at how normal everything seemed for her aunts, too. She'd wondered if she was going to wake up to Deirdre screaming or a neighbor banging on the door to tell them about someone else gone crazy. Instead, everyone had slept through the night.

And then a regular morning like any other. The same surreal rhythm of the monotonous necessities of life needing to resume as usual had droned on after her parents had died, too. The true agony for Emme hadn't been during their funerals, but after, realizing that she had no choice but to walk through the minutia. Sometimes she thought the routine nearly killed her and sometimes she thought it was the only thing that saved her.

Breakfast continued with its familiar cadence, complete with Emme chiding Fi and Deirdre for trying to get her to finish everything on her plate when she normally just had coffee. The only part that was strange for Emme was when Deirdre asked Fi about her Italian. Fi recognized the perplexed expression on Emme's face and explained before her niece had a chance to ask.

"Emme, Mama was talking about my new Italian thing. We visited Bowling Green a few months back and went to this ginormous bookstore. I wanted to look up some new canning books. We had record tomatoes this summer."

"I take it you had luck?"

"I found more ways to fix tomato sauce than I thought possible. They love growing fresh things out of the ground in Italy, too. I have jars and jars of Italian-style sauce sitting back in the pantry and maybe tonight I'll make some homemade pasta to go with . . ."

Deirdre interrupted her daughter. "See, you can teach an old dog new tricks."

"Hush, Mama. As I was saying, I found all sorts of new things there, all those Italian recipe books. Then that sent me all over hooty's goose in the other sections of the bookstore since I wanted to keep hunting for more on Italy. I found . . ."

Deirdre interrupted again. "We hunted all damn afternoon. I thought I was gonna drop over dead."

"Mama, you know you loved it as much as I did."

"So now my daughter thinks she's gonna be going to Italy."

"I'm gonna drag you with me, Mama, kicking and screaming if that's what it takes. We just have to have a better year with the crops to afford it."

"So, you two have started learning Italian? Even Aunt Deirdre?"

"We got a bundle of them Italian lesson tapes for only two bucks. Even Mama's been listening to them with me."

Before Emme responded, she closed her eyes and imagined her aunts in Italy. She found it enchanting. "Italy was incredibly beautiful. I should go back with you, when everything is . . . is . . ."

"When everything is right with Kelly. You gotta be heading out soon to see her. Mama and I were expecting it."

After Emme made sure she had everything she needed, she left Fi and Deirdre with seven simple words. "Thank you. I love you. Be safe."

Lochlan Community Hospital was small because Lochlan County itself was small. Red River only had a population of around five thousand, and all of Lochlan County still had less than thirty thousand. Since Red River was the county seat, that was where they put the hospital. From having her tonsils out to her parents' time there, Emme knew the hospital well.

The fifteen-minute drive from Aunt Fi's was more of the bizarre normalcy that had defined Emme's morning. Emme loved October in Red River, when every house had a jack-o'-lantern. She especially adored the square, with its historic courthouse smack dab in the middle of town. Vivid mums of varying hues sat atop hay bales that perched on every corner around the courthouse. Cornstalks tied together with autumnal ribbons stood sentry by the front door. Even the hospital was decked out with fall wreaths on the main entry.

Emme had no doubt that she would see ten people she knew before she made it to Kelly's room, and that was a soothing thought. But she was petrified when, after she glanced down to put her keys in her purse, she looked up to see Mrs. Maddox coming toward her.

Mrs. Maddox didn't petrify her: it was the little girl holding her hand. Emme knew exactly who she was and tried not to stare at the child while she was hugging Mrs. Maddox.

"Emme, I knew you'd be coming home for Kelly. Of course they wouldn't let me in to see her, though. I was here for Sissy Blankenship. She's recovering from a broken hip and I came to drop off a get-well basket."

"Mrs. Maddox, I'm sure Mrs. Blankenship was happy to see you. I'm happy to see you, too."

"Thank you, dear. I wondered if I might run into you at some point. I don't think you've ever officially met my bright little one, Mattie, have you? Mattie, say hello to Miss Emmeretta Finnegan McLean. Your father, who knew Emme in high school, always liked to call her by all her names. I guess it stuck with me, too."

Mrs. Maddox seemed to be having trouble catching her breath, which made her words come out in strange little phrases with tiny stops after every few words. Emme was surprised she used her full name because it seemed particularly difficult for Mrs. Maddox to spit out all the consonants. It made Emme wonder if Evan's mother was as uncomfortable as she was.

"Pleased to meet you Miss Emmeretta Finnegan McLean. I'm Mattheson Jubilee Evelyn Maddox. I have four names, one more than you, though I promise I'm not bragging. I'm four years old, another four, and you can call me Mattie. That's less of a mouthful than Mattheson. At least it's one syllable less."

Emme was more than stunned. But not because Mattie was so articulate. Mattie was like Evan and Evan had been a genius. His daughter's brilliance seemed only natural. Emme was, instead, almost made speechless by how much Mattie looked like Evan. Of course children look like their parents. But Mattie looked more like Evan than Emme could have anticipated. Not so much with her gorgeous skin, which was clearly a fusion of the skin of Evan, who had been African American, and Mattie's mom, who had been Chinese. It was Mattie's eyes, pale green with aqua-blue and brown flecks, the colors converging unlike any shade Emme had ever seen before or since Evan.

Mattie's hair made Emme tremble, too. Evan had always kept his hair short, but Emme still had seen a reddish tint in the black. Emme had no idea what it would've looked like longer, but she imagined it would be exactly like Mattie's brunette curls that shone with the same vermillion.

Those curls! Those impossible reddish-black curls that sprang out of Mattie's head and had already grown long, down to her shoulders, even though she was only four. All of it shook Emme. Of course Mattie would be cerebral like Evan. Of course she would be uniquely beautiful like him, too, with those rare eyes and hair.

And yet, Emme was so shocked that she had to start gnawing on the inside of her cheek. She had to draw blood to stop from breaking down right there in the hospital parking lot. She didn't want to frighten Mattie or cause Mrs. Maddox any more pain than she'd already suffered, but Emme's agony slammed her so hard she felt as if she might never be able to take a breath again, let alone speak.

In a matter of seconds, while her eyes were drawn to Mattie's little fingers, Emme remembered verbatim a conversation she'd had with Evan. They hadn't dared sit together in the same seat on the way back from the track meet in Logan County their junior year of high school, but they'd managed to be in the same row with only the aisle between them.

They hadn't looked directly at each other, but they'd talked the whole way back. They'd been friends for the previous two years of high school, when they took all the honors and AP classes together, but it was the first time Evan had shown any kind of vulnerability. They'd both joined the same rock band and talked often during rehearsal, but even then, Evan kept his feelings to himself.

The night on the bus, though, everything shifted. When Emme had complimented Evan's eyes, he brought up the red in his hair, too. He'd sarcastically asked, "I wonder how that happened?"

Emme innocently said, "I don't know." Evan sighed.

"Emmeretta Finnegan McLean. I've heard Kelly call you by all three names when she's frustrated with you, and I'm frustrated now, too."

"I'm sorry, Evan, but I have no idea what you mean."

"You're so naïve. How can someone as smart as you miss so much?"

Emme honestly didn't know how to respond, so she said nothing, and Evan continued speaking.

"Of course I know I'm black. And my parents and grandparents are black. But, look at me. There's some Irish in me, too. And those two things together make it not okay, Emme. You know the only way I could wind up looking like this, the genetics of it. And it sure wasn't my mother stepping out on my father. This goes way back."

"But, Evan—" Emme couldn't finish her sentence before Evan charged ahead.

"Emme, come on, you know what this means . . ."

"But, Evan—" Emme didn't finish her sentence. Evan wouldn't let her.

"You know how genetics works, how a few generations ago, when things were beyond difficult for my family, for my people . . . you know what had to have happened . . . Don't play dumb, Emme."

Emme felt dizzy as she listened to Evan talk about genetics and how difficult things had been for his family.

"I'm so sorry, Evan. I don't know what to say. I've never really known how to respond to all your math talk. But this is, well . . . I don't have the words."

"Horrific. That's all you can say."

"Just horrific?"

"Yes. You know the world is horrific sometimes."

Emme had turned to look at him, saying she was very sorry. She also told Evan that he was truly beautiful to her. She said that the most important part wasn't how he came into existence, just that he existed at all. But Evan had simply warned her to face forward.

"You know that even in 1989 no black boy is allowed to date a white girl in Red River. We can't talk like this. You better look forward."

Evan then started talking about numbers, his favorite subject, while he looked straight ahead. Emme looked straight ahead, too, and listened to his eloquent description of the Fibonacci sequence. But she kept sneaking glances sideways whenever she could.

As the lights they passed shone through the bus windows, Evan's hair glowed more red than usual. When Emme turned ever-so-slightly to look at it, her mountain gift started and she heard the Red River song her mother used to sing. That time, instead of her mother's voice, though, Emme heard a single cello. Emme listened to the cello cry out the old tune while she herself cried all the way back home. Even through tears, Emme couldn't help but still marvel at Evan's reddish-black hair. To Emme, there had never been a more perfect color combination of both fire and darkness.

"Miss Emmeretta Finnegan McLean, do you like my book? It's *Charlotte's Web*."

Mattie's question yanked Emme back to the present. Mattie held a book up for Emme to see. Emme had never been more thankful for a distraction from her memories.

Emme loved hearing Mattie enunciate every syllable of her full name and did the same thing back.

"Miss Mattheson Jubilee Evelyn Maddox, the beautiful girl with four names, but Mattie for short, I love that book."

"Me, too," said Mattie. "You may not believe me, but I read it by myself. I know Charlotte had to die, too. But there was a special plan for her. Isn't that what you always say, Grammy?"

Emme knelt down so she could look directly into Mattie's eyes. Evan's eyes. "You know what? I do believe you read that book. I knew your father and he was incredibly intelligent like you."

Emme wasn't merely flattering Mattie. She believed the little girl was very much like her father with his dazzling mind. Nothing Evan had accomplished ever shocked Emme.

Mrs. Maddox then told Mattie she was so tired from her hospital visit that, if she wanted to stop by the library before they went home, they'd better run along.

"Yes, ma'am, Grammy. It was wonderful meeting you Miss McLean. Since Grammy's tired, I suppose I should be brief, shorten your name and just say 'Miss McLean,' though Emmeretta is new to me. I hope to see you again and we can talk more about books. And your name."

"Yes, most people have never heard of my name. It's from a great, great, great-aunt who lived in Eastern Kentucky. Her name was Emmeretta, too. Emmeretta Clark. And Mattie, it would be my pleasure to see you again. Mrs. Maddox, I hope you get some rest. It was lovely seeing you."

Emme didn't know whether to shake Mrs. Maddox's hand or hug her. She wanted to hug her but didn't know if that would be right, if it was asking too much. Emme knew there was no way Mrs. Maddox could be with Emme and not think of Evan.

Luckily, Mattie decided it for her and wrapped her arms around Emme before quickly grabbing Mrs. Maddox's hand and pulling her to their car. Emme started walking toward the hospital again when she heard Mrs. Maddox faintly say, "Emme, you still look so beautiful," before their car doors shut and the engine started.

Emme took the elevator up to the second floor and quickly made her way to Kelly's door. She couldn't go in because Rowdy Denkins was guarding it. Fi had warned her. About how bad Kelly would look and how there was a guard outside the door. Since everyone knew and loved their family, Fi was pretty sure they'd break the rules and let Emme in to see her cousin like they had Fi.

Emme, despite the unease she felt getting ready to face Kelly, had to smile at Rowdy. The fact that he was a cop now but still had his Rowdy moniker from high school right there on his uniform was silly to her and she laughed loudly enough for the nurses sitting at their station nearby to look up. Emme was pretty sure one of them was Denise Harris, whose family had a farm just down from her aunts', but her hair was highlighted blonde. If it was Denise, Emme knew she'd be able to get away with making noise.

Rowdy's face lit up as vividly as the fireworks he'd gotten in trouble for setting off every year in high school, months after the Fourth.

"Emme, I knew you'd be back sooner or later. And, yes, I'm gonna let you in, but you gotta make it fast or Everett'll fire me."

"No one could fire you." Emme walked quickly over to her old friend.

"I don't know. There's already been such hoopla about this case, people calling from states I barely remember existed since it's been so long since I had social studies. Not that I was ever good in that class."

"Yeah, social studies wasn't your strong suit."

"I ain't been out of Lochlan County but three times and the last time was just up to Cincinnati to see the Reds. Give me a hug quick and tell me what you were laughing at."

"Oh, Rowdy. Of course I'll hug you. I was laughing because I love how after all this time you've kept that nickname and now here you are a man of the law."

"A man of the law. Who would've thought it?" Rowdy's smile was as full of joy as ever.

"I always knew you were one of the good guys. Okay, the fireworks weren't always the best idea. And I'll never forget how you got that name in the first place."

"Scoot on in there, Emme, but stop by soon at the station or down at the house. We can swap old stories about our former bootlegging pals and that time we got kicked out of the Mexican restaurant down in Clarksville. El Palacio."

"I'll always remember that restaurant."

"Where I got my name. Damn, that was a fine place. They never carded us. Double damn that was fun. Pardon my language, ma'am."

Then Rowdy tipped his hat at Emme, actually tipped his hat. Charming as ever.

Emme had an arm around him as she whispered in his ear before she opened the door to Kelly's room. "Thank you, Rowdy. I won't forget this."

Emme had never considered herself melodramatic, and usually she wasn't. But ever since she'd heard about Kelly, she'd imagined her cousin beaten so badly that she wouldn't even really have a face left. But there was still a face there. Maybe not her cousin's, but someone's.

As bad as it was, the damage to Kelly's face didn't frighten Emme as much as what she sensed. The air in the room felt electric and heavy, dangerously charged like right before the tornadoes came and the sky turned an unreal greenish gray.

Thinking about greens and grays together reminded Emme of what Deirdre had told her of the witches and banshees she believed were haunting Red River. Emme quickly grabbed Kelly's hand, the one in cuffs, and looked at her fingers.

Emme had always thought her cousin had the most beautiful fingers in the world. They were long and sophisticated, with nails she never polished, but somehow managed to keep pristine even though she often painted. She mostly painted still lifes for herself. Emme knew they were excellent and had urged her to take them to a gallery in Nashville. But Cy had convinced Kelly she didn't need to sell her paintings, so they had stayed in their attic.

Then Emme glanced up again at Kelly's face, staring at the cuts on her lip, her cheek, and above her eye. It'd been two days since it happened, but her face was still red and purple and badly swollen, with only the bruise above her eye having started to fade.

The stitches were the worst, though. Emme knew from Aunt Fi that skilled surgeons had taken care of her cousin, including a plastic surgeon they'd called in to help with her face. But the sutures were barbed wire sticking out of Kelly's skin.

Then Emme looked at her cousin's shoulder and arm, the one not cuffed, which was completely wrapped up above the elbow. The smaller part of her arm, wrist, and hand that was free from bandages was swollen to twice its normal size. Emme kept rubbing circles with her thumb on top of Kelly's thumb until Kelly opened one eye, the eye that was only partially swollen. Even though Emme might never have recognized her cousin with her eyes closed, there was no doubt it was Kelly when she looked into that single, pale blue eye.

"Wellllll, about da . . . damn timmmmme, don't ya th . . . thinnnnk?" Kelly gave a lopsided grin because she could only move one small corner of her mouth. And even doing that made her grunt in pain.

Emme couldn't believe Kelly was able to smile, even if only a tiny bit. She slurred her words and stuttered, but Emme could understand her. Emme realized her cousin was on powerful painkillers, though they could only kill so much of the pain. Emme would've asked the nurse to get her cousin more meds right then, but she knew she had to keep Kelly awake to ask her questions.

"Honey, I got here as soon as I could. I only have a few minutes, though, before someone kicks me out. I'm lucky it was Rowdy out there."

Emme forced herself to keep on talking to Kelly, even after Kelly moaned.

"I should've worked harder to get Cy locked up . . . after—"

Emme knew there was no way she could end the sentence.

"It's o . . .o . . . kay, Em . . ." Kelly stopped talking. Emme wondered if she'd fallen back asleep, but then realized it was just the pain.

"Kelly, I know you didn't do it."

"I did s . . . something. I clawed himmmmm. I hit . . ."

Kelly moaned before talking again.

"When he p . . . pushed me . . . I pushed b . . . back. I wanted to save m . . . myself. That's why I told Everett I did it when I woke up."

Kelly's speech started to grow clearer with less stuttering, her last few words nearly perfect. She also tossed more on the hospital bed, as much as the handcuff would allow. Emme knew her painkillers were almost completely worn off.

"What exactly did you do? I called Everett from DC before I got on the plane. He said Cy was found slumped on the floor, part of his body still sitting up against the wall."

Emme had to pause before she spoke her next words, words she knew would be harder for Kelly to hear than for Emme to speak.

"Everett said he could see where Cy's head had been smashed against the top of the wall and slid back down. They took pictures and I'm going to look at them soon. I don't think there's any way you could've done that."

What Emme didn't tell Kelly was what Everett had said about the gray matter hanging from Cy's head. About how a large part had been smeared across a wide space and fragments of discernable skull bone were still sticking to the upper part of the wall, near the ceiling, in multiple places over several feet. Not just vertically where he slid down, but several feet wide. Everett said he'd never seen anything like it.

"There's no way you could've thrown Cy. He was six foot four and over two hundred pounds. The other women in our family are tall, but you're barely five feet."

Kelly didn't answer her. Emme didn't want her to be in such pain, but she knew if she called the nurse, she might get kicked out. She had to keep on going.

"Pushed him? Punched him? Sure. But you couldn't throw him up that wall and then slam him around from side to side up at the top of the ceiling. The new house he built you had a two-story entry. That's, what, twenty feet up?"

Kelly shook her head. At least she tried to until it hurt too much for her to move at all.

"There's not a man around here who could toss Cy up there like that, either."

Emme went from looking at Kelly's matted hair to her one blue eye when it fluttered back open.

"He broke two ribs, snapped your clavicle in two, and broke your humerus. Do you know how hard it is to break that bone in your upper arm? I covered the crime beat for a while. I had to talk to a ton of doctors and police. It's tough to break that bone."

Kelly managed to shake her head a little, but Emme couldn't tell if it was for a yes or no.

"Fi told me that everyone here said, despite all that Cy did to you, you'll still be released from the hospital in a day or two. But for what? To go to a jail cell? For confessing to something we both know you couldn't do?"

Emme knew she had to push on. "Do you even remember what happened? When Curtis found you and called 911, you were unconscious. Everett got there before the ambulance because Curtis, bless your neighbor, called the cops before he even went over. He knew Cy well enough to know he had a temper and he heard you both screaming all the way next door."

"I was s . . . screaming. Sometimes I feel like I still am." Kelly spoke almost perfectly.

"You're safe now . . . and I'm so sorry to rush this, but I have to before someone comes in. Everett said you were just waking up when he got there and that you confessed. He said it didn't make any sense, but you kept saying that you'd killed him, so he had to arrest you."

Kelly didn't respond, so Emme went on. "They took you to the hospital for surgery because your broken arm bone damaged the artery. I know you never wanted to live in a new house near town, but it saved your life being near the hospital. But Kelly, there's no way you could've done all that to Cy, so why confess?"

Kelly spoke through gritted teeth, but without slurring. "After he beat me and almost ripped my arm off, everything stopped. He'd dropped my arm and just stood there. He looked afraid of me."

Kelly whimpered and the sound of it became bird bones jabbing into Emme's ears. Then Kelly rallied. Emme realized pure adrenaline must've been pushing out her cousin's next words.

"I looked at his eyes, just nothing. He had no soul, Emme. But then I saw my right hand, on its own, pointing at him. I swear I didn't make my hand do that. He'd stepped away from me. I still had my back against the door. I'd been trying to run out when he'd come after me. I started screaming that he'd go to jail and I'd divorce him."

Kelly's one open eye went wild. Not just with pain, but with memory.

"Then he snapped out of it. It only took one step and he was on top of me again. But my right arm somehow punched him, Emme. All by itself. I remember it punching him in the face. Then . . ."

Kelly stopped. She didn't even breathe for several seconds. Emme hated it, but she had to urge Kelly on.

"I'm so sorry, but you've got to tell me the rest of it."

"I woke up with Everett above me and I could hear the ambulance. Curtis was there, trying to help. Everett said he was gonna have to pull me over a bit, and it might hurt, but that the EMTs needed to get the stretcher over to me."

Kelly shuddered then in a way than made Emme shudder, too.

She had kept trying to pull her arm out of the handcuff as she'd been talking and there were bloody marks around her wrist.

"Then I saw Cy. I could barely talk, but I told Everett I'd done it. I figured it was all my fault one way or the other. If I'd never threatened him, never told him he'd end up in jail . . . if I'd never punched him . . ."

"You don't remember him hitting the wall, almost up to the ceiling, right? I know you don't. Everett said there were multiple prints from the back of his head up there, like someone kept bashing his head over and over, but twenty feet in the air. No one could do that, Kelly, but especially not you."

Emme hoped her cousin could hold on for just a minute more.

"Everett said once they'd looked everything over, it didn't make sense. But you confessed. And with Cy sitting there dead with his face smashed in and the back of his head smashed in worse, well, he said he had to arrest you. They didn't finish analyzing the photos until hours later, but first they had to act on your confession."

Emme took the briefest breath possible to get enough air so she could finish and let Kelly rest.

"Your arrest, you being handcuffed to that bed, is only bad timing. With all the other crazy things happening, everyone's watching our town. Everett had to follow the rules. But it's a couple days later and you're still in handcuffs."

As she became angrier, Emme let go of Kelly's hand so she could wave her arms.

"Everybody keeps calling this a ruckus. It's the most insane thing I've ever seen. And that's saying a lot, since I've been in DC. You couldn't have killed Cy that way and you know it. They should know it, too."

Kelly shuddered again. Whether from her pain, fear, or exhaustion, Emme couldn't be sure.

"I don't know how to tell you."

"What?"

"There was something in that room, something angry. It wasn't just me and Cy. No, I don't think I could've thrown him up that high, but there was no one else there. Not in a normal way, but that makes no sense."

Emme heard two taps on the door and Rowdy poked his head in. "They just called me on the walkie. Someone's coming soon to relieve me. You've gotta skedaddle quick. I'm sorry."

Rowdy shut the door.

"I have to go. I'm so sorry. Before I do, though, please tell me what you mean by 'something in that room.'"

"I wish I knew. There wasn't another person in that room with me other than that son of a bitch. But there was something. Not a someone. Or maybe a lot of someones. I could feel them when everything slowed down. You believe me?"

"I do. We'll figure it out. I promised Fi and Deirdre that I'd make things right. I'm promising you the same."

Kelly closed her eyes and her body was relaxing when she jerked her eyes open again.

"I remember something. Someone else. Aunt Della wasn't really there . . . but I could hear her singing in my head, like you always say you hear songs."

Emme nodded her head yes.

"She was singing and then she said to come back to her. I want to, but I can't. You have to get back up that mountain to Della for me." Kelly thrashed on the bed more.

"I will."

Kelly moaned again, but she managed to get out some last words before she clenched her teeth together in agony. "Promise me, Emme."

Emme said she promised it true as she squeezed Kelly's beautiful fingers one more time and then rushed out of the room to the nurse's desk.

"Denise, I know I wasn't supposed to be in there, but Kelly needs more meds. Please, a lot more."

Denise got up immediately and started running toward Kelly's door. She looked back over her shoulder and said, "It's okay, Emme."

Emme yelled a "thank you" to Denise's back as Rowdy opened the door for the nurse. Then Emme moved as fast as she could to her car. Before she shut the door, though, she leaned over and threw up in the parking lot. She closed the door and started driving. She didn't stop until she was across the state line. Emme had run from Kentucky more than once, but never faster than that day.

CHAPTER 3

AFTER AN hour wandering around the antique mall in Goodlettsville, Emme slowly stopped crying. She didn't care if people stared at her as she went from booth to booth, pressing tissues to her face. She just kept on walking around and looking at the leftovers from other people's lives. An old wooden bucket. Some hand-crocheted doilies. A pretty little doll dressed in pink Victorian garb. A dining-room table with what looked like ivory inlay. A small stool painted blue with yellow sunflowers on it. Endless plates of various patterns.

When Emme could finally breathe normally again, she headed home via the shortest route on I-65. She didn't want to see the trees on the backroads anymore. They would make her feel something and she couldn't bear it yet. She refused to let herself think of anyone she loved, especially Kelly, until she crossed back over into Kentucky. But then Emme quickly created a plan and that was all she allowed in her head until she was back home.

Fi was still on the front porch when she got there, even though the sun had already gone down.

"This whole mess has me fretting so. I was starting to fret over you, too. Glad you're finally home."

"I'm so sorry. It took me a little while to gather myself after seeing Kelly."

"I haven't gotten over seeing her like that, either. But things might be worse with Mama. She's still too spooked to stay out here long, so she went in and heated up leftovers. There's a bowl for you, too, more of the This 'n That and the last of the cornbread."

"I know things are not good here if Aunt Deirdre's not sitting out on the porch."

"It's definitely not good if Mama can't stay out here for long. It's frightening me to my core is what it is, but I can't let myself be thinking too much about it now. Can I get you that cornbread?"

"No, thank you. I don't think there's time."

"Sweetie, I don't understand."

"We have to take Deirdre back up the mountain to see Della. I know she doesn't want to go back up there, but it can't make her more upset than staying here right now. And I think if there's anybody who can make her feel better, it's her sister. Kelly said I have to see Great-Aunt Della."

Fiona started to talk, but Emme was determined. She wasn't purposefully rude, but she felt as if she had to talk right over her aunt in order to maintain her resolve.

"I know it doesn't make any sense. Kelly didn't do this, and I don't know who did. But if she wants us to go back up the mountain for her, we will. I don't even want to stay here tonight. I want to go inside, pack up, and drive until I can't drive anymore. Then we'll stay at a motel until we leave at first light. Don't fight me on this, Fi, please. I know you won't want to leave Kelly, but she needs this. We all need this."

"I understand, I really do."

Fi spoke in the soothing tone Emme always found comforting, though her voice still held a shard of anxiety, too.

"I shouldn't dare to try to sneak back into the hospital again to see Kelly," Fi said. "I don't think I could bear to see her busted up like that again anyway. Plus, those boys already risked everything to let me in the first time, and now you, too."

"I was glad to see Rowdy."

"Me, too, and I was thrilled to see Denise. She was on shift the day it happened and after the doctors came through. After Kelly's lawyer came out to question her more, Denise was in there checking her stitches and all that miracle stuff nurses do. I surely thank them."

Emme loved that even in the middle of the hard times befalling her family her aunt could still maintain such a grateful spirit.

"Our Kelly begged her to let her make a phone call, so darling Denise done give in and even helped her dial Cecil down the road. For some reason, that's the only number she could remember at the time. Cecil drove on up here and took me next door to Merle and Kathleen's. All so I could call her back at the hospital."

Emme couldn't help but laugh as she imaged the circus. Half the town was involved in trying to help Kelly, who wasn't supposed to be making calls, get a phone call through to Fi, who had no working phone in the house.

Fi laughed with Emme.

"Yes, Emme, a whole lot of effort for all of us for one call, but I got to talk to Kelly. Now that Cy's dead and won't be calling and cursing us all the time, I better get another phone."

"That's probably a good idea."

"Kelly wasn't making sense, though. I know she'd just seen you, but she was still real agitated and I suppose the drugs didn't help. The one thing I got was she said that you gotta take us back up that ol' Black Mountain to see Della. She begged me. We're already packed. Mama, too."

Emme had half a mind to ask, "Will wonders never cease?" just like her mother used to, but she could tell Fi wasn't finished.

"You'll be shocked. Even Mama said we gotta go. As much as she loves her sister, and however much beauty lives up there, she hates being back up that mountain. She feels like the coal's gonna get her. But she said the answers, at least the start of them, were up there."

"What answers?" Emme genuinely hoped all the answers were up on Black Mountain.

"I don't right know exactly, but Mama started talking about the old ways again, how they could fix things better than any police or even you, Emme. She said there was healing powers in the Red River songs wherever we sang them, but up on that mountain with Della? That's the source, the closest we can get if we can't go all the way back to Scotland and Ireland."

Fi put her hand to her face in a thoughtful way.

"I swear, I thought for a second she was gonna say she'd finally be willing to get on a plane and go all the way across the ocean to see where we all come from. But she said that going to the mountain would be enough."

Emme knew it was finally time to ask Fi, "Will wonders never cease?"

"I don't know about wonders, but we already packed up your stuff, too, and made some sandwiches for the road. Mama had already made that peanut-butter fudge you loved as a young'un, so that's coming with us, too."

"Oh, Aunt Fi. It was hard to come back here, but it was also the most beautiful thing to me, too. I missed you. I didn't think I'd end up back in Eastern Kentucky, though. But there's no other way."

They were out of the house and on the road in less than thirty minutes. They ate the food and drank the thermoses of tea that Fi had packed earlier. They didn't even need to get more coffee, even as the hours of driving started accumulating. In many ways they were more awake than they'd ever been, and caffeine was not only unnecessary, but it seemed that it would make them more addled.

For a group of ladies from Kentucky, known storytellers, they didn't say much. When they started the trip, they listened to WSM, the country station from Nashville, whose signal was strong enough to reach up into Kentucky until it faded out as they moved east.

Then they sang one of their favorite ballads, "Barbara Allen." When they sang the line, "Oh mother, oh mother, go dig my grave. Make it both long and narrow. Sweet William died of love for me and I will die of sorrow," Emme stopped singing.

She saw Evan, but not with her mountain gift. Her images were ones from the past. Memories of a girl who had lost someone she loved.

"Please, I can't sing this song right now."

"Don't you be fretting. We can find a better one."

They put in an old tape, *The Best of Porter Wagoner and Dolly Parton*, and they played it over and over while they drove, not singing along. The three women quietly drew strength from simply listening to the songs until Deirdre surprised Emme by mentioning someone out of the blue.

"Emmeretta, have you talked to that Aidan again yet?"

Emme turned the tape off. She was shocked. Aidan, the boy Emme had envisioned as soon as she'd pulled onto the road that led to the farm. Aidan, the boy who had transfixed her at the wedding years before. The one she still dreamed about every few months even though it made no sense to her.

"Mmm . . . no, ma'am. Why would I?"

"Listening to Dolly somehow reminded me of that wedding. Do you remember it?"

"A little bit." Emme remembered more than a little bit.

"Tonight ain't the night to be getting into it, though. I was just curious. I think I need some more music now."

Emme turned the tape back on and tried to figure out what wildness had crept into Deirdre to make her bring up Aidan like that.

Emme didn't have long to contemplate it though, because when the tape was done, Fi started to sing on her own. Neither Emme nor

Deirdre joined her because they wanted to listen to Fi's solitary voice on "Jolene."

When Fi started the chorus again, the first "Jolene" came out delicately. But when Fi's voice expanded to nearly a guttural howl as she repeated each "Jolene," Emme's mountain gift began again. She saw the strangest thing.

Emme saw Kelly, as if they were physically in a room together. Kelly, covered in paint, reached out to one of her canvases. The colors seemed to swirl and Kelly was trying to catch them before they rolled away. Emme went over to peer more closely into the canvas. She was in awe of the undulating colors that Kelly had been trying to tame.

Despite the paint moving, Emme easily recognized the images depicted. It was one of Kelly's still lifes with several kitchen objects. There was a simple white teacup, an aqua-hued Ball jar, and an old brown jug. The jug was plain except for a few streaks of brilliant yellow that ran from its top to its bottom. The yellow swirled even faster than before. Emme touched it, but when she did, the vision stopped. Emme was back in the car with her aunts. Fi was no longer singing words. Her gentle hum was the only sound.

But Emme couldn't dismiss the vision, the strongest she'd had in years. The effects reverberated in her. It seemed as if she closed her eyes, she'd be right back with Kelly at the canvas, trying to tame its teeming paint colors. Her fingertip crackled with sensation from where she'd made contact with the yellow. And all because Fi had sung "Jolene."

Emme had seen things when she heard music, and heard music when she'd seen things, for as long as she could remember. But she still didn't know what to make of her mountain gift. Was it really a version of the sight in which her family believed? Or was it only her particular form of synesthesia, where one sense morphed into another because her brain circuitry got mixed up?

Emme rarely talked about her mountain gift to people who

weren't her kin, even after she went to college and had access to the libraries at Georgetown. It was there Emme realized that what she experienced was probably the genuine medical phenomenon of *synesthesia*. That meant her mountain gift was not likely to be something mystical.

Despite learning its technical name, Emme continued to refer to it as her *mountain gift*. At least to herself and her aunts. A form of synesthesia or a mountain gift? It wasn't possible to know. Either way, it made Emme experience the world uniquely, even wondrously.

The frequency of Emme's mountain gift had changed. It had always come sporadically when she was growing up, but from the moment she left the farm, it arrived even less often. And when it came, the sounds and sights the gift produced were subtler, as if Emme were experiencing everything through a thin scrim. Her Aunt Deirdre had warned her before she moved that if she stayed away from Kentucky too long, she'd eventually lose her ability.

"Emme, most everyone from the mountains in Kentucky done got magical gifts. You ain't no different," Deirdre had said.

"I believe the mountains themselves are the source of your gifts. You can't be doubting it, child, and you ain't got no business moving so far away from them. From us. Your power will get weaker if you leave the mountains. You need them, Emme."

Deirdre and Della had admonished Emme many times even after she left for college.

They had also reiterated to their niece that her mountain gift was just that, a gift. Sometimes the gifts took on different forms, they said, and not everyone had them as powerfully as everyone else, but they were always there. Because of her aunts' constant belief, Emme had faith in her gift for many years, even when it frightened her.

When Emme had researched it at Georgetown, she began to question if her gift might only be a neurological misfiring. That's how the books and medical articles described it. Even with that knowledge, Emme still didn't often tell outsiders about it because she was afraid they'd think she was insane. Even if it was only synesthesia, it was so rare that most people had never heard of it.

Sometimes when she experienced something astonishing in DC, Emme could've sworn her family was right all along, that it was too stunning to be some brain mix-up. When she'd visit back home, or even when she just called or wrote, Emme would share her experiences with her aunts.

Emme's kin never wavered in their belief that Emme witnessed a magical world. Long after she'd moved, they wanted her to describe the peculiar but transcendent way she heard and saw things. It was most vibrant when Emme heard music. The melodies, or sometimes the tone of someone's voice, could birth a brand-new world. But it also happened in reverse, where what she saw, colors in particular, would make a sound or an entire song. Sometimes what she saw grew into a symphony.

Emme felt so strongly about music, especially the Child Ballads from Europe, that the scenes her mind created when she heard them were lushly detailed. She particularly loved Scottish murder ballads with their tales of ghosts, hangings, and lost loves. Many people in her family swore that the Child Ballads were true. They always made Emme see startling images, no matter how many times she'd sung them.

Emme didn't see the stories described in the Child Ballads; instead, she envisioned new things. Highly detailed scenes played out before her. This happened with other types of music, too, but the Child Ballads made the most astounding images. When Emme first noticed that some of the things she saw later started coming true, she couldn't reconcile it. She didn't believe it was possible to tell the future, though many of her kin claimed they had that mountain gift, too.

As Emme contemplated the scene with Kelly she'd envisioned while Fi was singing "Jolene," she knew she would find no easy answers. She didn't bring up her experience with Fi and Deirdre. Without a doubt they'd assure her she'd seen the future, or some form of it.

Emme chose to not think about the future for the rest of the car ride, even while she wondered about the significance of Black Mountain. Was it coincidence that she'd seen the clearest vision in years as they'd drawn closer to Della's home?

Emme, Fi, and Deirdre decided to stop only fifteen miles from the mountain. Even though they had been driving over five hours as fast and as hard as they could, and it was close to midnight, they didn't feel the need to sleep. But they didn't want to try to get to Della's in the dark.

Della lived three-fourths the way up the mountain, off the main road. The old dirt path to her house was heavily wooded and had no lights. Thinking of the mountain made Emme wish she'd driven Fi's truck instead of her rental car as she pulled into The Whippoorwill Motel, right off of 119.

Even though Della wasn't at the very top of Black Mountain, it was, at an elevation of 4,145 feet, the tallest mountain in Kentucky. They'd have to drive up over two thousand feet from where they were. Even in the day there would only be brief holes in the trees that would let the light in, but that would be much better than going at night.

They were glad to be sleeping in the same room again, with Fi and Deirdre in one bed, and Emme in the other. Check-in went quickly and they still weren't sleepy. They stayed in their clothes. They knew what they were wearing had to see them through the night, up the mountain, and back down it, too. The idea of undressing, even when they were safe in the same room, made them feel vulnerable, an odd sensation that they all felt together and didn't need to articulate.

The strange energy keeping them awake wasn't completely fear, either, although there was plenty of that. It was also a whirring of anticipation. Of seeing Della and the mountain again. Of learning something they felt they already had the answer to, but couldn't bring up out of themselves to know consciously. It was moving powerfully inside their chests, what they both did and did not know.

Deirdre hummed for a few seconds before she spoke. "I know Della sometimes feels like I done betrayed her by coming down the mountain. But I also know she understands at the same time. Just like I know why she stayed. You know I begged her to come down with me, after Alton died. Never knew one finer than him except for my own beloved."

Deirdre paused for a full minute. Emme knew her reverie consisted of bittersweet memories of her husband, sister, and brother-in-law, the loss of one turning over and into the other.

"Could there be two more beautiful things than Della and that mountain? Since she no longer has to deal with the horror of Alton digging that coal, I bet she believes it's the most magnificent place on earth. That's why she stayed. She's probably right, too. I only wish we were coming back for something good."

Emme set her straight. "Aunt Deirdre, I think this is for something good. To save Kelly. Maybe to save us all. I haven't had the chance to ask you all the details yet, but I know things were even worse than all this mess with Kelly. As if things could be worse than that. Maybe on the way back home tomorrow I'll be able to talk to you about it. Until then, I'm going to believe that it will be okay. We're going to see Della and the mountain tomorrow. Good will come of both."

Then they sang more songs together. A little Patsy Cline. Then Patty Loveless and Dwight Yoakam. More mountain ballads. They ended on The Judds, who Aunt Fi always called "the pride of Kentucky."

Emme joined in as loudly as her aunts. Since she started singing again, Emme had fallen back into the habit of just opening up her mouth and breathing music. All the songs poured out effortlessly like air.

Emme's mountain gift blossomed again, too. While she sang with Fi and Deirdre in the motel, Emme envisioned a whole museum's worth of paintings. Instead of detailed scenes, Emme glimpsed impressionistic bursts of color moving in front of her as she harmonized. They sang until they could bury their worries for the night.

CHAPTER 4

EMME AND her aunts were never so happy to see a Waffle House. It was a block down the road from their motel. They knew they couldn't take long, but it was morning and they finally needed coffee. And enough food to help them make it up the mountain and face all that it held, the beauty and grief of it, too.

After breakfast, Emme was determined to drive. She knew she had Black Mountain running through her veins, but she was still afraid to drive up it. Fi and Deirdre, partly to tease her and partly to keep their minds off everything that was wrong, made fun of her in a lighthearted way.

"You were practically raised on this mountain. You spent all your holidays here and half of every summer when you were growing up. How could you possibly be afraid to drive up it?" Fi chuckled as she spoke.

"For starters, all the time I came up here as a kid, I never drove. Mama and Daddy would speed along like lunatics, happy lunatics mind you, and you know the roads didn't have guardrails back then."

Emme's face blanched as she remembered peeking down the side of the mountain as her parents had raced to reach the top. On the way up, she could only look out of the car for a few seconds before her fear of heights took over.

"I know you both love to tease me, but I had to bury my head in the seat until we reached Della's. I'd get sick from all the curvy roads. That's what made it so bad."

"I done always liked that it was so high up and all them curves to get there. Half the fun of it."

"That's great for you, Aunt Deirdre, but not for me. Sometimes we'd be completely covered in trees on either side and that wasn't so bad. But sometimes we'd be out in the open, practically hanging off the side of the mountain."

"Hanging off the side of the mountain? You're exaggerating."

"No, ma'am, I'm not. But once we got up there and stopped swerving around those crazy curves, and I didn't feel like I would throw up, it was heaven. It's gonna be worth it now, too."

And Emme told herself exactly that. She repeated, "It's gonna be worth it," at least ten times before they made it to their destination.

Della's land was on a part of the mountain three-fourths of the way up. It was flat enough for the house and even a little garden behind it. The house itself was almost completely surrounded by trees, but the garden was placed in an open, light-filled area. Beyond the forested part of the land, you could stand clear of the trees enough to look down to the undulating hills below.

On this clear area, Emme had written her first songs and taken her first photographs. Unlike the wildly winding roads on the way up, Emme wasn't afraid of the flat space on that part of the mountain. It didn't even seem that high to her once she got there. Every time Emme saw the view she couldn't help but say out loud, even just to herself if she was alone, "It's something."

She knew there wasn't a word perfect enough to convey exactly what the *something* was. Each time Emme looked down from atop Black Mountain, a sense of peace she didn't know she was capable of grew into a lavish warmth rippling over, then under, her skin, building until the sensation was so startling she thought it would burst out her fingertips as light. Then there was only music left.

Emme would start to sing "The Cuckoo," the tune sounding more ancient as it echoed around the mountains. When she started with the lines, "The cuckoo, she's a pretty bird, she sings as she flies. She bringeth us good tidings, she telleth us no lies," Emme sang tentatively.

But as she got to her favorite part, "Going to build me a log cabin on a mountain so high," Emme sang so powerfully that when the words echoed back they nearly knocked her over. Whoever was with her would join in. If she was alone, she'd sing louder. She never had to wait for her mountain gift when she saw that view. Emme started singing on her own first, and she sang until the song wasn't only coming from her, it was her.

As the car finally reached Della's part of the mountain, Emme was already humming "The Cuckoo." She parked and opened the door, but then sat still, even though she wanted to run to the cliff so she could see the verdant splendor laid out before her. Even up on the mountain, fall hadn't shifted into full force yet, and she knew there would be more green than autumnal hues everywhere she looked. Emme loved the Kentucky mountains, what her aunts called *their Highlands*, whatever color they were, but the green was most thrilling to her because it was the most alive. She could breathe it in, fresh and thriving.

Emme, if she'd had the time, could have stood outside of Della's place for an hour doing nothing more than inhaling. Della had written her several months back and told her that outsiders might rip the mountain's top off. Long before what happened to Kelly and Red River, Emme had considered going back to Kentucky to photograph Black Mountain before it was gone. She wanted to breathe it in deeply in case something happened to it.

Emme took one huge breath and realized that was all she had time for. As important as savoring the mountain was, saving Kelly took precedence. And it was going to be hard.

Before they'd even gotten out of the car, Della came out of the house to meet them. She'd gone partially deaf, so she couldn't have heard the car pull up. But Della knew things. Like so many of Emme's kin. And Della had the sight the strongest out of all of them.

"I knew you was here. I knew it when you started up the mountain. I could feel you even before that, actually. You know I could, too, so don't be doubting me."

Emme and Fi stood back and let Deirdre embrace her sister. Deirdre took her hands and put them on either side of Della's face and looked at her.

"I'd never doubt you. You practically raised me as much as our sweet ol' mama. I tell people, don't I Fi and Emme, that my sister is the smartest woman in the world. Book learning, how we fought for at least some of us to get it, don't mean a thing next to pure intellect. A mighty mind and a heart even greater, that'd be my sister."

Emme was thrilled to see Deirdre's cheeks pink up as she spoke to her sister. Emme touched her own cheeks as she felt a sudden warmth come to her face, too.

Deirdre seemed to have slipped off her cantankerous self, for which she was notorious, and put on a brand-new coat of graciousness just for her sister. "Della, you are magnificent. That I get to call you sister, well, it's a blessing I don't deserve."

"Oh, dear one. You never judged me. Me and my refusing to use all the fine grammar. I was more comfortable with the old talk. Still am."

"I hear you. I'm so proud our young ones, like Emme, talk so clear and perfect with all that education. It's a miracle, but I'm glad I don't gotta be worrying about you judging me for speaking the old style, either."

Della smiled the sweetest smile, similar to Emme's, though Emme could never see the strong resemblance like others did.

Della and Deirdre reached out their hands to encompass Fi and Emme for a bit. Then Della started pulling everyone inside.

"We have to be getting to it, don't we? There's never enough time, but especially not now."

Although Della's place looked like nothing more than a very basic small house from the outside, more a cottage than anything else, inside there were certain luxuries. Nothing ostentatious, but subtly beautiful pieces were in the living room, which, other than two tiny bedrooms and an even tinier bathroom, was the bulk of the place.

At the back of the living room, opposite the door, was a small kitchen. The farm-style dining table separated the living area from the cooking area. But the feeling of a rustic grandeur was visible: there was a velvet blanket in a deep burgundy hue and damask pattern thrown over a rocking chair and a tall dark-wood china cabinet with intricately carved details, full of transferware in different patterns and colors and small crystal glasses etched with a petite floral pattern.

Perhaps most stunning of all was part of an old stained-glass window that hung suspended from the ceiling by leather straps. When the sun poured in the east-facing window, light would shoot through the glass and splinter into dancing colors.

When Emme had visited during her childhood, she'd always stood still in the middle of the pooling hues, letting the colors cover her from head to toe. With her mountain gift, she'd heard the most remarkable symphonies when she'd glimpsed the refracted light at the right time.

Also in the room was a small brown couch, a settee, really, that held only two comfortably; one clawfoot chair in a brown plaid pattern; and a wooden rocking chair on which sat a hunter-green pillow decorated with a bouquet in needlepoint. It was the perfect number of seats for the four of them.

As everyone got settled, Della started speaking her straightforward way. "Emme, I know you been dreading coming up here to see me."

"There's no use lying. I did dread this. But I was also overjoyed at the thought of seeing you. I missed you more than you know. I just wish it was under better circumstances."

"I done known for ages how you missed me and home. So many nights for so many years I been sending you my thoughts, sharing what you need to know. What you already knew if you'd just accepted it."

"Aunt Della . . ."

"Child, let me speak it true. Don't get me wrong, though. I don't think I done know all. I'd never say something like that now, because the older I get, the more I know I don't know."

"What do you mean?"

"All the mystery being in every nook and cranny. It's done been everywhere this whole time of my long life, but I see it more and more now. The mysteries ain't no one ever gonna figure out."

"Which mysteries? There are more than I can count now."

"Yes. More things of mystery I don't know than what I done figured out. Some magic that can't never be truly held. I've done gotten so long in the tooth and learned plenty, but that don't mean I have the answer to everything."

Deirdre piped up, some of her sass back. "I never thought I'd live to see the day that Della would be admitting she don't know everything. Don't you get your feathers ruffled, sister. You know I'm teasing."

"You're right, though, Deirdre. Pride done got to me like it does everyone sooner or later. But I've got many years now, humbling years, that I can finally be admitting what I don't know. That's my biggest truth and I gotta speak it."

Della looked at Emme. "Does that make sense, child?"

"Yes, ma'am. A little bit."

"But that also means when I say I really know something, then I done be knowing it clear to my marrow. So you gotta be trusting me."

Della didn't need to wag her finger at Emme. Emme's self-imposed guilt brought shadows to both women's faces as Della continued admonishing her niece.

"You better be coming back soon, Emmeretta, I done said over and over. But you shut me out. I even tried thinking it all in a song. You heard it sometimes, I know you did. You stopped singing, but every time you done take one of those photos, you heard the song, too. I know it. With that there mountain gift you have done been blessed with."

Listening to her great-aunt, Emme felt a mammoth loss. She'd missed too many opportunities to spend time with Della. "I promise when this is all over, when Kelly's out of the hospital and free, I'll come back up here. But we have to focus on Kelly today."

Della harrumphed in a way that sounded exactly like Deirdre.

"Yes, we do. But you ain't gonna wanna hear what I think about Kelly."

Fi laughed—a laugh full of melancholy as much as mirth—before she spoke. "And why do you think we came running back up this big old mountain? This ain't one of those reunions we wrote about having for so long, full of 'shine, singing, and goin' hunting for a brùnaidh. I keep expecting one to steal something out of my purse any second."

Della, being so old, took Fi's words literally and gently scolded her. "Fi, dear, you don't have the sight strong like I do, like your mama has it, and Emme in her own way. So I doubt you'll be seeing any broonie. I think only them hobs steal things, anyway. They the evil ones, remember?"

"Oh, Aunt Della, I remember." Fi knew better than to try to convince her aunt that she'd just been teasing about the broonies.

Della continued talking, "A brùnaidh will help me out some-times. I don't have to work to believe. It's easy for me since I done seen them for so long. But since you believe, maybe you'll see one even if your gift ain't strong."

Della spun her head around as if she was looking for a spritely creature to pop up any second, right there in her living room.

"More likely up here where the magic's stronger. I think the mountains is like a spring cave keeping meat cold in the old days; things are still fresh here. They don't fade like they do down where y'all moved. That's why I stayed up here. The old ways aren't old ways, they're now ways."

Emme had expected all the old tales and had anticipated being frustrated by them as she had been when she was growing up, but for some reason she was listening more keenly than ever. Emme could feel herself leaning in, her body being pulled closer to Della even as she fought it.

"Della still believes. Fi believes some, too. But Emme? With every generation it slips away. The old ways. The believing in something beyond you. Bigger than you, too. It's fading down where you live."

Deirdre had to chime in. "You know I believe."

"I'm sure you do, sister. It's Emme here that don't."

Della turned to look directly at Emme. "I don't know whether to tell you what I think, Emmeretta. I ain't talking about the brùnaidhs and hobs, though I swear on my beloved's grave that I've danced with many a brùnaidh in my day. I'm worried about whether you truly be wanting to hear what I know. It might scare you bad."

Emme, if she was honest, was afraid. But she also wanted to reassure her aunt. "I've come this far. And you didn't see Kelly. Or everything that I've witnessed in DC. I've seen more bad things than you know."

"Darling, I do know. I know what you see because I see it, too, or feel it in my way. But this is more than all that. The banshees are back. The banshees or some sort of angels or I don't know exactly what, as I keep getting confused. But everything unresting came with them. Well, I think they been here all along, but sometimes they rested."

Emme knew that the time for pleasant catching up had quickly passed. So Emme put both of her feet on the ground. Somehow that position seemed to steady her, not only physically, but in her mind, too, as she waited for Della to continue.

"This thing here now, is one of the things you got to know, something that will help you. You gotta realize that not all angry things are evil. I'm a little confused, but not about this part."

In the past, Emme fought against believing her aunt whenever she brought up the old ways, especially once she moved to DC. But with Kelly and everything else, Emme knew she shouldn't argue with Della anymore.

"Go on, Aunt Della. I'm listening." Emme's whole body wanted to hear. She could feel each part of her open up, waiting for answers.

"Not all spirits walking this earth are evil. And Deirdre, I know you is scared the most by them, but you not listening right, not seeing right with the vision. You be twisting it."

Della, unconsciously illustrating her sister's point, twisted her hands together in a way that looked painful to Emme. They suddenly looked like the gnarled roots of a very old tree.

"They not out to get you, sister. They be speaking to you and to all of us with the sight. They want us to know they're mad. Now they done reached a point of fury and someone had to pay. You tried to warn Cy, Emme. But he never listened. So he paid. For all of them. Every single last one."

"What do you mean 'for all of them'?" Fi asked, starting to breathe heavier from following Deirdre around the room. Deirdre had gotten up and started pacing as Della spoke. Then Fi got up to try to get her mother to sit back down, but Deirdre kept pulling away from her and wanted to walk around, even though the room was tiny. She kept circling the room, so Fi had to circle behind her.

A look of wonder had come across Emme's face as Della mentioned Cy. She paused before she responded. "It shouldn't surprise me that you know I tried to warn him years ago, Aunt Della, but somehow it still does. I know I never told anyone, and Kelly didn't tell anyone. I sure know Cy never came up this mountain to tell you."

Della sighed. It was the sigh of a woman who was not only very old, but very tired of having to explain what to her was the simple truth.

"Emme, if you could ever go on and fully believe, every last thing would be better."

The sense of wonder that had taken over Emme morphed into irritation. She felt her body close off, her shoulders hunching down.

"Do you mean believe everything you've told me all my life? In all the old ways? In brùnaidhs or broonies, or whatever you want to call them? In haints and banshees? And that you can see the future? Do you really want me to still believe, right now, in magic?"

"But you already believe. You all do, you just forget what you already know sometimes."

"I love you more than life itself, Aunt Della. But, no, I don't believe, not fully. Not enough for you."

"Yes, you do. I know it true, no matter how much you fight me." Della spoke with no frustration in her voice, only weariness.

There was frustration in Emme's voice, though. "No, I don't. Respectfully, no. That's why I left Kentucky. All these things you want me to believe in. I never could see them. It was only my brain misfiring all along. Synesthesia."

Della, Deirdre, and Fi looked back and forth at one another when Emme mentioned synesthesia.

"And if I did ever believe in what I saw, where did that get me?"

"Emmeretta . . ." Della couldn't finish her sentence, so Emme went right on speaking her mind. She realized she sounded more like Deirdre than she ever had, her defiance adding a pointed quality to her tone.

"None of the old ways helped me at all. Did they save my parents? I couldn't keep hanging on to things that were murky at best. I wanted to go where things were concrete. I could capture them in photographs. I wanted, and still want, to document the truth. Right now, not ancient stories from hundreds of years ago. I went away to fix things. Real things. I don't want to be haunted by anything ever again, so, no, I don't believe."

The entire time Emme spoke to Della, she popped her knuckles, a habit she knew drove all her aunts crazy. It wasn't that she was trying to get back at them, only that Emme felt herself becoming slightly unhinged, and popping her knuckles soothed her.

"But you're still haunted. I know you see things. You hear them, too. You did as a child and you still do, even if it got weaker when you left home."

Della took in one of her enormous breaths. Then she smoothed her hair down, even though it had never come out of place.

"Just because you stopped talking about all the magical things you seen and heard don't mean they don't still exist. Mountain magic is the strongest magic of all."

Della glanced at Deirdre and Fi before she turned back to Emme, more determined than ever.

"Are you gonna sit right there in front of me in my own home up on this here mountain and lie to my face?"

Emme looked right at Della but didn't say a word.

"Are you gonna swear to me that you don't hear and see nothing special? You used to tell me all about the wonderful sights you seen and heard when you was but wee. I know you done seen and heard the same things still to this day. The mountain gift you have never died, Emme. It might've done come less and less while you were away, but it ain't gone."

Emme buried her face in her hands and sat still for a minute. Deirdre and Fi stopped pacing. No one said a single word until Emme looked back up at Della.

"No, ma'am, I can't say that I haven't experienced strange things. But I researched it in college. I have something, what I said a few minutes ago. It's called *synesthesia*. I studied it. And I'm an artist. Of course I see the world uniquely. That doesn't mean that all the things you believe are true, either, though. But since I can't prove that they don't exist, I won't fight you."

Della smiled softly. "I ain't worried about you fighting me, but about you fighting yourself."

Emme's next sentences started having a sputtering quality.

"But what does all of this have to do with Kelly anyway? Let's say I believe you and go against all the education I received. Graduate school. All my research. Let's say while I'm back in Kentucky trying to help Kelly that I leave logic and tangible things out of it. I'll forget the modern world."

Emme took a breath almost as large as the one Della had taken before she continued speaking.

"Instead, for a minute, I'll give in and try to one hundred percent believe everything you're telling me. Everything you've told me all my life. But how can that possibly help Kelly?"

"It's a balance. One season full of life, all green with movement in every direction, babies being born and flowers of every color in every direction standing up and waving at you. Then the other."

Della gestured to the window as she spoke. Everyone turned to look at the trees that, with their leaves mostly green but with the smallest tint of fall color, told the same story Della was telling.

"Another season dead and gray, hardly any creatures moving, just things in the wind. Brittle things. Blowing away in the storm. They balance each other. Both those seasons. Life and death. Good and evil. Even some of your science laws, I read it in the encyclopedias we got for Charlotte before we sent her down the mountain, the thermo-dynamic laws. No energy made or destroyed. Balanced."

Fi, despite all her worry over Kelly and her mother, was tickled by seeing her aunt talking about physics.

"I tell you, Aunt Della, I never thought we'd come up here today and hear you speaking about physics. Emme had a friend that taught us quite a few things, even thermodynamic laws. Maybe I learned them in school, but then I forgot. Evan helped me remember. Evan, right Emme?"

For the second time in two days Emme had heard Evan's name after having not heard it for years.

"Yes, it was Evan. I can't believe you remember that after all this time."

"Of course I do. Evan had a way of merging the old and the new. He didn't think all those science laws disproved mountain magic. He thought it proved them."

Emme could tell Fi was about to start on one of her rolls, full of helpful information, enthusiastically so despite everything life was throwing at her.

"Aunt Della, Evan said math was the code to the entire universe and I believed him. I was impressed by that young man. He sure was a star at everything, wasn't he? Sports, math. Music, too, with that band you had, Emme. Went to some mighty fine schools. Even finer than Emme's Georgetown, and that's saying something."

Instead of again mournfully thinking about Evan, remembering his math genius as described by Fi made Emme feel something closer to peace. The tension in her face dissipated.

"Yes, Fi, Evan was . . . special. He got a scholarship to Columbia and stayed on there for his PhD. He never stopped loving math and science. I think he loved them even more at Columbia. He met his wife there, too."

"Real shame about them. Nice couple like that dying in that car crash. So young and with a baby. When I get into town sometimes, I see his mama with that baby girl looking just like him. Just as smart as him, too. I heard her a couple times talking like a grown-up."

Emme remembered meeting Mattie. Despite all that was going on with her family, Mattie hadn't been far from Emme's mind.

As she began to speak again, Della lifted her arm up, as if she was going to touch Emme, even though they weren't sitting close enough to reach each other.

"I can see it still pains you. Evan dying. I could feel you feeling him gone. But like that balance, there's something of him, some piece of his life still walking on this earth, ain't there? He's not completely gone."

Emme could see Mattie so perfectly in her mind then that the image drew out her mountain gift. This time the music was simple and sweet. A bright carousel song. She could smell cotton candy.

"See, Emme, balance. All them seasons with death turning back to life again. I lived so long I done see it time and time again. But sometimes to keep that balance, someone's gotta do something. It's you whose gotta do something now."

The carousel music Emme heard stopped abruptly.

"I came back from DC and I saw Kelly. One of the most difficult things ever, but I did it. Then I drove up this mountain today. I know Kelly didn't kill Cy, but other than helping prove she's innocent, in a concrete way, I don't see how I can help. But I want to with all my heart."

"Oh, honey, I done known that. You ain't perfect, none of us is, but you so good. I don't want to beat around the bush no more, though. As much as I wanna break bread with you and sing the old songs, I know you got to get on down this mountain. So I'm just gonna say it straight, but you gotta believe me and promise to do all I say."

Emme knew there was no use arguing with her aunt.

"Yes, ma'am, I promise it true."

"I know. All these years away and you're still the same person, good through and through. I know I'm repeating myself now. You just gotta let an old woman repeat herself, though."

Emme didn't know why, but tears came to her eyes. Maybe it was

Della acknowledging that she was old. Emme knew they'd all been lucky to keep her so long.

"This is gonna be hard. You gotta convince the law that things gotta change, because if they don't, all the banshees and whatever else is out there is gonna stay around forever and more people will die and more people will go crazy. You have to do something else, too."

Aunt Della paused for what seemed too long to Emme and it made her nervous.

"What?"

"You gonna have to search real deep to be able to do it. I know you believe, even with all that fighting me and fighting yourself, you believe. In the old ways. In mountain magic being more powerful than all that's evil. You gotta trust it, though."

Emme looked straight into Della's eyes. "I trust you."

"That's good, but you gotta trust yourself, too."

"In what way?"

Emme found it comforting that, despite her being so old, Aunt Della had enough strength left to speak more, and with vim and vigor, too. Any other person her age would've grown silent by then, napping away.

"The mountain gift, Emme, that's the way you is powerful. But also know when it ain't enough. Our powers can't undo all of what came before. Folks dying. All those that you done loved so much. I won't call them gone, but they changed and you can't be with them now in the same way, so you is still grieving. But you got to make peace with it before it kills you."

"Why? I'm doing okay. I've had enough peace to go on."

"Not enough. You gotta have more. So you don't be going around haunted all the time. You can't never turn back the days. Them seasons keep turning and keep seeking their own balance. You gotta face it, your mistakes, what you missed before you go missing more.

You gotta go get that girl. The itty bitty one just like her daddy. You know which one."

Emme knew Della meant Mattie.

"I seen her. I seen you with her, too, all twisted up, dying a little right there when you first saw her. You were haunted and crazy with grief almost like half your town done gone mad. I know how many done gone crazy, even those not speaking about it. Don't I, Deirdre? You haven't told everybody, have you? What you seen, sister?"

Fi turned to her mother as Deirdre made her way to the stained-glass window. Deirdre reached up and touched it, rubbing her fingers over the panoply of colors until she became still. Emme watched her and thought she looked ten years younger, the way the colors from the stained glass touched her face.

Everyone watched Deirdre as she started to speak.

"Yes, Della, I went a bit crazy, too, but didn't tell no one. Fi knew. Part of it. I done known you felt it all the way up this mountain, though. Knowing you was with me was one of the things that helped me through it."

Emme bristled. If she was willing to admit it, on some level she, too, had known about Deirdre losing her mind the night that half the town lost their minds, too. Right before Cy died. She couldn't explain any of it, but Emme knew she was going to have to share it with her family, even if it defied all logic.

Damn, Emme thought. Della's always right.

"Sister, I was with you, it be true. I'll be with Emme when she goes to all the town leaders, too. Not in the flesh mind you, but I'll be there in the way you know I'm always with you. She's gotta convince them. It's the only way to stop the madness."

Fi started crying. She intuitively knew what was coming, what Della would tell them about Kelly.

Emme swallowed. She felt sick again, but didn't want to throw up in the middle of Della's beautiful little house.

"Aunt Della, convince them of what?"

Emme was still in awe of Della as she once again started to speak and so many words poured strongly out of her mouth in what seemed like one breath.

"They got to believe the women. Believe every woman from now on. They didn't believe Kelly. You know that, Emme. Cy forced hisself on her. You tried to tell them at the police station, but they didn't do nothing about it. This is man's sin right here. Or I should say men's sin. Not only the men who hurt women in the flesh, but the men who pretend it don't exist. They been hurting the women, too, by not believing them."

Emme stared, dumbfounded, as Della spoke.

"They gotta change and you gotta make them. That's the right thing to do, even if Kelly can't go free. I suspect it'll help with that, too, but even if she's locked away forever, the haunting will stop, the killing will stop if you can convince some of those leaders down there to do the right thing. If not, more shades and revenants will be coming around the bend."

Fi kept crying. She hadn't known the worst thing that had happened to her own baby. At least not consciously. She'd seen when Cy had hit her. Fi had tried and tried to talk Kelly into coming back home every time he beat her. Fi finally talked her into coming back home at the end. But she didn't know about the rape.

Something occurred to Fi then and she stopped crying. She realized that Kelly hadn't told her because she thought it would've likely killed her. After Fi'd lost so much, her husband and all the others. The thought of Kelly being so brave for her sake was almost more than she could take. Fi knew she couldn't completely fall apart, though. Kelly needed her more than ever. So she just gritted her teeth.

Emme stood up. "Aunt Della, of course I tried to do that before. To convince them to lock Cy up. It didn't work."

Della didn't seem angry when she spoke next, but she was forceful.

"Well, now the Red River done bled all over the whole town and

Cy's gone, good riddance, and half the town is crazier than anyone's ever seen, so they'll listen this time. You just gotta be strong enough to stir up the hornet's nest again. That's the only way to get the balance back."

Emme wanted something more concrete. The journalist in her demanded answers.

"But who killed Cy, Aunt Della? We all know Kelly didn't do it, even if she confessed. She couldn't have. Not with the extent of her injuries. And they told me about what they found at the crime scene. There's no way she did all that."

Emme could tell that Della was finally getting tired, as her words were softer, even though she still spoke at length.

"Oh, honey, you done known it all along. You know what happened to Cy. You felt it all the way in DC just as I did up on this mountain. Now you gotta let yourself believe it."

Emme wanted to completely understand what Della was saying, so she leaned in even closer to her great-aunt.

"That's part of the balance, too, Emme. You gonna be off-kilter until you admit all the truths you done known deep down for so long. But that's all I can tell you now. I'm tired. You gotta go back now and get your house straight. Balanced. Come here and kiss an old woman goodbye like it's gonna be the last time we meet this side of heaven. Tell me you love me true."

They had all congregated by the door near the end of the conversation and were standing in a circle, holding hands. Fi and Deirdre broke the circle first to kiss Della on the cheek. They wrapped their arms around her and told her they loved her true.

Then they opened the door and stood just outside it as Emme wrapped herself into Della. She didn't wrap her arms around her great-aunt, but let herself be enveloped by the woman she believed was wiser than anyone she'd ever met.

Emme could smell rosemary on her and a bit of chicory coffee. She loved those smells. Emme didn't want to leave. She didn't want to have to keep the promises she'd made, either, but she always kept her word. As Della unwrapped Emme from her arms and walked her great-niece out the door, she smiled and cried at the same time. All four women looked around at each other and spontaneously started singing Bill Monroe's version of "Wayfaring Stranger."

When they finished, Della had her eyes closed, as if it was too much to bear to watch them drive off. She put her fingers to her lips, about to blow them kisses, but instead kept her hand on her mouth, keeping any last words locked in.

They all repeated, "I love you, Della," and "Thank you, Della," before they got in the car. The moment they started driving down Black Mountain, they stopped talking, and let Della's words resonate within them.

CHAPTER 5

UNLIKE THE silent trip to Della's, driving back to Red River everyone chattered. There was simply no other way to bear the burden of all that had happened and all they still had to do. Fi and Deirdre told Emme they knew she was glad to be down on flatter ground. They swore, yet again, that they didn't know how a girl half-raised on a mountain could be afraid of heights.

Then they let Emme pick a radio station and she found one that played a mix. They heard Annie Lennox, U2, and an old Elvis song. Then came the Indigo Girls, one of Emme's favorites, and she sang along to "Closer to Fine." Emme contemplated the Indigo Girls's ancestry.

"I believe they're from Georgia, but listen to that harmony. I get chills. Don't you think they could've been from our mountains? I wonder if we went far enough back, we'd find out we were kin?"

Then they heard Madonna and an old Queen number, then an even older Stones song, then right back to country crossover with Shania Twain's "You're Still the One."

"Aunt Deirdre, I can't believe you're letting me get away with listening to all these modern songs."

"I ain't got time to be explaining it all to you, but you know it deep down anyway like you know everything else."

"And what's that?"

"Sometimes the styles be different, sometimes these folks seem mighty modern, but most of what we been listening to, they got old souls. I can hear the ache in them songs. I know that ache."

"I can hear it, too. When I hear it the most, that's usually when I see . . ." Emme paused for a good long while.

Deirdre laughed. "Go on and say it. No use denying what Della done called you out on. Say it loud, child."

"When I hear that ache the most, that's when I see more things, too."

"Della knew that. Fi and I knew it, too. Just one person in this here car be needing to know it better."

"Yes, ma'am. But it's time for some more songs. I'm going to crank up the radio, so get ready."

They listened to loud music. After a while, despite Deirdre and Fi having taken it all in easily, Emme knew her aunts had had all they could take of the modern sounds. She put in another tape. Carter Family songs. Emme thought that there had never been a recording that beat the Carters' version of "Can the Circle Be Unbroken."

The cantankerous Deirdre departed as she sweetly said, "Oh, Emme. I do be loving the Carters." Then she sang joyfully.

Emme and Fi joined Deirdre with enormous voices that aligned so perfectly with those on the tape that they, too, could have been members of the Carter Family. Their blood harmony was tightly interwoven, and they knew they were somehow distant kin.

Emme thought that maybe, then, the Carters and the Indigo Girls could be kin, too. Emme imagined them harmonizing flawlessly with each other. So many people from Eastern Kentucky could trace their families back to Scotland and Ireland, just as so many folks in Virginia, Tennessee, and Georgia. Like the Carters. And the

Indigo Girls. Everybody was kin around the Appalachian Mountains if you traced it back far enough. It made Emme realize that everybody everywhere was kin if you traced it back far enough.

Even though they hadn't stayed for lunch at Della's, they didn't want to stop for a long time. No one was really hungry until the sun set. They still had a couple hours before they got home, so they pulled over at a Cracker Barrel. They had old-fashioned meatloaf, mashed potatoes, and greens with coffee.

Despite feeling a push—almost an actual physical force—propelling them forward, to rush back home and fix things for Kelly and the whole town, they needed a bit more space between them and Red River. They had to get their minds and hearts situated so they could face what they needed to face. Especially Emme. To her, it seemed as if ever since she'd first heard about the sickness in Red River, everything had been rushing forward. The past couple of days weren't only starting to blur, they were making everything and everyone blur, too. Emme most of all.

So they sat quietly for a spell after supper with their coffees. They let all the movement of the waitresses and travelers coming and going speak for them. But before they got back in the car for the last leg of their trip, Emme knew she had to tell them what they all knew now from Della, but from her perspective.

"You know I couldn't tell you. Kelly made me promise. But, yeah, that's why I came home four years ago. When Cy attacked her so badly. Please forgive me for not telling you."

Color drained from Fi's face.

"There's nothing to forgive. I know why she didn't want me and Mama to know."

"Aunt Fi . . ."

"It's okay."

"Are you sure?"

"Yes. Kelly thought it'd kill us, knock us flat over if she told us or if you did. Now, though, we're all having to fight to save Kelly, so I suppose I have no choice but to deal with it."

Fi's next words were spoken with the voice of a wounded animal. She sounded as if she were the only person in the restaurant because the keening quality of her words, while not loud, rose above all the other noise. Sharp grief cut through everything else.

"Oh dear God, this mess, this horrific mess. I guess I knew on some level, though. I have to confess that. I'm a mama. Sweet Kelly's mama. I knew something horrible had happened. But I also knew she couldn't bear to talk to me about it, so I had to let it be, for her sake. Though it about killed me."

Emme was afraid of what her aunt would say next.

"Now Cy's dead. Thankfully. That helps. Though why I let Kelly go back over to his house alone to fetch her paintings, I'll never know."

"I'm sure Kelly talked you into it. I think we all wanted to see her get back to her painting and take it seriously."

"I honestly don't know. I can't hardly remember. I think I've tried to block that whole night out of my mind. I do know, though, that you don't need forgiving, Emme."

"I hope that's true."

"I'm the one who needs to be forgiven, for thinking such a thing. I'm glad Cy's dead."

Deirdre, her rage blatant, added, "That bastard. Ain't no use mincing words, Fi. Damn him!"

Emme wasn't shocked by the cussing or that Deirdre would take a hard stance against Cy. Emme loved her ferocious aunt.

"Sometimes there ain't no other way, Emme. None of us would've blamed Kelly if she'd done killed Cy. Not for what he done to her and for what she knew he was gonna do to her, kill her dead for leaving him. But we know she didn't do it."

Emme realized she had to tell them everything then.

"The time before. Before Cy died. When she eventually moved back in with you. She called me in the middle of the night. She waited until Cy had drunk himself to sleep and then she snuck to the phone. I knew it was something horrible because it was one in the morning. She said that I needed to come home. Somehow I knew and didn't need to ask for details."

Emme was, in that moment, resigned to admitting even more of what Della had told her about her mountain gift.

"Della's right, I guess. We know things. I certainly did then. I told her I was on my way. I'd never packed faster. I thought if I started driving straight through, I could be there before I could catch a flight out. It was supposed to take over eleven hours. It took me ten. I stopped twice for some gas and coffee and to go to the restroom. I made it by midmorning Friday."

Emme shook her head in disgust.

"Cy had gone into work like nothing had happened. Just told her she needed to straighten up. I asked if she needed to go to the hospital, but she said the bleeding had stopped."

Emme started rearranging the salt and pepper shakers on the table.

"Are you sure you want me to tell you all of this? It's horrible."

Fi and Deirdre both quickly said, "Yes."

"Kelly told me it was such a good thing she'd been taking birth control pills. Cy had been yelling at her for failing to give him an heir for so long. But all along she'd been sneaking birth control pills. She said almost from the beginning he'd been attacking her, and, as much as she wanted a baby, no baby should come into the world that way."

Emme didn't want to start crying again, so she started pounding on her own leg underneath the table. The pain helped to distract her so she could finish telling her aunts what they needed to know.

"It took me two hours to convince her that the only thing to do was to go to Everett. We all thought he was good. Practically family.

He'd had to lock Cy up for public drunkenness before and the neighbors had called the police more than once when they heard Cy beating Kelly up."

Emme stopped and Fi urged her on with the slightest nod.

"We knew Kelly hated being in that neighborhood with all those huge houses on tiny lots so close together."

Deirdre nodded vigorously. "She done hated it there, but go on."

"Kelly always said she didn't have breathing room. She didn't care about luxurious finishes or anything like that. She wanted more trees. Ponds. But I swear, having neighbors so close was good when it came to them hearing Kelly screaming as Cy beat her."

Emme, as hard as it was, looked directly into Fi's eyes.

"I don't have to tell you that she never pressed charges, though. She'd go home to you for a few days after every time he beat her. Up until the end."

"You're right. She'd be back home and I'd try to talk her into pressing charges, beg her to leave him."

"I would, too. Every single time she called me. But then he'd come sweet-talking his way back and she was over there again in no time. I know you all thought he was the devil, the way he could be so charming with Kelly when he wanted to be."

A little color had come back into Fi's face. Emme knew it was rage over Cy.

"Somehow, though, the last time she called me in DC, I knew she was finally ready to turn him in. Or she wouldn't have called me, at least not so late. Because the wounds were so much worse that time, the ones no one could see."

Emme had to pound even harder on her leg before she spoke her next words.

"Kelly could never tell you all of it. It was as if she loved you too much, knew it would hurt you too much."

Emme glanced at Deirdre. She imagined her great-aunt taking a pitchfork after Cy.

"I also know Kelly thought one of you would want to kill him and she didn't want that, either. So I took her to Everett. She just flat out said Cy had raped her. No mincing words. No crying. Just 'Cy. Raped. Me.'"

Fi banged her fist against the table. Emme thought her aunt's hand was surely going to be bruised from the force.

"Everett didn't believe her, did he? That's what Aunt Della said."

"It's not that he didn't believe her. He'd been out there himself on a few of those calls to their house. He knew Cy was a son of a bitch, violently drunk. It's just that, according to him, them being married made it difficult. The rape part. He said he didn't know how that could ever stand up in a court of law."

Fi lifted her hand to beat the table again, but Deirdre reached over and gently stopped her.

"Everett kept saying, 'But you're married to him. Maybe if you'd divorced him and then said this happened. But you're married to him. I don't think that constitutes rape. Not in the eyes of the law. It'll be 'he said, she said' in the courtroom. You'll never win the case. No DA would even pick it up to begin with. Cy and his family, you know they own half the county."

Emme wanted to jump up and run away from the table. Instead, she kept smoothing the hair behind her ears. She fidgeted more with the salt and pepper shakers. The thought of what Kelly did after she heard Everett made Emme feel sick again. But she had to forge ahead. She had to tell her aunts all of it.

"I told Kelly that it was time to get a divorce. That she could move back home. But, instead, she collapsed onto the floor."

Fi looked like she, too, was going to collapse on the floor, but she told Emme to go on.

"Everett tried to catch her. I tried to catch her. I had one of my visions then, so, yeah, I saw something. Even without hearing any music at first, I saw something. I'm tired of holding that in. Della's right. Of course I still hear and see things."

Deirdre, unusually tentative, gently asked, "What did you see, Emme?"

"I could see some part of her spirit float up out of her. It was dazzling. Then I heard a song, too. I heard my old friend from school, Jackson Malloy, on the banjo, clear as day. They all have their own fingerprints, no two musicians play the same way. I knew it was Jackson immediately."

Fi simply asked, "And?"

"But the music stopped, and I couldn't see her spirit anymore when she was in that heap on the floor. I don't know where her light went. I looked around the whole room for it. I still don't know how she wound up on the floor. We couldn't catch her. She didn't want to be caught. She looked up at nothing for a second, up into space like we weren't there. Then her eyes focused on us as we bent over to help her up and she said she couldn't divorce him. That he'd kill her."

Emme's voice got quieter as she went on.

"Everett said they wouldn't let that happen, but Kelly said no one could stop him. As she got back up off the floor, she said there was nothing else to be done, she was better off going back. The crazy thing is, she didn't even cry then. Nothing. She simply walked out the door."

Gnarled words came from Fi. "My sweet girl. Giving up like that."

Emme tried to reassure her aunt.

"You both know I then stayed the longest I've ever stayed on a vacation at home. Cy wouldn't let me stay with Kelly. I knew there'd be more violence than before if I pushed on that matter. I told you guys that I wanted to start a side photography project, remember? Something more along the lines of the art photographs I'd done in graduate school before I started for the paper. With the two series, one of the old barns and the other with the musical instruments."

"Child," Deirdre said. "We knew you was lying to us. You only took a few photographs, but kept going over to Kelly's or begging her to come to us. I knew something was going on, something real bad. But I kept my mouth shut and figured Kelly wanted your help with it, not ours."

"Those three weeks about killed me, Aunt Deirdre. I couldn't understand why she was resigned to staying with him. He was good again, for a while, I believe. Same song, different verse. He could always become almost calm again, the gallant gentleman, even after one of his rage binges. That's what I called it. A rage binge."

"Hell yes, a rage binge. Damn the bastard and his rage binges."

"Mama, normally I'd scold you for the cussing. But not now. What else, Emme?"

"I knew it wouldn't last. Cy being good. Eventually, and this is what I hate myself most for, I think some part of me gave up on Kelly just as Kelly gave up on herself. I couldn't keep fighting with her. That's when I left. It's one of the things I'm most ashamed of."

"You ain't been back since. Now I know why. I knew it wasn't all Evan getting killed."

"Yes, Kelly was why. Part of why."

Emme started talking in fragmented sentences. "But . . . despite everything I love home. All of you. All these people who are my family, not only my blood kin, but the whole town. And the land itself, too. I know I come from this soil as much as I come from all of you. The people and the land. I love it."

"But?" Deirdre asked.

"But I saw what was wrong. All kinds of violence, not only against women like Kelly. So many prejudices that people somehow ignore after all these years. It went all the way back to Evan in high school. And then Evan died."

Emme weighed a salt shaker in one hand and a pepper shaker in the other, then held them up as if offering them to her aunts.

"I guess I gave up in a way just as Kelly did. I felt powerless to change anything. I felt helpless with my own memories. Everyone keeps talking about being haunted, all these banshees and witches running around. I'm haunted, too."

Emme put the salt and pepper shakers down, stared at them before she picked them up again, and then looked directly at her aunts.

"Della's always right, damn it. I really was haunted. Probably still am. Everything in Red River is a memory I can't bear. I wear memory like a second skin, flesh rubbed raw. So I stay in DC where I can peel the past off for a little while, where I can change something."

Deirdre got up, walked around the table and took the salt and pepper shakers out of Emme's hands. Then she took Emme in her arms.

"But did you, Emmeretta? Change things in DC? You probably ain't got the answers yet, do you? Surely you did change some things there, yes, I don't doubt it with you being the spitfire you is. But could it be making up for what you left behind?"

"I honestly don't know."

"There's been deep sadness in your voice, so much broken. Almost as much as Kelly's. I think you done been wearing your memories in DC, too."

"You're right. I haven't forgotten anything there. And I haven't been able to change much for other people, either, to help them. Not really. Not enough. Sadness begets sadness. Here I've been trying to fix the world and I can't even fix myself."

Deirdre gently shook Emme by the shoulders.

"Don't you think that's what you're doing right now? You're fixing Kelly and you're fixing yourself, too."

"I hope so."

"I believe it true, Emmeretta."

Deirdre stretched up as tall as she could, making her height even grander. "We're gonna go now. We'll drive right on back to the farm and sleep a good sleep. I can still feel Della with us like some soft shawl wrapped around me in winter. Let her comfort you, too. She believes in you, child. We all believe in you."

CHAPTER 6

WHEN EMME went back to Red River the next day, she realized that, while she'd talked to Everett on the phone after Kelly was arrested, she hadn't seen him. Not since Kelly had collapsed on the floor.

Although Emme knew Everett hadn't purposefully chosen Cy over Kelly, she was still angry. As sheriff, he should've done more. And now with Kelly handcuffed to a hospital bed, Emme was even more riled up. She didn't want to be too hotheaded, though, so she stood outside looking around.

The police station was in an old building on the square across from the courthouse. The former courthouse structure housed the library. Emme remembered the fair the town had put on in the fall when she was little. All of downtown had hosted a series of booths, even one for apple bobbing. There was also a large dunking booth. Both her parents had still been alive back then. Emme remembered them volunteering, and that they hadn't minded being dunked: they were laughing the whole time. The folks in Red River had gotten together to work on the fair in order to raise the funds to convert the courthouse into the new library. It was one of the memories of Red River that Emme cherished.

That October felt and looked very much like the current October. Emme surveyed what was new and what was still the same. Sadie's Restaurant was now Tilly's, but there was still Lochlan Bank and Loan on the south side of the square and Cece's Hair Salon was on the north side. All the way around the square were the businesses that had been not only the center of life for Emme, but for every single person in Red River. Jessie's sewing store. The only department store, Haskins'. Modene's Malt Shoppe. Stevens' Hardware.

Emme let her eyes rest the longest on Stewart's Drugs, where her mother had gone to get her maxi pads when Emme first started her period. Mrs. Stewart herself was working the counter that day and had a long talk with Emme about becoming a woman. Red River was like that, a place where the drugstore was owned by a sweet family whose wife not only regularly worked the counter but was also your Sunday school teacher. An older lady who felt it was perfectly fine, no, she believed it was her duty, to encourage you and your burgeoning womanhood. In a very polite and dignified way, of course.

When she looked around, Emme didn't only see storefronts. She could picture all the people who owned and ran those stores, and her friends who had worked part-time in them on the weekends. She knew that most of the buildings had been around almost as long as the town itself when it was first founded in 1820.

Some of the houses up and down the four main streets that shot out from the courthouse were that old, too. Emme had witnessed the architectural splendor of historic Washington, DC, had traveled to Boston and New York, and even overseas to London and Milan in college, and more places while she worked at the paper. But Emme knew the simple beauty of her home's downtown was unequaled.

People always said Red River's historic area looked like it belonged on a postcard, especially the picturesque courthouse. And, although it had been a library for almost two decades, Emme still called it *the courthouse* as everyone else did.

Emme knew that Mrs. Maddox was probably working in the

library right then. Knowing that if she contemplated Mrs. Maddox for long, she'd inevitably be overwhelmed by memories of Evan, Emme realized it was less painful for her to go confront Everett, however frightening that was.

She'd barely gotten in the police station door when Porter Mills had his arms around her. Emme wasn't surprised to see her musician friend there because all the news in a small town got around to everyone. The news about Porter had even reached Emme all the way in Washington, DC. She knew that he'd finally given up playing bass guitar in his band and any other group that needed him, though he still did occasional session work in Nashville when he was offered the opportunity. Like Rowdy, seeing Porter in a uniform was comforting. It made Emme hopeful that, despite how little Everett had helped Kelly, there were still a few good folks serving in blue.

"Emmylou Harris and Loretta Lynn . . . Emmeretta, you beautiful lady who has a name that is the perfect combination of two of the finest female musicians the world has ever known. How the hell are you?"

"You are looking mighty fine in that uniform, though I never thought I'd see the day when you chopped off your mullet."

"I miss it, may it rest in peace."

"Fi told me you were gigging less and less and that you finally jumped on over to being a grown-up with working for Everett."

"I don't know if I'm quite a grown-up yet, but I'm trying."

"Good for you. I know Shelby is about to have another baby, so, what, this makes three? No wonder you needed a steady job, though you know I think you're the finest bass player in the world."

"Actually, Shelby is carrying twins, so we'll be having a total of four little ones. Can you believe it? Me with all those kids. Eight and under."

"Heavens, Porter."

"Here I thought I'd tour forever and be picking up the ladies in towns across America, but nobody could ever hold a candle to Shelby. I've been all over and never met a finer lady, other than you."

"Really, I can believe it, you with the wife and kids. You beat the cliché to hell. You were a wonderful musician who didn't use that as an excuse to get in girls' . . . um . . . undergarments."

"Before I was married, maybe once or . . ."

"Okay, so maybe you played music for the ladies a little bit. But you were the real deal. You mostly played for the soul of it."

"So did you. You would bang them keys like you were in a desert banging a stone to get water out. Remember how most of the other musicians back then couldn't get over it that we'd let a girl in the band? But damn if you didn't play better than any dude. No wonder Evan demanded we give you a try."

Porter grinned. His grin was still huge and Emme had missed it. "I loved our band. Those other musicians were sexist pigs to doubt I could play rock music simply because I didn't have a, well, a male part."

"A 'male part'? Penis or no penis, you rocked the keys and everything else."

"I appreciate that." Emme, even though she'd known Porter all her life, felt shy and looked down.

"I still to this day don't know why you had to go off to DC and leave us. And Evan to New York. If he'd left to play guitar, I'd have understood it. But for math? Nope."

Porter rubbed the tiny bit of stubble on his chin as he talked.

"But, look at me talk. I suppose I'm finally leaving music, too, for a steady paycheck to feed all those babies. Really, it's *paychecks* with an *s*. Red River is still too small to need more than a few deputies beyond the sheriff, so me and a few others are part-time. I also work for the fire department and the rescue service."

Emme looked back up at Porter and said, "That's a lot of jobs, but I'm proud of you."

"Yeah, Evan would bust a gut if he could see me now with so many real jobs. Still can't get over it, though. Him in New York for math."

"You of all people know that Evan did everything his own way. He always had his feet in two worlds at the same time. But to him, music was math and vice versa, so it was all the same, gigging or math formulas."

"Evan and you, you two were . . ."

Porter was going to elaborate on Evan and Emme together until he saw Emme's face, how it tightened. Then he started fumbling for words.

"Well, I mean as in Evan and you, well, I guess . . . and me . . . but . . . no, no, shouldn't forget . . . and the, Toad and Munchy . . . I mean, uh, Todd and Mikey."

Emme was grateful to be able to tease Porter because it helped her forget Evan. "Porter, I can't believe you'd still call them that. Calling Todd that was mean, well, I know you were kidding, but it wasn't your funniest joke. And Mike gave up the weed a long time ago. A preacher now and everything is what I heard."

"Yep. You heard right."

"I was just looking around the square and thinking that hardly anything had changed, but I guess it really has, hasn't it?"

"Plenty's changed. Some better. Some worse."

"Some much worse. Which is why I'm here."

"I'm so sorry about Kelly. I don't believe for a second that she did it."

"Thank you."

"If she did, between you and me, I don't blame her. I know I'm 'the law' now and not supposed to say that, but come on. I know what Cy was like. Everybody did."

"Worst kept secret in this town, the way he beat her. See, another thing that's never changed. Lots of folks know other folks' business around here, and that's not always good. But when everybody knows something bad is going on and no one does anything about it? That's despicable."

Emme rubbed her hands together as if she were trying to warm them before she spoke again. "But I don't want this to get too negative. Not with you."

"You do whatever you need to do."

Emme's face brightened. "I just remembered . . . my aunts and I were listening to the original Porter the other night. Is your daddy still nuts about him?"

"Absolutely. Though you'd be surprised. He's taken a liking to some new folks, too. Well, they still sound old to him or he wouldn't like them. He sure does love Travis Tritt."

Porter cleared his throat a little then.

"I could talk with you all day, but I know you have to be here to see Everett. He's out, though. I can have Sharlene leave him a note saying you stopped by. He's expecting you."

"I bet he is. Fearing me coming is more like it. But before I get into that, could I ask you for a favor real fast, please?"

"Sure."

"Could I use your phone to make a long-distance call to DC? I promise to make it quick, but I need to call my editor."

Porter walked Emme to his desk and handed her the phone. "Be my guest."

Emme then called Richard. Sitting in the police station with Porter had reminded her of her time at the paper when she'd covered the crime beat. She realized she hadn't touched base with Richard and she knew he would be frantic, though she wasn't worried about that. She just needed to end it all with him. She'd made up her mind on the way down the mountain after seeing Della. She knew she'd never work with Richard again and she didn't care that everyone in the police station could hear her tell him that. As she neared the end of her conversation, he tried to convince her to stay at the paper. She told him no, she was quitting, that she wouldn't snoop on her own town, her own family. She wanted to find another paper to work for, a place with integrity.

When Emme put the phone down and walked back to Porter, she still looked angry. "And I'm coming for Everett next, so he best be ready."

Porter shuffled his feet.

"I know you really want to talk to him, Emme, but I don't know how much he can do."

Porter stepped over to his desk. Emme leaned against it while he sat in his chair.

"That's the problem," she said. "He's never been able to do much."

"This whole thing is just so weird, though. Kelly confessed. But there's no way she could've done it."

"I definitely agree with you on that."

"A whole bunch of us have been out to the crime scene, and there's no way in hell that Kelly's guilty. That's my professional opinion, too."

"I believe you're right. But why exactly do you think that?"

"We saw the wall. It's tall, two stories. One of those modern things. Well, you know, you've been there. I personally can't stand them, even if I could afford them. Too weird looking with entryways being two stories. Give me an old house any day of the week."

"Kelly felt the same way about that house."

"I'll say it again. No way Kelly did it. No woman—or man for that matter—could've done it, either."

"So why she's cuffed to her hospital bed?"

"Because she confessed. But I guess you know that, or you wouldn't be here."

"Her confession is ludicrous. She was delirious, beaten half-dead when she 'confessed.' It's complete bullshit!"

Emme didn't curse much, but when she did, her voice didn't become shrill. It became more resonant and commanding.

"Hell, Porter, everybody knows she didn't do it. But if she didn't, and you say nobody could've, not even another man, then why is she still in cuffs? What actually happened?"

Emme had to move again. Porter got up, and they walked together out the front door.

"That's the big question. This is just one more bizarre thing happening. All this weird shit. Oh, sorry for the language."

"You just heard me, so I'm not one to judge. Especially not with Aunt Deirdre cussing up a storm, so go on."

"All this weird stuff has been happening. Half the town claiming they saw or heard ghosts and witches. People going insane. Really insane. I even thought Shelby was going to have the baby early."

"What?"

"She had real bad pains, worse than even her labor pains with our first baby, when the other women got sick. She was afraid, anxious even before everything happened, and that's not like her. Shelby says she's from sturdy stock, and she's right. She didn't see anything herself, but she keeps saying she felt something. When I ask her what, she says she doesn't know."

"I'm so sorry. Please tell Shelby I'm thinking about her."

"Thank you. But you know, it's no wonder news trucks have been over not only from Bowling Green, but up from Nashville, and all sorts of places."

"Word definitely got out fast."

"No one's ever seen anything like it here. People up from Atlanta and the CDC checking the water, thinking there could be some mass poisoning or something like that."

"That's part of the reason the news made it to me at the paper, before I found out about Kelly. Crazy stuff."

"Mass poisoning is less crazy than me believing that we're being haunted."

"That's what I told my editor, too." Emme suddenly realized how free she felt being rid of Richard for good. Now, if she could only help set Kelly free, too. Emme knew that would really make her feel better.

"But this thing with Kelly. Bizarre as shit. Oh, sorry. There I went again. You know I could hardly ever control my language."

"You don't have to apologize to me. In DC I have editors who drop a swear word because they think it's a lovely descriptive word. It doesn't offend me."

"As weird as it is now and as weird as it was before, with all that happened with Evan and everything else, I still don't think Red River could ever be as weird as Washington, DC."

"Like every other place, DC has its good parts and its bad parts."

"I played up there once, in a blues group I had on the side. We played at the 9:30 Club. Aw, shit, you remember. I called you when I got there, but you were on a story."

"I'm sorry, I really was working. I would've loved to have seen you."

"It's okay. Anyway, DC was weird. In its own way. Not that I hate it. I just don't see how you could've stayed there for so long."

"We don't have enough time for me to explain all of it. So you just have to trust me."

"But it's not you. All that noise. For some people, that's heaven. But I know you. You love trees, rivers, farmland, and mountains."

"I could get to trees and rivers when I needed to."

"But you didn't sing anymore, either. I really don't get it. I'm not trying to be mean. You're the sister I never had. It's just I never got it and I still don't."

"You're not the first person to give me that speech. This isn't even the first time you've given it to me. I think it's the third time you've asked me how I could've stayed in DC."

"I guess I've lost count."

"I have the same answer for you now as all the other times. I had no choice. Like I said, I keep fighting myself on this. Sometimes convinced I did the right thing. Sometimes not."

"Honestly, in the end it's your choice. No pressure. I trust you. Always have, always will. And I know it was so tough with Evan."

Emme had to turn away from Porter when he mentioned Evan again. She stood with her back to her old friend with her eyes closed until she could turn back around.

"I love you, Porter, you know I do. But I truly can't talk any more about Evan. I've got to focus on Kelly."

"I miss him, too, you know."

"But I've got to hunt Everett down and talk some sense into him. To try to get Kelly out of those handcuffs. It's insane."

As they talked, Emme and Porter left the front of the station and started walking around the square.

"You are preaching to the choir. But there are all kinds of legal technicalities. Because of all this bizarre stuff, everyone is watching Red River. Everett can't slip up in any way. The reporters are out to get him. At least that's what it feels like."

"Oh, I know that part. I fought hard with my editor and you heard the fallout. I never in a million years thought he'd ask me to cover a story in Red River."

"No one ever paid us much attention until now, did they? Well, not since the car accident . . . all those semis and everyone else. That got a lot of news. I remember . . ."

"Porter . . ."

"But, um, I won't bring that up now. Sorry."

"You know why I can't talk about it."

"I understand."

"Thank you."

"So, the thing is, Everett and the DA are in a tight spot. They're trying to follow all the rules, what with everybody watching us so closely."

"Why exactly are they watching Everett, though? The town I get. But him specifically?"

"The outside powers that be found out pretty quickly that he's friends with your family, which means he's friends with Kelly."

"Everybody's friends with everybody here."

"He can't show favoritism, and she did confess. Multiple people heard her."

"Ah, the 'confession.'"

"They have to go before a judge. But she can't do that yet, so they have to cuff her in the meantime. I know it's ridiculous, but that's the way it is."

"That's the way it is, is it?"

Emme had to stop herself from running back to her car. Or into a store. Anywhere. But she turned instead and glared at Porter.

"You and everybody around here have always loved to say, 'That's the way it is.' You want to know why I left and never came back much?"

"Of course. But I think it's more than just me wanting to know, Emme."

"The answer to that question is obvious. I can't stand the status quo. The idea that time keeps marching forward but all the bad things in this town keep on being the same. Yes, there's more beauty here than anyone in a big city could ever understand. But there are still so many things wrong, too. Everyone just rolls over and accepts it."

"Is DC really any better? Aren't there good and bad people there, too?"

"I don't know. It always felt like I could do more in DC."

"Then why come back now? If you really believe you can't change anything here, then why waste the time to come back? Ever?"

"Because this is my family. Even if I can't do anything, I should be here. I could never live with myself if I weren't. Not with what happened to Kelly."

"Then how could you live with what happened to Evan?"

"I can't believe you just said that."

Emme smoothed down her hair frantically, as if it'd been disheveled by a windstorm.

"I know you were close to him just like I was. You thought he was family. That's all. I know I should drop this."

"Yes, you should. Please."

"Maybe you can tell me what you love about DC so much, maybe that'd help."

"I certainly wouldn't stay there if it was all bad. Do you want to hear some of its good parts?"

"Okay."

"When I went to college, I had roommates. Some of them are still dear friends. They were from all over the world. Georgetown is international. My friends were Jewish and Muslim as well as Christian and Hindu. Some were atheists and agnostics. They were black, brown, white, and every other variation. All living together, working together. Loving each other. Don't laugh at me for saying that, either, Porter."

"I won't laugh, I promise."

"Good, because I'd hate to have to slap you."

"I'd probably deserve it, but go on. No laughing from me."

"The closest we got to that kind of thing, with everybody working together and being close no matter what their ethnicity, was in high school with our band. With Evan being in there with us. And we both know that caused problems. But most of the time it was good."

"Yeah, and half the time I forgot that anyone was a different color than anyone else. We concentrated on the music."

"That's how all of DC was for me. One of my best friends in college, Sammy, was the finest painter I've ever met. He encouraged me more than anyone else with my photography. I probably wouldn't have had a career without him. If I ever had gotten married, I would have had him in my wedding. And you know what?"

"Let it out, Emme."

"He proudly proclaims from the rooftops that he's the gayest man ever and tells me all the time that he's prettier than I am. And he is. Let me tell all of Red River. I'll shout it. Sammy is prettier than me!"

Porter had to smile when Emme spread her arms out wide as she described her friend.

"And you know I go way back with Jimmy and cousin Beth right here in Red River. I never turned my back on him when he came out, even though I thought our tiny town was going to explode with the gossip from it all. Or maybe even kill him for being different. But not in DC. So many people in a great big melting pot like we studied in history. That was Georgetown."

Emme stopped waving her arms around, but her words were still loud and large.

"Honestly, it was glorious. I learned so much, to trust and love people who were very different from me. Here in Red River, for all the wonderful people, you know it's very much still segregated."

"I don't know if I'd put it exactly like that." Porter transferred his hat back and forth between his hands.

"How would you put it, then? It's been years since things legally changed."

"Yeah, segregation has been illegal for a long time. Everett wouldn't tolerate it. He'd arrest anyone at any business that tried that shit."

"But in our actual everyday lives there's still tons of segregation. There are white churches and black churches. Black people live in one part of town and white people in another. Most of the top jobs belong to white people. No black people live in the northern part of the county. The one time a new black family moved in, it didn't end well. Remember when we got a new science teacher, Mr. Tyler?"

"Of course."

Porter scowled because he knew what Emme was going to say.

"He thought he could rent property in the northern part of our county. But the folks up there, they burned a cross. Porter, the KKK came out and rode around the square here, then turned north and burned a cross in Mr. Tyler's front yard. He had to move. He never came back. Our county scared off a fantastic science teacher. All because of the color of his skin. That was in 1987. Not 1887."

Porter had to fight smiling at Emme, who had practically stomped her foot when she said 1887, as she had back in high school when they disagreed over how to play a song.

Porter opened his mouth as if he was about to speak, then shut it. Then he opened his mouth again, then shut it again. Finally he shook his head and spoke.

"I honestly don't know why things are the way they are. I don't know why there's still so much bigotry or this type of segregation. I certainly don't want it like that."

"In DC I not only was allowed to be friends with people of every color, but I lived with them, and they became my best friends. No one burned a cross in their yard for trying to live with a white girl."

Emme and Porter were standing close together, but neither could look the other in the eye.

Porter rubbed his chin hair stubble some more. "I just don't know how to fix it. At the end of the day, I got less answers than you."

"Just because I talk about the problems in this town, you've got to believe that I know DC has issues, too. I really do. Please trust me that I don't think I'm better than anyone here. I love my home."

"I know you do."

"I'm glad. I promise I didn't abandon y'all. At least not on purpose. I wasn't able to make Evan feel safe, let alone save him or my parents, so how could I stay?"

"No one expected you to save everybody."

"That's good, because I can barely save myself. I thought I had a better chance to make things right in DC, though. Maybe I was just too afraid. Maybe that's my biggest flaw."

"In what way?"

"I don't even think I've begun to scratch the surface of my fear. It's something I've really gotta work on. I'm trying to figure it out, though."

"Then what?"

"All I know for certain is that I love everyone here. But that's all I got for sure at the moment. Maybe I'm not such a great person if after all this time away, that's all I've got to show for it."

"Emme, I'll be believing you're good until the day I die. But how do you feel about yourself?"

"What do you mean?"

"I know I'm just a small-town boy named after an old country singer and I don't know much, but I know you. Or I did. After Marshall was born you sent that present and a sweet letter to me and Shelby."

"I remember."

Emme and Porter started looking at each other again, even though both had difficultly making eye contact.

"But it wasn't you in that letter. You weren't rude, you weren't . . . you. You were polite, but it was just that. Polite. No joy. No sass. That was way before Evan died, too. Over the years there's been so much of that."

"What?"

"You disappearing. And I'm not just talking about you living in DC."

"I don't know what's wrong with me. Sometimes when I feel confused or afraid I get all polite. Not in a good way, but a distant way. I'm sorry."

"I know you don't do it on purpose, but it certainly wasn't you at Evan's funeral, either."

When Porter brought up Evan again, Emme could no longer look at him. She turned her back to him and stepped away, then pivoted back to face him again.

"You can't stop yourself, can you? You have to bring up Evan all the time." As much as Emme loved Porter, she heard the anger that punctuated her words.

"Yes. For Evan. For you. You weren't just sad and grieving like all of us, it was something else. That distant thing you said."

"Maybe."

"But I was too much of a stupid man to figure it out or even be able to ask you. Sometimes I don't have the right words. I don't have them right now." Porter's long arms hung down lax beside him, and it made him look like a boy again, which softened Emme's anger.

"It's okay."

"But I love you. You know I do. I said it before and I'll say it every time I see you. I know you're good, or you're always trying to be."

"I still wish I had more explanations for you. For myself. About the choices I've made. This is all so complicated, though. I guess it was complicated before this hell with Kelly, too."

"I think it's been complicated for a long time."

"Honestly, I think in many ways it's been like that since Evan died, even before. Some time I'll tell you about the day he came to visit me when I was at Georgetown. But I know you probably have to get back now."

When Emme mentioned Porter getting back to work, his body, which had seemed to droop to match the sadness in his voice, sprang into motion again. His arms came up, and his shoulders went back. "Yeah, I actually do. Before I lose my job. You know, me with all those kids and Shelby. I gotta hang on to all the jobs I got."

"I thank you for the time you were able to give me."

"Give me a holler if there's anything I can do."

"The only thing I can think of right now is for you to promise that you believe me. That Red River is still my home. I never stopped loving any of you."

"I believe you, Emme."

CHAPTER 7

EMME HUGGED Porter goodbye and watched him walk back to the police station. Then she went to sit on an old bench in front of the courthouse. There was much to do for Kelly, but talking about Evan had done Emme in.

She reached into the zippered pocket inside her purse and took out the small eight-sided die Evan had given her when he came to visit Emme in DC years before. She hadn't even remembered packing it when she left to help Kelly. The die was blue, but not plain blue. It was cerulean with specks of metallic aqua. She'd always thought it looked like a pyramid sitting on the surface of a lake where its image was reflected perfectly in the water beneath, twinning it.

"Emme."

The way Evan said Emme's name had never left her. In band, in AP Spanish, when they'd rested after track practice. Emme didn't understand why Evan tried to keep their relationship secret when it was obvious he loved her. It came out every time he said her name. Emmeretta Finnegan McLean. Or even when he simply said "Emme." However he said it, it ceased being merely Emme's name. It transformed into mellifluous flowers Evan presented as a gift.

And that's all Evan had said at first, her name, when he walked off the bus. He'd traveled from New York to see Emme in DC. He'd gotten into MIT, which was his first choice, but Columbia had given him a full scholarship, so that's where he'd gone. It only took him a few hours by bus to reach Emme, though. And the moment he walked out, Evan had presented two gifts. Her name and a velvet bag.

Evan had loved working on random number generators and constantly brought different kinds of dice with him. He knew the die he'd brought was Emme's favorite color. He'd never found one exactly that shade of blue, with the aqua bits, until he went to New York. The die had come in a small red velvet bag.

"I hope this will do until I can afford a ring. We're finally out of Red River. We can get married now."

He said it just like that, as soon as he arrived. He quickly pulled out the bag as he was descending the bus, looking at Emme with each step down. He'd never even hugged or kissed her. He said her name once, then grabbed her hand and put the die in it.

Emme thought it was somehow more intimate that way. That he didn't need to say much. Despite that, she didn't answer Evan right away. He stood there waiting for a reply. When Emme finally spoke, she couldn't believe the words coming out of her mouth.

"Evan, no."

Evan didn't respond, he turned and started to go back up the bus steps. Emme had to practically tackle him to get him to come back down and talk to her.

"We haven't even been on a date. You never asked. I would've said yes. Even today you still didn't say you love me. You just proposed. Not even really a proposal. Just a statement that we could get married now. How could I possibly say yes to that?"

"You know I love you. You've always known. Like I've always known you love me, too. You know why I couldn't ask you out in high school."

Emme, still uncomfortable, forced herself to keep looking Evan right in the eyes, in his remarkable, anomalous eyes.

"No, I don't know why. Was it really impossible?"

"When we started in the band together, Brad Dawson cornered me in the boys' locker room. He told me I better not be thinking of mixing the races. That's what he said. 'Mixing the races.' And he had been my friend before that."

"You never told me that."

"He said bad things happen to black boys who mess with white girls."

"I'm going to go back to Red River right now and kick Brad's ass for telling you such a despicable thing."

"But, Emme . . . my own mother told me I better stay away from white girls or I'd be strung up."

"Evan . . ."

"I wish I hadn't been such a coward, but I thought if I waited it out, we'd go away and then our lives could really start. I didn't want to get killed."

"I wouldn't want that, either. Not ever."

"Not that I wouldn't die for you. But then what good would it have done? We wouldn't have been together that way, either. So, here I am now. Both of us in college on the East Coast. Anything is possible now."

Emme had never heard Evan say so many words together, unless he'd been talking about math or music. Emme looked at the buses pulling in and out, staring at the endlessly blurring silver shapes. She let her eyes stop on a red, white, and blue logo of a bus idling nearby until she looked back up at Evan.

"But we can't even get married right away. We don't have any money. We have to finish school. We have to keep our grades up so we don't lose our scholarships. I love you. You're right. But can't you slow this thing down a bit?"

Emme kept looking at Evan, but he couldn't maintain eye contact.

"Come down every weekend, or I'll take the bus up to see you. We can switch off. We can finally go on a real date. You could actually kiss me. I'd even let you talk about math for the entire date."

Emme tried to laugh as she said the last words, but felt kicked in the stomach. Emme loved Evan, but she was afraid. Not afraid of what people would think, but afraid of the speed things were going.

Emme thought back to when Evan had helped her with physics, how he'd explained acceleration. Emme believed that was the basis of her stomach pain. The fast rate at which Evan was switching the direction of their relationship was shocking to her. Emme liked to plan things. She felt safer with details. Evan was moving faster than the speed of light.

And just as swiftly as Evan had come and radically altered the path of their relationship with his abrupt proposal standing outside of a Greyhound bus, he disappeared from Emme's life.

After Emme had talked about dating instead of being engaged, Evan kissed her on the forehead. He looked her right in the eyes and said, "I'm sorry. I was wrong to do this. Just never doubt that I loved you."

Then Evan got back on the bus. Everything about him, his straight back, the tight muscles in the side of his neck, his clenched jaw, all of it said he didn't want Emme to talk to him anymore that day. He didn't want to compromise.

So Emme let him go. She'd thought they'd work it out later. But he'd never returned her letters or phone calls. When she went home for Christmas break, she heard from Porter that he was seriously dating a girl he'd met at Columbia and was still in New York with her. By spring break, Porter told her that Evan had asked the girl to marry him and she'd said yes. They married the summer after their junior year. Emme wasn't invited to the wedding.

After coming back to Kentucky and hearing everything Della had told her and now Porter, too, Emme realized it wasn't only practicalities that had stopped her from saying yes to Evan's proposal.

Emme could finally admit that she had simply been afraid. Afraid of what a life with Evan would be like, at least if they ever returned to Red River. She didn't want to live in fear, waiting for some horrible thing to happen to Evan all because he was black and she was white. Emme also didn't want to worry about what people thought of them. Finally admitting it all to herself, Emme knew she should feel ashamed. And she did.

Emme stood up, but immediately tumbled back onto the bench. Her legs gave way. She rested her head against the back of the bench. To anyone looking at her, it must've seemed as if she was taking a rest, sitting on a bench outside on a perfect fall day.

Emme stayed like that for almost an hour, not even crying, just letting the guilt of her stupid, immature fear weigh her down, trapping her on the bench. To Emme, her guilt and fear weighed ten thousand pounds. Emme didn't know if forgiving herself would ever be possible. Della had told her she had to, but Emme couldn't see how.

Emme finally got up from the bench. She knew she needed to stop thinking about Evan because she couldn't change the past. She had to hunt Everett down and fix things for Kelly. But she knew she wouldn't be able to focus on her family until she spoke with Mrs. Maddox again. Emme realized it wouldn't be the same as talking to Evan, but it was as close as she could get. So she got up off the bench and walked over to the library.

Inside, Emme went to the front desk and asked if Mrs. Maddox was in. Mrs. Kerner, in her gray skirt and lavender sweater, her typical uniform, was volunteering just as she'd done several days a week for the past forty years.

"Mrs. Maddox is back in her office. I hope Kelly's doing better."

"Thank you, Mrs. Kerner."

Emme maintained her politeness even though Mrs. Kerner's eyes had squinted as she said Kelly's name. Emme could tell that Mrs. Kerner thought Kelly was guilty, but wasn't offended. As sweet as

Mrs. Kerner could sometimes be, it didn't surprise Emme that Cy's murder had brought out Mrs. Kerner's less-than-empathetic nature. Every town had a few busybodies.

Emme went to the back of the library and knocked on Mrs. Maddox's door for a while with no answer. Emme got worried and opened the door to check on things. She found Mrs. Maddox on the floor sitting with her back up against the wall. She opened her eyes and looked directly at Emme.

"Now don't you go being all worried, Emmeretta. I'm alive. I was just resting down here. I got a little dizzy and took a tumble, but we got the new carpet in here last year and it's so nice I thought I'd just sit here a spell. Making sure I was steady when I got back up."

"Oh my heavens, Mrs. Maddox, please let me help."

Mrs. Maddox started shaking her head no.

"Emme, dear, I didn't know it was you when you knocked. I was hoping it was Mrs. Kerner and she'd assume I was deep into a book. I was a little winded for a few seconds and couldn't quite get the words out to say, 'Please come back in a few minutes.'"

Emme went right over to Mrs. Maddox. "Do you think you're steady enough to sit up in your chair if I help you?"

"I think that would be mighty fine. Yes, please." Emme helped lift Mrs. Maddox up and walked her the few steps to her chair. As soon as she sat down, Mrs. Maddox reached for the mug that was on her desk and started drinking from it.

"I think I only need some of this water. And, please, if you don't mind, would you bring that chair around here? I'll put my feet up and that'll surely help, too. Thank you, dear."

Emme got Mrs. Maddox situated.

"You might think I fibbed the other day after seeing me like this. I really was at the hospital to see a friend from church, though. But I might as well get it all out now, because you'll hear soon enough anyway."

Emme had always heard of people holding their breaths while

they received bad news, but had never consciously done it herself until that moment. She gulped in air and then held it as Mrs. Maddox continued.

"I'll say it plain as day. I've got leukemia. I also was at the hospital to see Dr. Branham, God bless that saint of a man."

Emme could find no words in response, so Mrs. Maddox continued.

"He told me it's not looking good. I've got six months. Maybe less."

"Mrs. Maddox, I don't . . ."

"There's still hope, though, perhaps a bit. He drew more blood to run a few other tests. He also said he was going to look into some other chemo, more trials and things like that, but I just don't know. I'd rather spend my last months really living, spending time with Mattie and getting her situated. She doesn't remember her mama and daddy. I want to make sure she remembers me."

"I'm so utterly sorry, I don't . . ."

Emme had stopped speaking and even breathing again. She tried to breathe normally as she attempted to respond to Mrs. Maddox. She was unable to finish a sentence. As much as she fought to look neutral, Mrs. Maddox saw through it.

"Don't you go being all sad, Emmeretta. I'm gonna see Evan again and his daddy, Evan Sr. If there's reading in heaven, I'm gonna be strong enough to stay up all night reading again like I used to. There's a reason I've worked in this library all these years. I love me a good book. I want to read them all."

"I bet you do. But aren't you scared even just a little bit?"

"Of course I'm scared. Not gonna start lying now. I just gotta go by my gut, though, that everything's gonna be all right."

"I'm so sorry. I honestly don't know what to say."

"I don't quite know, either. What to say or do. Especially about Mattie, but I tell you, that child is special. She's gonna not just survive, but flourish in a way none of us can even imagine. Whether I'm here or not."

All the grief about Mrs. Maddox, on top of Evan, Kelly, and the death of her parents before them, everything Emme had kept wound up tightly inside her, sprung out. She went and held onto Mrs. Maddox and cried. As she cried, she didn't make a single sound, but her whole body shook. Mrs. Maddox kept on saying, "Oh, Emme, it's okay."

After a few minutes, Emme was able to talk again. "I'm so sorry, Mrs. Maddox. You're the one who should be crying, not me."

"Most everyone deserves their tears. You certainly do."

"I don't mean to hijack your grief, though."

"All of Red River knows that you've suffered and here you are suffering again over Kelly, and me, too."

"You're the one who's really suffering. And Kelly, too. I wish I could help both of you."

"We both have work yet to do with the time we have left on this earth. I know you want to help Kelly. You couldn't save Evan, and you can't save me, but you can save her. That's what you have to focus on now."

"I'll try to, but it's tough. I'm so truly sorry. That you're sick. I'm so sorry about Evan, too. Just today I was thinking about him, how he proposed and I turned him down."

"Yes, he told me."

Emme, in that moment with the dying Mrs. Maddox in the library, recognized that death was a clarifier. She would never have been able to talk so openly to Mrs. Maddox if Evan hadn't died and if Mrs. Maddox wasn't so sick, too. However horrible death was, Emme knew she needed to make the most of the clarity it had given her.

"It wasn't because I didn't love him, but because it was all so complicated. I was afraid and stupid. That part's not complicated, though. I'm more sorry than I have words for, about Evan and now about you, too."

"Evan loved you. Even after you turned him down. But he was meant to go on and marry someone else, so they could make Mattie. He loved his wife, too, though in a different way, I suppose, from you, but he loved her."

"Yes, he must've. I wish I'd been able to know her." Emme had always wondered about Evan's wife. As weird as it might've seemed to others, Emme knew they'd have been friends if they'd spent time together. But she never got the chance.

"And they really did do something wonderful together, my Evan with his bride. Mattie's a light in the world. I know you felt it, too, when you met her. She glows. Everyone who meets her knows it."

"I did feel that when I talked to her. At the paper they never want us to use big words and it drives me crazy, because sometimes the perfect word will never be printed. The perfect word for Mattie is ebullient."

"Yes, she's ebullient, shining more than anyone I've ever met. And, Emme?"

"Yes, ma'am?"

"You have to trust that if it didn't work out yet, your life, Kelly's, it's gonna work out soon. And Evan forgave you, I know it. Now forgive yourself."

Emme remembered Della telling her to do the exact same thing. She wished that Mrs. Maddox could meet her Great-Aunt Della. She would love to see the two of them together, talking about anything, everything.

"No wonder Evan was the miracle he was, Mrs. Maddox. Here you are exhausted from cancer, your husband and only son gone, but you're comforting me. Not the other way around. Evan got his gargantuan heart from you. And Mattie . . ."

When Emme pictured Mattie, a tiny musical trill accompanied the image. "Your Mattie, too. She got her heart from you."

The music stopped and the reporter in Emme suddenly kicked in.

"Mrs. Maddox, I worked on many stories back in DC, some of them medical. I can make calls for you."

"You have enough to worry about, so don't go working yourself into a tizzy over me."

"But there's got to be something, a trial no one around here knows about, not even Dr. Branham. I went through this with my family. I'll run back over to the hospital and discuss it with him, if that's okay with you. He did wonders for my mother and I know he'll do his very best for you."

"Yes, Dr. Branham is a fine man."

"I'll ask him about more solutions. And if you need anything, anything at all, please let me know. I mean it from the bottom of my heart."

"I know you do. And I thank you."

"You are very welcome."

"Just let me rest a tiny bit more right now and then I'll get on home to Mattie. All this talkin's made me tired again, so I better hush and rest up so I can get back. She's with Ginnie next door until I get home. Don't you be fretting about me."

"Yes, ma'am."

Mrs. Maddox's smile was tired and brief, but it soothed Emme's heart to see it. She kissed Mrs. Maddox on the cheek and told her she'd see her and Mattie soon.

CHAPTER 8

EMME KNEW she shouldn't try to sneak into Kelly's room again, so she made her way to the second floor of the hospital instead. The oncologists had their offices there, and she wanted to see if Dr. Branham was in. She didn't know if she'd see him, but when a receptionist let him know Emme was there, he came right out into the waiting room and took her back to his office.

"Emmeretta, it's a real honest to goodness pleasure to see you."

Emme reached to shake his hand, but Dr. Branham hugged her right up, just like her father used to.

"It's wonderful to see you, too, sir."

"I knew I'd see you eventually. I've been thinking about Kelly. I know she couldn't have done all that nonsense. I only wish I'd known more of what was transpiring with her. I would've tried to assist. Maybe I can help now?"

"There's nothing anyone can do for Kelly right now, sir. I've been trying, but not accomplishing much. But I do have some questions for you."

"I'll certainly try my best. You know I go far back with your father and with Kelly's, too. We all used to fish together. But what am I saying? Of course you remember that. So, what can I do for you?"

"I'm here for a couple of reasons. Some to do with Kelly and some to do with Mrs. Maddox. I know you can't break patient confidentiality, but she told me she has leukemia. She says it looks like there's not much hope. I told her I'd try to help, so I'm here to mainly ask about her. Please, sir, is there anything I can do? I could make some calls back to DC, look into new research trials. Anything."

"You always were so wise. And, yes, it seems like you are quite up to speed with Mrs. Maddox, so no one's breaking any rules. Still, I will try to talk generically about the logical steps in cases like this. You want to look into trials. and I'm doing the very same thing. When people's numbers drop, I start making calls myself. I then wait on the newest results after I retest a patient and I wait on the trial people to call me back. Then I go from there. You know I never give up."

"I know you don't. You never did with Mama. I know she's the one who made the decision to stop fighting, and I really don't blame her." Emme remembered that when her mother's breast cancer finally metastasized after two years, her mother was already exhausted.

Emme purposefully kept her voice steady. Even though Dr. Branham had seen her cry many times, she didn't want to start again so soon after the library. Emme knew tears were nothing of which to be ashamed, but they always exhausted her, and she needed to save her energy to help Kelly and Mrs. Maddox.

"Yes, your mother simply wanted peace at the end. She fought tenaciously for so long, but it surely did deplete her as it would anyone. She fought longer than most."

"Yes, sir, she did."

"As a doctor I'm supposed to be objective. But the best thing about working as a physician in a small town is also the worst. I know everybody. I care. It becomes immensely difficult when I have no more resources left to assist someone."

"I know you tried everything. I think close to the end she just wanted to come home and be with all of us. She didn't see it as giving up, but as moving on to the next phase of her life. You were good to her, to all of us. I'll never forget it, Dr. Branham. Thank you."

"You're very welcome. Your family, all of you, good people. No, great people. Salt of the earth as I like to say."

Dr. Branham was getting old. Emme could see his wrinkles, but he was also vital, full of energy. He seemed at least a decade younger when he started talking again.

"Tremendous people like your family and Mrs. Maddox, they're the reason I wanted to get into medicine, and oncology specifically. Some days it's hard, though. But when I can help someone, even if it's just to ease things in the end, it's worth it. But we're going to have to be patient to figure out the next steps with Mrs. Maddox."

"I figured that was probably it, but I had to come by and ask. Well, the main reason. We both know this is a small town and news travels fast here. So, you probably know everything . . ."

"Yes, I know some things. Ask away."

"Do you know what really happened when all the women came in? Before Cy was killed? Off the record, of course. Again, nothing that would jeopardize your position with patient confidentiality rules."

"I was actually here that night, called in to see one of my patients. But most of what I saw was just as an observer, since none of those women were my patients at the time. I can tell you that the whole hospital was frantic. The doctors and nurses were still professional, but it was blatantly obvious to everyone there that something of great magnitude was transpiring, something highly unusual. Chaos ensued."

Emme, despite her anxiety increasing in anticipation, was smiling. Dr. Branham was grandly articulate, the way he enunciated every syllable clearly.

"The ER was swarming and every doctor on call was consulted about what to do with the overflow. These were good women, Emme, not prone to hysterics. With so many of them sick, some of them vomiting and with high fevers, all of the moaning and shaking, it was as if we were in the middle of a natural disaster. Scores of people incapacitated."

The smile quickly left Emme's face as Dr. Branham continued to describe what he witnessed at the hospital. Dr. Branham started to nervously comb his fingers through his thinning hair, a gesture Emme had never seen him make, not even when his patients were dying.

"The most alarming part was how frightened all of them were. All speaking of the same things even though they came in from all over Red River and the entire county. They couldn't have conferred with each other or known what the other women were going through. Because so many were throwing up and had fevers, of course we thought there had to be some kind of illness, either food poisoning or a virus. We basically had to put the hospital on quarantine. Because there were so many truly ill with something we couldn't clearly diagnose, the CDC got called in. Of course they found nothing. They were here rapidly, within six hours from the time we called them, to investigate and they started running cultures. Nada. Not one single thing showed up."

"I think that's why word made it to DC so quickly. The CDC doesn't get called to rural Kentucky very often. Not for so many people."

Dr. Branham nodded.

"Eventually the women improved, and it was as if it never happened. They were all released the next day. Only one, and I can't name her, was actually officially sent to psych for a longer hold as she continued to exhibit erratic behavior."

Emme thought of Deirdre's erratic behavior.

"But the rest, while still frightened, just wanted to go home. When the fever broke and their fluid levels were back up, they stopped talking about the irrational things they'd been talking about when they arrived. No more screaming. Back to normal for the most part. Shaken up, yes. But crazy? No."

"No, I don't think a single one of them was crazy. So, what was it?"

"The best I can surmise, it was a twelve-hour virus of unknown origin, though nothing showed up in the blood work. We had to let them go and so did the CDC. But then we had to contend with the news trucks from all over. Our town has never seen anything like it, I can tell you that. No wonder it made it all the way to you in DC, Emme. Far too many reporters made too much out of the ghost talk, though, in my humble opinion."

"As soon as I heard about all the sick women, I was debating whether to come. My editor wanted me to. But I absolutely knew I had to get back once the call came in about Kelly. Even before that, though, when I heard just how many women in Red River were hospitalized, I was ready. It was frightening, even in DC."

Emme remembered the first news reports. How twenty-seven women from Lochlan County had, over the course of a few hours, been admitted to the hospital. It took just two hours more for the word to reach the newspapers and television stations in Bowling Green, which then spilled over to Nashville, which then went across the AP wire everywhere, even up to Washington, DC. Especially after the CDC was called in and temporarily put the hospital in lockdown, a real quarantine.

Emme had started making calls when she heard. Some to her friends back home and some to get a hold of the other reporters who'd already arrived in Red River. She offered herself as a resource and got all the inside information. Word leaked about the women not only being physically sick, but about their psychoses as well. "Mass Hysteria in Kentucky Cow Town" was splashed across multiple papers. That's what everyone described it as, except for the few sleazy reporters who wanted to play up the "haunted holler" angle of rural Kentucky.

Those trashy newspapers were calling it "a modern-day Salem." Not that there were trials or that the hospitalized women were viewed as witches, but there had never been more talk about witches and ghosts in one area of the United States since the Salem witch trials. All the women were screaming about witches and hauntings, and no one could keep it a secret.

Although most assumed it was group delirium, the worst case of mass hysteria they'd ever encountered, some thought there must be poison, maybe something in the water from new pesticides. But no one could avoid that all those affected were female. And from the same families.

All of them had started screaming at around the same time on the same night, around eleven-thirty. Their spouses or partners, or mothers and fathers, depending on the patient's age, woke up and thought their loved ones must have something horrible like a ruptured appendix.

It was the worst for Bobby Logan. Both his wife, Jenny, and his daughter, Sarah, who was seventeen and still lived at home, started screaming almost at the same time. His older boy, Bobby Jr., had gotten married the year before and wasn't there to help him. He was trying to get his wife to calm down when he heard Jenny's voice double.

That's when he realized Sarah, who sounded so much like her mother, had started screaming, too. So he kissed Jenny on the forehead and said he loved her and he'd be right back to help her as soon as he checked on Sarah. He couldn't get either one to stop screaming, and after running back and forth between their rooms for a few minutes, he went to the kitchen to call the ambulance.

Sarah and Jenny, along with Marjorie Rogers, the principal's wife and everyone's favorite English teacher, as well as Nancy Morrow, who worked at the bank, were the only four to be brought by ambulance. As all the calls started to come in, Pam in dispatch had to tell the people calling that she'd never seen anything like it, so many emergencies at once. And could whoever was calling just drive the women and girls directly to the hospital themselves?

As Emme read all the accounts and reached out to anyone who might give her more details, she could only imagine what it must've been like for all those families. Trying to get their screaming loved ones into cars and trucks. She imagined what those screams sounded like as they reverberated in the enclosed spaces of the vehicles.

It wasn't until they started arriving at the same time, with all the girls and women screaming and starting to say the same things over and over, bizarre things about witches and murders, that the doctors thought there was a mass hysteria or mass poisoning of some kind. Of course, all those doctors never thought that there was any truth to the stories, even after they realized that not all the victims, which is what they called them, were lunatics, alcoholics, poor, or uneducated. There was also a nurse, Amy Topkins; her cousin, Margo Tompkins, taking a few days off from getting her PhD down at Vandy to visit with her sick dad; esteemed teachers; a city councilman's wife; Maggie McIntosh, the first female city council member in Red River; and Emme's cousins on her mother's Logan side, the twins Shannon and Siobhan, who were barely thirteen. Most of the women, whether young or old, were trusted and loved by the entire community.

Only the Tompkins girls' other cousin, Christie, had a not-so-great reputation. She'd dropped out of school at sixteen, and worked at the Fruit of the Loom factory for several years before it closed, then went on the dole after she broke up with another boyfriend. But she didn't drink. She certainly wasn't crazy, on drugs, or anything untoward.

What Emme didn't read in all the reports was that Deirdre had been one of them. But Emme somehow knew anyway. She sensed it—not the full force, but something like an echo of it—even in DC.

When she had felt Deirdre experiencing the horror, Emme had hummed to try to calm herself. And that triggered her mountain gift. She had a distinctly clear vision. At first she could've sworn that she saw Deirdre, Kelly and Della, too, all in front of her. They were trying to say something, but no sound came out. Their faces were ghastly.

Emme only saw them for a second, but it'd been enough to scare her. She knew, in the way that Della knew things, that Fiona had been up late that night. She was reading when she heard Deirdre moaning and thrashing about. A few minutes later Deirdre calmed down, then told her what she had dreamed, only she swore it wasn't a dream.

Emme hadn't known all the details until after Fiona had called her collect from the hospital. Everett had had Porter drive out to the farm to personally let Fi know about Kelly, and Porter had taken her directly to the hospital to wait out Kelly's surgery. As soon as Fi had called her, Emme gathered her things and headed to National Airport so she could fly home to help.

"Thank you so much, Dr. Branham. After I get things sorted out with Kelly, I'm going to help Mrs. Maddox. I'll try to come in with her the next time she sees you, to give her some support. I know she has other people to assist her, but I have to try to help, too. For Evan as much as for her. I wish I could stay longer and catch up, but I have to go find Everett now. Thank you."

"You're most welcome. And, Emme?"

"Yes, sir?"

"I'm more pleased than I can convey to see you again."

Emme hugged Dr. Branham goodbye. "Thank you, sir. I feel the same way about you."

CHAPTER 9

"I KNOW you're here to give me hell."

"No. Well, maybe a little. Either way, I'm glad to have caught you."

Everett was on his way out, so Emme didn't have to ask anyone to let her into his office. Everett, despite knowing that Emme was there to chew him out again, couldn't help but smile. Emme's father had been dear friends with Everett. They'd been fishing buddies, and they'd both been in the Rotary Club. Everett loved her like his own child and greeted her that way. He had always secretly wanted her to marry his boy, Stephen.

"And I'm glad to see you. I wish things hadn't ended so damn badly on the phone, though. Would you let me hug you?"

"What would Mrs. Cecelia say about you cursing in front of me? And, yes, of course you can hug me."

Emme let Everett engulf her with massive arms. Right then, as she concurrently felt safe with and enraged by Everett, Emme saw the crux of all her issues with Red River. Why she'd been unable to return for so long. Things were not as simple as everyone in DC assumed. There wasn't a clear line of who was evil and who was good. Sometimes the best people made mistakes.

That was Everett. A good person who made mistakes, some of

them massive. Emme had told Richard that her home was complicated and she'd meant it. Red River was full of people who were loving and hardworking. But it also had people who were violent and bigoted. And it had many who were very much in the middle, decent folk who still maintained the status quo even when it was harmful.

"Cecelia knows that sometimes a bad word slips out. She's used to it by now. She wouldn't recognize me if one day I showed up all perfect."

"You know that I of all people will never think you're perfect. I can almost hear Daddy rolling over in his grave as I'm saying this, but you've finally gone too far."

"Emme, I . . ."

"No, let me finish, Everett. This is the most ridiculous thing in the world, Kelly still handcuffed to that hospital bed. And still accused of murdering Cy. Are you serious? We both know none of this would be happening if you'd locked Cy up to begin with."

Emme looked up. "Oh, Daddy, I know you're rolling now, but I can't stop talking, I just can't."

Everett took Emme seriously, but also thought her looking up to talk to her daddy sweet. The left side of his face turned up in the smallest of smiles, but that didn't stop Emme's rant.

"After years of silence, look where it's gotten us. Kelly is innocent. And Cy deserved some kind of punishment anyway. He beat Kelly repeatedly. And raped her, too. You know it just like I do. Nothing in this town is going to be right until you let Kelly go. If you don't do that for Kelly or for me . . . or for one of your best friends, God rest my daddy's soul, then do it for your town."

Everett opened his office door and let Emme go in, and he quickly followed and closed the door.

"I know you don't mean any disrespect, and I don't even think your daddy's rolling in his grave right now. But you know my hands are tied."

"You're the most powerful person in the whole county. Like hell your hands are tied!"

"Kelly confessed and multiple people heard her. She repeated it in the hospital, too, right before she went under for surgery. What else am I supposed to do?"

"But you told me that all the evidence, what you and the forensics team documented after they took Kelly to the hospital, all of it points to the fact that she couldn't possibly have done that. No woman could have done that. Probably no man, either, based on what you said."

"I know. And that's why I think if you just give it time, it'll be cleared up. It's not like she's even in jail right now."

"She's not in the Bahamas, either."

"But she is in the hospital getting Jell-O cups around the clock."

"After everything she's been through, to have her one good arm handcuffed, bolting her down to the hospital bed rails . . . you've got to be kidding me."

"Like it or not, that's the way it's gotta be for a while longer."

"Aunt Fi told me the doctor said she may never be able to use her left arm completely. And her face, dear God in heaven, Kelly's face. They let a plastic surgeon work on her, but there will still be scars. And you're saying you have to keep her in those handcuffs?"

"It's not even up to me now. I wrote down what she said. Everybody heard it. She confessed. Multiple times. How many times do I gotta repeat that?"

"Apparently you haven't said it enough times because it still makes no sense to me. Not one damn bit of sense."

"Now we have to wait until she's well enough to go before the judge. Her doctors told me it won't be too long. Despite all she's been through, she's still strong and healing quickly. Based on the physical evidence of the crime scene, I believe it might not even go to trial."

"Is that even possible?"

"Yes. And I'm gonna try to get some outside evidence to seal the deal, objective insight since I don't think anyone would believe me with our families being so close."

"Too little too late, Everett. But it's better than nothing."

"She's gonna have to stop confessing, or she's gonna have to explain it better. And how did you even see her? She's not allowed visitors. Don't tell me that I'm gonna have to fire Rowdy."

"You won't fire Rowdy and you know it. And I snuck into Kelly's hospital room. I had to."

"Why doesn't that surprise me?"

"And here's the thing. Her 'confession' isn't even a real confession. She doesn't have a single memory of anything that actually killed Cy. Yes, she tried to punch him to get him off of her. She admits that and she admits that she pushed him. But that's all. She remembers all of that perfectly, but nothing beyond it, so it can't possibly be a full or rational confession."

"For right now, though, given the circus that is Red River with all those sick women, all the papers covering us, it counts as a confession. Why are we going in circles now? I already told you all this."

"Because no judge, let alone a jury made up of people who know Kelly, described as the sweetest girl in the world since forever . . . damn, it even says that in the yearbook, 'sweetest girl in the world.' No jury would ever convict her, so you're wasting your time. And punishing her for something she didn't do."

"You gotta know that no one here is trying to punish her. We're just following protocol."

"Protocol? When will you stop the horror for her, for the town? For future women who are assaulted by their husbands?"

"Oh, Emme." Everett looked down at the floor.

"You are more powerful than you know. I didn't think I could ever fight you on this. Heaven knows I don't want to now. I don't want to hurt you or Mrs. Cecelia, but I will drag this in front of the whole town. I'll make sure it's on the front page of the newspaper."

"Emme . . ."

"I'll make sure my paper in DC and all the papers in the US get this story, how you let Kelly continue to be raped even though you knew Cy was guilty. How you let her get beaten again and again, only to have her, that sweet girl, be the one in handcuffs and not the rapist and wife-beater. I swear to God, Everett, I'll do it if I have to."

Everett had just started saying, "I'm sorry, Emme," when his phone rang. He mouthed "sorry" at Emme and picked it up. Then came a flurry of words, "Yes, yes, absolutely. Thank you. I'll come right up. I'm mighty grateful." Everett hung up the phone quickly.

"I can't give you details now, but I'm on my way to Louisville, back up to Bourbon County. I know you've got some kin up that way and I do, too. But I'm going for work."

Emme was exasperated. "You've got to leave now? Right now? In the middle of me chewing you out?"

"This is for Kelly. I need outside sources, I really do, if I'm gonna help her. Everyone knows I'm simply too close for my word to mean much, but I believe she's innocent. I'm gonna get someone else who can prove it, though."

Everett quickly kissed Emme on the cheek as she glared at him. Emme followed him as he walked out his office and over to Porter's desk.

"I'm gonna need you to pull some more shifts, Porter."

"Yes, sir."

"I guess you gotta get the other fire-and-rescue folks to fill in for you as you fill in for me. I'll be gone overnight, at least, if not more."

"No problem."

"You've got to hold down the fort. Crazy things keep happening in this town. I'll have Cathy make sure you get paid for it all, but you're officially on full-time with overtime pay for the rest of the week, if that's okay with you?"

"Yes, sir. I want to help and the extra money would be nice with all the babies we keep having. You can count on me."

No matter how mad she was at Everett, Emme couldn't help but smile when Porter saluted, even though she knew Porter had never been in the military and deputies in Red River never saluted their bosses.

"And one last thing, Porter. If you hear anyone start screaming about the Bell Witch, ghosts, or that damn Red River again, take them immediately to the hospital. But try to keep a lid on it. We don't need the CDC and all those reporters back here. We're a friendly town, but all those people gawking was too much."

"Yes, sir. Will do."

And with that, Everett briskly walked out the door.

Porter got a funny look on his face then.

"What is it? You look weird. No offense."

"Maybe it's because you were standing here in front of me while Everett said it, but I just remembered something."

Porter paused.

"What, Porter?"

"When all the crazy things started happening when all the women got sick, the night Cy was killed, too, well, I do remember word going 'round that they were all raving about the Red River and the Bell Witch."

"I know that."

"But I completely forgot about that time the band was supposed to go down the river to the cave. Of course, Munchy and I never made it. His mother grounded him at the last minute and I stayed with him to help with the extra chores. But I know you and Evan went down there and got really scared."

"It was awful. I'm still afraid of that place. I'll never go back."

"Evan never told me the specifics, just that it was bizarre. I know you used to hang out by the part of the Red River that came up on your property, too, and you used to sing the song about it. Your whole family did."

"That song keeps coming up. But what does it have to do with Kelly and the women?"

"I was just wondering if that canoe ride you took had anything to do with all the haunting nonsense now? I swear I didn't remember the trip you took with Evan until Everett said the words *Red River* and *Bell Witch* and you were standing right next to him."

"It was a long time ago. But I can't get that song out of my head, either. I've hardly had time to think about our canoe trip much, though, or its significance. I've been running all over the place hoping to help Kelly, but you might be on to something."

"Well, mark this day down in history. I'll tell Shelby I was the smart one for once."

"You've always been a genius in your own way."

"Aw, shucks."

"Since I've got to wait on Everett to get back, and I probably shouldn't try to sneak in to see Kelly again, I think I'll go home. I'll walk down there, to the part of the river that's on our property. I was always down there as a kid. I'll try to remember all the details of the cave trip. Thanks, Porter. I really mean that."

"You're mighty welcome. I hope we all have good news soon and everything goes back to normal. I'll do everything I can, though, to help."

"I know you will. Thanks again."

CHAPTER 10

ON THE drive back to Fi's, Emme left the windows open. She wanted to breathe in the farmland, manure and all, that increased the farther away from downtown Red River she drove.

She wanted to forget talking with Dr. Branham again about her mother's death at the hospital, with its pungent ammonia smell that wasn't strong enough to mask the death scent. She wanted to forget about her father passing away less than a year later in the same hospital. Emme's father had technically died of a coronary because of the heart disease that ran in their family. Emme and everyone else, though, knew that he died of a broken heart after his beloved wife had passed on.

Emme didn't blame him. Her heart almost broke in two from all that death, too. If it hadn't been for Fi and Deirdre taking her in and raising her practically as a sister to Kelly, who was only six months younger, Emme didn't know how she would have survived. Yes, she grieved, but Emme was constantly amazed at the amount of love that permeated Fi's farm, even amidst the loss. Every single one of those women there had suffered. All of them had lost someone. A husband, mother, or father. Or all of them.

Fi and Deirdre had been smart, too. They'd helped Emme sell her parents' house, which had been not too far from Fi's, and put the money away for college. When Emme got into Georgetown, she got a scholarship, but only a partial one. Emme really wanted to go there, and the money from the house helped. Emme majored in political science and photography so she could be a political photojournalist, something she'd wanted to do since she was a child and had seen photos of President Kennedy. She loved how one image could convey more than the best-written article.

But really, Emme thought going to Georgetown would allow her to major in life. Washington, DC, was the nation's capital. Emme thought politics was the answer to making the world better, and DC was the fulcrum of that. She would have gone even if she had no scholarship, but the money from selling her parents' house covered the rest, with extra left over. Emme would have gladly traded Georgetown to get her parents back, though. Since that was impossible, she had decided to gratefully accept the gift that Georgetown was, the last present from her parents.

Deirdre, Fi, and Kelly were gifts to Emme, too. Emme had thought that she and her parents sang often, but when she got to Fi's farm, everything was a song. They sang when they worked in the kitchen. They sang when they worked in the garden. They sang when the crops came in and when the crops were ruined. They sang "Fair and Tender Ladies," "Don't Be Cruel," "The Pill," and endless Child Ballads like "The Boy and the Mantle," "The Twa Musicians" and "Fair Annie." They sang "Be Thou My Vision," "Stand by Your Man," "Boogie Woogie Bugle Boy," "Sleeping Single in a Double Bed," "Ring of Fire," "Love Can Build a Bridge," and "Keep on the Sunny Side." They sang all the songs from the mountains and new songs on the radio, too. They sang it all, and the songs saved them.

Emme remembered every last song she had sung with Kelly and her aunts. And with her parents before. She remembered the singing up on Black Mountain with Great-Aunt Della and Great-Uncle Alton, too. Emme reached far back in her memory to when they had been picking tomatoes out behind Della's house when everyone she loved was still alive. Emme realized she must have been only two or three, but she could still remember looking up at them while they were working. They were sweating and wiping handkerchiefs across their faces and foreheads, but they were still singing.

They had sung "Wildwood Flower." When Emme got older, Della had told her about all the flora and fauna that were unique to Black Mountain. How it would be a sin for the coal companies to rip off the mountaintop because all those one-of-a-kind plants would be lost forever. Della had sung "Wildwood Flower" again with her.

But back on the day they were picking tomatoes, the song was not about stopping the coal companies, however important that was. It was simply beautiful to Emme. She had especially loved the lines, "I'll sing, and I'll dance, my laugh shall be gay, I'll cease this wild weeping, drive sorrow away," and had quickly memorized all the verses despite being so young. She had belted it out at the top of her lungs.

Emme started singing "Wildwood Flower" again on the way back to Fi's. She drove the long way home, taking all the side roads so she had time to go through the song's variations. "I'll Twine Mid the Ringlets," "The Pale Amaranthus," "Raven Black Hair," "The Pale Wildwood Flower" and "The Frail Wildwood Flower."

For a while, everything seemed better. But then she felt the inevitable circling her again and she knew there was no way around it. She had to think about all the people that she loved and how they died.

She had to remember Evan. Oh, Evan. She knew he would describe it all as a statistical anomaly, one permutation, one possibility. Him driving with his wife at exactly the moment when the other vehicles crashed. Everything had to line up perfectly, every vehicle passing through its specific place at a particular moment, every detail down to the last second. One small change, even a car being a foot ahead or a foot behind, and he could still be alive. She had not been there when he passed, but somehow, as she got closer to Fi's, Emme was able to see it all in her mind as if she had been standing right there.

Maybe it was all the articles. She had read every single one. There had never been a bigger crash in their area involving more cars and trucks and more people dying. No one in their county had seen anything like it, so there were many features in the newspaper covering Evan's death. Maybe it was hearing about it from Porter or other people. Maybe it was her mountain gift. All Emme knew was that she had tried to not think about it for a long time because when she did, she started to see it clearly. But there was no more putting it off. Emme was only half a mile from Fi's when she pulled off the road. She knew if she let herself focus on that day, she would see and feel it in such complete detail that it would overwhelm her view of the road. Emme parked her car and stared straight ahead. She did not see her aunt's farmland.

Emme saw Evan back in town for Mrs. Maddox's birthday. It was early evening on a Saturday. A few years into graduate school, Evan had come back to visit and had brought his wife, Xiuyang, along with his baby daughter. Mattie was not even a year old. When Mrs. Maddox said she would love some of Hank's famous BBQ for her birthday, she had offered to keep rocking Mattie so Evan could run out with Xiuyang and pick it up.

Emme remembered the details. How there had been a long line of semitrucks, one of the Jackson boys' uncles riding in his old Chevy pickup, a minivan with a family of seven, and Evan's car right in the middle, all of them crashing into each other in one massive wreck because a drunk driver in an old blue Ford Bronco, someone from a county over passing through, had jumped lanes and slammed into the first semitruck. But knowing the details as if they were police reports was not the same as experiencing them with her mountain gift. Emme knew it was time. She had to let herself feel it.

Emme saw them driving. She could see Evan's mouth moving as he talked to Xiuyang, though she heard no sound. She'd started humming when she pulled over on the side of the road and she hummed even louder as she saw him sitting there in the car, oblivious to what was about to happen. Emme's humming made up for the absence of the sound, the harsh silence, in her vision. There was no melody she recognized, but the tune came out of her easily, as if she had hummed it her entire life.

Emme smelled Evan. Not his cologne, but him, his good clean smell with the smallest amount of sweat, too, which also smelled good. She smelled the car smells, a bit of gasoline and some kind of leather cleaner. She felt the steering wheel in Evan's hands, the bumps where the leather was threaded together. Evan kept running his thumb along the steering wheel's bumpy seam. Then Evan saw, then Emme saw, only in the tiniest fragment of a second, a large shadow rising up to swallow their tiny car, the semitruck in front of them flipping back onto them. Then Evan felt, then Emme felt, the heft of the steering wheel in Evan's, in Emme's, chest, more pressure than pain at first. Evan knew, Emme knew, they'd crashed, but didn't understand anything else. Then Evan looked over, no, Emme looked over, they both looked over, and saw Xiuyang. She was lying with her head across the dashboard. She was perfectly still, with only a small amount of blood rouging up her left temple. The sticky maroon liquid was tangled up in her midnight-colored hair. Emme next felt the way Xiuyang's skin felt when Evan reached out his hand to touch his wife's hand seconds later. Evan tried, Emme tried, to pull Xiuyang down off the dashboard, so he, so Emme, could talk to her, to try to get her to wake up. Evan was, no Emme was, only vaguely aware that he couldn't move his left leg, that parts of the car, angry metal shards, were sticking up through his, through Emme's, left leg and that there was blood. His blood was everywhere, pouring down onto the floorboard. All Evan could do, all Emme could do, was think of Xiuyang. Evan and Emme tried to pull her down off the dashboard to save her. As Evan moved Xiuyang closer to him, he barely grazed her collarbone with his fingertips. Evan marveled at Xiuyang's delicate collarbone. Emme marveled at the sensation of Xiuyang's delicate collarbone, wondering how it hadn't broken in the car crash. That fragile bone, somehow still intact, when everything else around them, and in them, was broken. Xiuyang's collarbone was the last thing Evan felt and saw before he and Xiuyang died. And it was the last thing Emme felt and saw before her vision cleared and the farmland around her was visible again.

Emme had to have her camera. Right then. Experiencing Evan's death so completely had drained her. Instead of crying, it was more as if she was in shock. Emme desperately needed to feel the jolt of energy she got from looking through her camera and seeing things anew. She needed to go on a barn hunt. Emme had always wanted to do more art photography, including a series of images from all the barns in Lochlan County. Some sturdy, some dilapidated, but every barn beautiful in its own way. Beautiful enough to distract Emme.

Emme had another photograph series in mind, too. She wanted to focus on those images, anything but death. She threw herself into her plans. She wanted to take shots of her family's musical instrument collection. Then she wanted to go down to Nashville and ask Johnny Cash, Bill Monroe, Loretta Lynn, and scores of others to photograph their instruments, too. Emme loved the curves on guitars, mandolins, and fiddles. She called them dangerous curves. Sensual, siren instruments calling out to whomever saw them.

Emme sat on the side of the road for an hour straight and pictured all the barns and musical instruments she was going to photograph. She relentlessly ordered them in her head, which shots she would take first and why. Until she could recover from remembering the people she loved dying. Until she could go back to Fi's. Until she was strong enough to walk out to the river and remember all the details of the canoe trip that had haunted her, almost as much as the deaths of her loved ones, for so long.

CHAPTER 11

"YOU AIN'T never been a scaredy-cat before."

"You can make fun of me all you want, Porter, but I don't understand your obsession with the Bell Witch."

"Once you get down there, you'll love it. You'll forget you were the biggest scaredy-cat and you'll thank me."

"I doubt it. I can think of a million other things I'd rather do than go to the Bell Witch Cave."

Emme hadn't wanted to ever remember the canoe trip to the Bell Witch Cave. But standing on Fi's dock and looking out at the Red River, she knew she had no choice. All the details came back quickly.

"You have a real thing for ghost stories, don't you? I remember you would sit right in front when the storytellers came out at Halloween for the fall festivals, whipping everyone into a frenzy."

"I loved them. They were convincing, promising everything they said was the God's honest truth. I believed them. Still do."

"Trying to freak us out on purpose is more like it."

"But, Emme. You know the Bells in Red River. They swear they're distant cousins to the ones in Adams, Tennessee. They swear all the stories are true, too."

"Oh, I know all the stories they tell. Know them by heart. Back in the 1800s, cousins down on their Tennessee farm had been haunted by the ghost of a girl, Kate Batts. Kate was supposedly still angry, even after her death, that Betsy Bell had married Kate's love, Joshua Gardner. Kate, who came to be known as the "Bell Witch," continued to let Betsy and her family know of her displeasure. Sometimes violently so. The Bell Witch had a temper."

"You got it right. And it's absolutely true."

"If those stories are really true, then why would I ever want to go?"

Emme loathed ghost stories. But for some reason she could not remember, she had agreed to drive down to Tennessee with her friends in the band. Porter wanted to start closer to the part of the river that went through the Bell farm, where the cave was. Porter wanted to see it. There were many caves around those parts in Kentucky and Tennessee. Emme always suspected that if you went deep enough into them, they would reach all the way back to the massive Mammoth Cave out past Bowling Green. Emme thought the tiny caves in Lochlan County and nearby in Tennessee were kin to Mammoth. She loved caves, but hated ghosts.

Still, Emme had agreed to go with the band. Probably because she wanted to spend more time with Evan. It was the only time they ever drove anywhere just the two of them. They were always too afraid to be alone. They never said it out loud, but the fear of that was a living thing between them.

Despite her misgivings, Emme asked Evan to pick her up and take her down to the canoe rental spot in Tennessee. It was right on the Red River, not too far of a ride from the Bell Witch Cave, where Porter and Munchie would meet them.

Except Porter and Munchie never showed up. But Evan convinced Emme to rent a canoe with him and paddle out to the cave. Emme voiced her trepidations repeatedly, but Evan told her it was empirically impossible that ghosts were real. He promised Emme that the ghost was not tormenting anyone because she did not exist.

Evan could believe in a higher power because he said the universe had an elegant design that was visible everywhere, proof of something creating it. But he could never believe in ghosts. The math didn't add up, he said, though he never explained the specifics to Emme. Emme never told him the reason she was afraid of ghosts was because so many of them showed up in the Scottish murder ballads her family sang and swore were true.

Instead, Emme pushed down her fears and rode in a canoe with Evan to the Bell Witch Cave. They didn't see any other people renting canoes, and Emme thought that was a bad sign.

When they got to the cave, Emme tried to sing. Her anxiety rose, though, and she could not get enough breath to do it. So she hummed. She kept humming as she got out of the boat. Evan tied it to the dock. Emme thought humming would call up her mountain gift and she would see something beautiful. Something to distract her from feeling like hundreds of slugs were sliding over her body as they walked into the cave. But there were no astounding colors or visions. Once she was in the cave, Emme was not able to even hum anymore.

Emme's vision turned brown, as if someone had covered her eyes in mud, sepia-colored slime dripping over everything. Evan grabbed her hand for the first time, but Emme could not revel in it, the way love vibrates between people's skin. She was too afraid. When they got to the part of the cave that people had spray-painted, Emme became terrified.

Emme saw her own name immediately. Someone had written "Go Home!" That was to be expected. Probably other teenagers predictably writing things to scare people. Stupid pranks. But other people had signed their names, too. Most of them were drawn through. But four of the names that could be seen—Gene, Emma, Margaret, and Zeke—had one letter that was completely unmarked. The *e* in Gene, the *m* in Emma, the *M* in Margaret, and the *e* in Zeke. And it was right above the "Go Home!"

Emme started hyperventilating.

"Emme, it's okay."

"So you see it, too?"

"Yes, I see your name, but it's a statistical anomaly. It could have just as easily have been my name. If you have enough monkeys pecking at typewriters, eventually one of them will type out a novel like *Great Expectations*, every single word, randomly. It's all mathematical, nothing else."

But coming so soon after her parents had died, Emme was working hard to even breathe right. There was always a heavy fear, an albatross atop her chest, crushing her lungs. And when she saw her name in the Bell Witch Cave, Emme's albatross grew to hundreds of pounds.

Emme ran out of the cave. She almost flipped the canoe as she fought to get back in it. Evan wordlessly helped her. Then he paddled the entire way back by himself because Emme was shaking.

Evan would pause every few minutes, stop rowing, and reach forward and touch the back of Emme's head. He never stroked her hair, but he cupped the back of her head and gently patted it. At first it was in rhythm to Emme's shaking. Then he pushed a little harder and the pressure of it, the heat of his hand on her head, calmed Emme and she stopped shaking.

They made it back to the rental place, turned in the canoe, and Evan drove Emme home. It was the only time he ever ate supper with Emme's family. Emme begged him to stay, told him he had to, that she was still too afraid. So Evan had given in. She asked him to never speak of the cave again, and he obliged.

Back at the farm, one of the most frightening times of Emme's life turned into one of the most wonderful. Evan blended into Emme's family better than she could have dreamed. They loved to hear him talk about math and music. They loved the way he bragged about how brilliant Emme was in the AP classes, at track, on the keyboard in the band. They loved the way he loved Emme and they loved Evan, too.

Standing at her family's dock, Emme realized she had been holding her breath as she remembered the Bell Witch Cave visit from years before. She exhaled, inhaled, and exhaled again as she looked at the river. It was not boiling as it did before a storm came. If the water was white-capped and raging, she knew she better get back to the house. The river was simply sliding along gently then, though.

Emme thought again of the message in the cave and wondered if it was tied to what had been happening in Red River. She wondered if ghosts were real. Or was Deirdre, and every woman who went mad, being influenced by the myths and lore from Appalachia, and from the old country before that? Blending fact and fiction. Surely Deirdre wasn't really seeing ghosts and banshees. But if it was all true, what did the ghosts and witches want? Had they been there when Cy was killed? Is that what Kelly had felt? Was it the same thing Emme had felt in the Bell Witch Cave?

When Emme could not stand to think about the Bell Witch anymore, let alone Cy being killed, she started to sing "The Ballad of Red River." The melody was in a minor key, but it had never seemed so sad before. Over and over Emme sang parts of the chorus, each version growing darker. "Many a lady will lose her love. Many will drown in sorrow. Many a lady will ride the Red River. She'll go to her death on the morrow."

She sang it the way her family had taught her, switching up the pronoun so it changed from "She'll go to her death on the morrow," to "You'll go to your death on the morrow." And eventually to "I'll go to my death on the morrow." When Emme sang, "I'll go to my death on the morrow," everything around her turned brown and her mountain gift started. It was the same sepia film, mud covering everything, that Emme had seen in the Bell Witch Cave.

But Emme refused to move. She was not going to run anymore. She closed her eyes and tried to think of something else. What popped into her mind was the "Tinker's Lullaby" that she had first heard at a wedding right before she left for Georgetown. It was a jubilant Tinker wedding, like all Tinker weddings. A distant part of Emme's family was made up of the nomadic Tinkers, who were still very tied to their Irish ways even after coming to America. The lullaby, by Pecker Dunne, was a relatively new but popular song, and had quickly made it over from Ireland to the States.

Emme had always thought the song was sweetly alluring. She loved the lines, "When your mother died and left you, you had to fend all alone, all in this land of saints and scholars, and still you have not got a home." Those lyrics had made Emme feel better when she first heard them. Even though she was still mourning her mother, just like the singer of the song, Emme also knew she was different. Lucky. Despite missing her parents terribly, she felt grateful to have a family and a home.

When everyone had sung "Tinker's Lullaby" at the wedding, Emme had expected Aidan to show up. Ah, Aidan. Full of music and mystery, even as a child. Emme had believed Aidan would appear in the middle of the dancing celebration, but he never came. She had not seen him since the first time they met, at least not in the flesh. Emme remembered seeing a version of him in her car when she neared her family's farm, though. Her immediate reaction to remembering that was that she'd wished he'd been there so she could talk to him. When Emme finished singing the "Tinker's Lullaby" out on the dock, she opened her eyes. The frightening brown world was gone. But Emme's thoughts of Aidan were not.

CHAPTER 12

"I HEARD your car pull in, but you never made it inside."

"I'm so sorry. With everything going on, I should've let you know I needed to go down to the dock."

"You're safe now, no worries. Can I get you anything?"

Emme didn't mean to be rude, but she forgot to answer Deirdre. Once she'd remembered the "Tinker's Lullaby" on the dock, she couldn't stop thinking about her distant cousins. All the Irish ones that lived in Cumberland County. Before her cousin, Brady, married his wife, Colleen, they'd all danced together at a sprawling, festive wedding in Marrowbone, Kentucky, when Emme was a child. Colleen, a girl herself then, had been there with her Tinker-Traveller kin. Emme remembered them all together, singing, dancing, wearing brightly colored clothes.

"Emme?"

Emme remembered that she'd adored the Travellers' ease with themselves. They talked openly about their mountain gifts amongst the other Irish people at the wedding and it was one of the only times Emme had talked to people outside her immediate family about hers, too. She felt at home with them. She'd never danced so long and laughed so much than at that wedding. Colleen had told Brady that night that she knew they were going to get married some day. And sure enough, years later, it happened. Emme had lost touch with most of that part of the family after she moved away.

"Emme, honey . . ."

"Oh, I'm so sorry. What did you say?"

"Can I get you anything?"

"No, thank you."

"Fi's back at the hospital, so I'm sure glad to see you. You look exhausted."

"It's been a long day."

"You also keep forgetting your camera. It's been sitting on the sofa all day again. I can't imagine you without it."

Deirdre pointed to it, and Emme realized, since she'd been home, she hadn't taken a single photo. For someone who'd made her living through photography and who genuinely loved the art of it, too, she couldn't believe she'd left it behind. It had become a natural extension of her body, but in a few short days she'd stopped carrying it, and had reverted back to singing. And maybe even believing again in her mountain gift. Or at least not outright rejecting it and the rest of her family's ways.

"Thank you. I've nearly forgotten it. So much has happened and keeps on happening. Everett says he's going to help Kelly and he's off to Louisville to do it. And I found out that Evan's mother, Mrs. Maddox, has leukemia. It feels like everyone in Red River is in a war."

"That's horrible. The part about Mrs. Maddox. But I like the idea of Everett gone off to help Kelly."

"It's better than nothing from him."

"It's about damn time."

"Yes."

"And Mrs. Maddox. Such a shame. I always have the best talks with her when I'm at the library. Still a shame about Evan, too."

Surprisingly, Emme didn't fall apart when she heard Evan's name.

She did feel guilt, but something was shifting. She was also exhausted and let out a big yawn.

"You done been going and going since you got back to Kentucky. I think you forgot that camera because you are tuckered out. Rest for a bit while I heat up some biscuits and ham in the oven and maybe a little watermelon preserves on the side."

"I can never say no to your preserves."

"I've already been cooking them pole beans on the pot with a tiny bit of bacon all day long, so those flavors are getting acquainted real nice. I know you like them like that. Go rest. I'll call you when it's ready."

Emme picked up her camera and put it on the coffee table so she could lie down on the sofa. As soon as she closed her eyes, she wasn't asleep and dreaming, but she wasn't fully awake, either. She was a child dancing with the Travellers at the wedding again.

And there was the boy she'd seen in her car. A grown-up version of him at least. Emme remembered him well from the wedding. Aidan, Colleen's brother. They were too young to be romantic with each other, but there was something about him that pulled Emme to him.

Right in the middle of everyone singing and dancing to "I'll Tell Me Ma," one of Emme's favorite Irish songs, she and Aidan stood still together in the middle of the revelry. Aidan was Black Irish with dark wavy hair and gray eyes. He was handsome in a way that seemed so pretty he could've been a girl. Emme stood not six inches away from him looking straight into his pale eyes.

Aidan looked back with a half-smile on his face. He took Emme's hand and held it, very politely. The entire wedding party and all of the guests whirled around them, but Emme and Aidan were still. Emme didn't feel what everyone described as butterflies in her stomach, but something fiercer. She felt as if she opened her mouth that some kind of animal roar would come out, so she closed it.

While Aidan was holding Emme's hand and the music continued to play, Emme's mountain gift created a second world right on top of the first one. She saw the young Aidan in that moment staring back at her, still clasping her hand. But she also saw an older Aidan, too. The older Aidan played a guitar and sang. Emme couldn't hear the song's words, but she didn't need to. More than she'd ever known anything in her life, she knew it was a love song.

Then it was time to cut the cake. The young Aidan let go of Emme's hand as the music stopped. At the same time, Emme's mountain gift stopped. The second, older Aidan from her vision ceased playing guitar and started to walk away, but not before he turned back to look at Emme. Emme could've sworn she saw the Appalachian Mountains, with all their mystery, in Aidan's eyes.

CHAPTER 13

EMME'S REVERIE was broken when Deirdre called her to supper. After Deirdre said grace, Emme asked her about cousin Brady, his wife Colleen, and Colleen's family. She didn't mention Aidan specifically, but Emme saw him in her mind. Both the child Aidan and the older Aidan she'd witnessed in her vision at the wedding many years before. And the same one she'd seen briefly in her car.

"It's too bad we don't see more of that part of Kentucky. Marrowbone's just a couple hours away. If I'd known you wanted to see them, we could've dipped down south a bit on the way back from Black Mountain."

"I forgot how close it is."

"Marrowbone's fairly tiny, but it's full of fine folks. Colleen's family, with our Brady now, lives on a pretty stretch of land on Hominy Creek. I been there once, many moons ago. Some of them are Travellers, you know."

"Yes, ma'am. I remember."

"There be all kinds of rumors about American Travellers, like our Irish Tinkers from the old country. Some say they're all thieves."

"Are they?"

"Maybe a few are. There be good folks and bad folks in every group, but I promise you true that those in Marrowbone be good. Most are still out this time of year, working their trades. But they have a home base there on Hominy Creek for the winter."

"What else do you know about Colleen's family?"

"Many of their Travellers are like the Romani. Sometimes people even call them the Irish Gypsies. They even have a similar way of talking, their own language, though I don't know much of it. Brady, as you know, married Colleen O'Hagan."

"I was just thinking about them."

"On occasion I done got a letter from that kind boy. He joined in with Colleen's family and their traveling. The O'Hagans are famous for the best moonshine in Kentucky. It's full of magic, too."

"Magic moonshine? Aunt Deirdre, I've barely begun to accept we might actually have real mountain gifts. But magic moonshine?"

"I swear it true, Emmeretta."

"I don't need to remind you that we're Baptist. I know Fi brought out the 'shine when I got here, but that's unusual. I don't think we're supposed to like drinking quite so much. Maybe a teensy bit, but not . . ."

Deirdre, being Deirdre, interrupted her great-niece. "We're Baptist here in a dry county. I think they're dry there, too, in Marrowbone. But they don't make it for everyone to be getting drunk."

"What's it for, then?

"It's medicinal. At least one version they make is just plain ol.' I've had some on occasion and I know Della still has a few bottles of it up on that mountain for when she gets real sick. It helps, it does. I tell it true."

"But what about the magic kind?"

"There's supposed to be a special brew. Extra magic in it, able to pull out our mountain gifts and help us see things more clearly. Almost like a truth serum."

"A truth serum? Hogwash."

"I thought you was done sassing me, that you believed things now."

"No sassing from me. Please go on."

"I remember sitting for a bit at a few of our family weddings where the Scots, and Irish, and all the Scots-Irish from all over Kentucky and Tennessee come to celebrate."

"I remember those weddings, too."

"At one wedding I was talking with Colleen's grandmother, Aileen. Aileen Carroll, if I done be remembering right. Brady said she's the only one left at home most of the time, back on Hominy Creek."

"Sounds beautiful."

"She got too old to travel. I don't blame her for wanting to stay put. The rest come back at winter, though, and park their RVs on Aileen's property and wait out the cold with her.

"Up in DC people think that because Kentucky's in the South that we don't get cold. But we certainly do, as you well know."

"Yep, and when the frost first comes, I done heard they make some extra 'shine, too. I could use a sip right now. Don't know why I didn't go and find some of it earlier when things was so bad. I should see if we still got any of their kind. Even better than our good 'shine, but Fi's gonna have to root around for it."

"I can help you with that. To think there could be 'shine better than ours . . . that'd be something. I'm willing to try anything at this point."

"Why are you asking about them now?"

"I guess I'm having a hard time processing everything. All the new things going wrong, Mrs. Maddox's illness on top of Kelly's arrest."

"Heavens yes. This new mess with Mrs. Maddox done be bad."

"I feel like I get close to being able to fix things, or at least myself. Then something else goes wrong. And then the old things come back worse."

"Dog chasing his tail around in circles. Happens to everyone."

"Just this afternoon I was singing the old Red River song and it made me remember horrible things from a long time ago."

"Best not be dwelling so in the past."

"Exactly. So I sang "Tinker's Lullaby" and it reminded me of that part of our family. I remembered how natural it was for them, with their mountain gifts."

Emme paused and Deirdre eyed her up and down.

"What else you be remembering?"

"I remember a wedding. It's when I felt most comfortable being me, being able to see and hear the things I see and hear."

"Why was that?"

"I don't know exactly. Maybe because the weddings they had were fantastic celebrations and everything seemed more possible. I guess now I want to go back to those people and see if they can help me figure things out. I think I have to visit Marrowbone."

"And Aidan's there. He's been waiting for you."

Emme realized she probably looked like a cartoon character. She knew her mouth was hanging open in an exaggerated way. Emme couldn't believe that her aunt had brought up Aidan again.

"Shut that mouth of yours before a fly gets in. I know all about that boy and you."

"I was going to ask how, but you'd tell me what you always do. It's our family's way, right?"

"Yep. Everyone's always known that someday y'all would get together. I know you loved Evan. But that wasn't your path. At least not in the way you thought it'd be. Just now you realizing things what all us old folks have known for a long time."

"What exactly do you know about Aidan?"

"At that wedding. Aidan standing still in the middle of the room with you like there was gold around you, a golden circle lassoing the two of you in together. Just children, but already linked. All of us with our gifts, we could actually see you two encircled."

"Why would you never tell me that?"

"We been waiting for you to get back here to Kentucky. You had to come on your own. I wouldn't wish what happened to Kelly for anything in the world."

"Me, either."

"But good has come of it. You're home. And you'll see Aidan, too. It's about damn time."

"You cuss more than any old woman ever should be allowed to get away with. Aren't you afraid you're going to taint my precious young mind?"

Emme started laughing so hard that she knocked over the jar of preserves Deirdre had put out.

"Yes, young you is, but not that young, Emmeretta Finnegan McLean. You're old enough to know I ain't gonna change my language."

Deirdre laughed as hard as Emme as they finished eating and put the dishes away. Then they waited for Fi to get home so they could make plans for Emme's trip to Marrowbone.

CHAPTER 14

EMME WAS back in her rental car. When she'd made up her mind to go home for Kelly, she had assumed she'd spend most of her time in Red River. But she was again driving across the state, back into the Appalachians. Marrowbone was much closer than Black Mountain, though, just over an hour east, so she arrived midmorning.

The land around Marrowbone was dotted with mountains. And there were hollows everywhere between them. Shaw Hollow. Barnes Creek Hollow. And Hominy Creek Hollow where Emme was going. She'd followed Fi's directions and gone through Bowling Green, Glasgow, and Willow Shade before she reached Marrowbone. She'd turned off Route 90 onto Hominy Creek Road, then driven down the dirt road until she got to the Carroll homestead.

Emme saw a small house nestled between magnolia trees. It was white with black shutters and looked newer, more 1920s than a turn-of-the-century farmhouse like Deirdre's place. A large brown camper and old blue Ford pickup truck were parked in front of a garage that was right next to the house.

Like Fi, Aileen Carroll didn't have a phone. But unlike Fi,

it wasn't because she got rid of it. She'd never had one, so Emme wasn't able to call and let her know she was coming for a visit. Emme knew Aileen would receive her like family, though, because Emme's cousin, Brady, had married Aileen's granddaughter, Colleen. To Aileen, that would be enough. Emme only knocked once on the door and Aileen came right out.

"What do we have here? It's one of those beautiful Red River girls!"

"Yes, ma'am."

"I remember you from the wedding, even though it's been quite a while. Come on in. What's your name again, young one?"

Emme hugged Aileen and went inside with her.

"I'm Emme McLean and I'm sorry to come here like this without an invitation, but we've had troubles back home. And my cousin, Brady, always says that you treat him like he was really related to you, not just an in-law married to Colleen. So I knew you wouldn't think I was rude to drive out here with no invitation."

"Hush now, of course I don't mind. Besides, every single one of the Irish in Kentucky is kin if we went far enough back."

"That's probably true."

"Brady's a fine boy, marrying my Colleen and taking good care of her. You're kin now, too, young lady."

"Thank you so much."

"Brady and Colleen are still out, though. There's good working weather and they won't be back to bed down for winter until the end of November. But I'll do anything I can to help. We heard of the troubles going on in Red River and we've been bringing out the Rosary more because of it, too."

Emme had forgotten that some of her Irish family and friends were still Catholic. The big schism that happened ages ago in Scotland and Ireland, when so many of her family became Protestants after the Reformation, was still talked about as if it'd happened yesterday. Much the same way the Civil War was. People still arguing over it, many of them in the same family. But Emme didn't care about whether someone was Protestant or Catholic. Certainly not after living in DC with its amalgamation of beliefs.

"We all appreciate that, Mrs. Carroll."

"Emme, I'm Aileen. I'm serious, call me Aileen."

"Yes, ma'am, Aileen."

Emme felt at home. Aileen sounded so much like Great-Aunt Della and Deirdre. And her grandmother before she'd passed.

"I bet you could use some reviving with refreshment. Could I get you . . ."

Aileen couldn't finish the sentence because Aidan walked through the door to what Emme could see was the kitchen in the background. He walked right up to her. He didn't say anything to Emme, but stood in front of her smiling.

"Here's my handsome grandson, Aidan. Emme, I don't know if you remember, but this is Colleen's brother, Aidan Walsh."

Emme didn't say anything, so Aileen kept talking.

"My daughter, Darby, married Stuart Walsh. Aidan's their youngest. I love this here boy. Sometimes I call him Duffy, his middle name, because that's my middle name and I love thinking of all the Duffys back in Ireland."

The whole time Aileen spoke, Aidan continued looking at Emme and smiling.

"It cheers my soul the way he's an honor to us all. He finished his degree, one of the only ones in our family to get a college education. Did you know that?"

"No, ma'am, I don't think I did."

"We're so proud, a degree in literature at Berea a few years ago. Then he came back to help me on the farm while he keeps writing away, though I think he writes more songs than stories now. I think his stories are worthy of Joyce, though, if I say so myself."

Aidan broke eye contact with Emme for the first time. Emme

was pleased to see color humbly rush to his cheeks when his Grandmother bragged on him.

"Oh, Meemaw, you need to stop filling Emme's head with such tall tales. I do love to write. I'll write anything, but I'm no Joyce."

Emme would've recognized Aidan even if she'd met him somewhere far away from Kentucky. Same dark hair, practically black, and same gray eyes.

"Hello, Emme. How are you? It's been a very long time. What brings you out here, if I may ask?"

Emme hated clichés more than just about anything, and she certainly didn't want to be one, but for a second she was speechless. Aidan looked exactly like in her vision when she'd seen his older version superimposed upon the boy she stood with in the middle of the wedding reception.

"Hey," was all she could say.

"I was just about to start some lunch. Why don't you come on back in the kitchen with me and tell me everything while Aidan goes out to the springerator and grabs a few things?"

Emme must've looked puzzled because Aidan told her what a *springerator* was.

"It's better than a refrigerator. Hominy Creek stays cool year-round. The small part of the spring that comes up on our property, not too far behind our barn, has a partial cave that's dry and cool because of the water always flowing around it. We keep things in there. Everything always tastes fresh and it's great for when the power goes out. I swear things could stay good in that cave forever."

"Oh, I get it now." Emme smiled at the thought. Finally, a cave that didn't scare her half to death.

"Aidan keeps some of his 'shine in there, too. The good stuff that'll cure any ill. He's got his own still where he makes the finest stuff. It doesn't have to be cold, but sometimes we like it on the cool side, so we keep a bit in the springerator."

"My Aunt Deirdre was telling me how wonderful it was."

"We're a dry county and the nearest drug store is thirty miles away, so it's such a blessing to have Aidan back here making 'shine again. Just like his papaw did, God bless my sweet Johnny's soul."

"Aileen, I might have to take you up on that. I don't drink a lot, but if it's medicinal, well, why not?"

Emme sounded more eager than she'd wanted to.

Aileen and Aidan laughed at Emme's enthusiasm. After they made their way into the kitchen, Emme saw that Aileen was just like Fi, a whirling dervish flying around making lunch. Then Aidan reached over and touched Emme's shoulder. She turned to look at him. They were standing there looking at each other much the way they had many years before.

"Are you sure you don't want me to get the kind that tells the future, too, Emme?"

"The future?"

"That's what folks around here say it does. I'm not sure about all that, but it does taste the best. That part I'm sure about. We don't give that one out much. Most people don't even know we have it. But since you're practically kin, and with all that's been going on with your family, I'd make an exception for you."

As Emme stared at the grey mist in Aidan's eyes again, her mountain gift flew out and she couldn't help herself. She started immediately singing the song that was in her head, a melody she'd never heard before. Spontaneous lyrics came out of her, too. "Mist rolls down the mountain and covers the ground. The fog carries my spirit and what's lost is found."

Aidan didn't seem shocked or even surprised that Emme burst into song.

"Those are some mighty fine lyrics and a pretty tune, too. Is that one of the old ones I just can't remember? It sounds old. I like them old."

"Me, too."

"I write new ones, but they always come out sounding old. Don't know if they'll ever sell because of that, but I gotta write what I believe in."

Emme had found it easier to sing than to speak to Aidan.

"Honestly, I have never heard that song before. I just . . . I just . . . it just came to me. With so many crazy things happening, I don't suppose my singing a brand-new song, reaching up and grabbing the lyrics and melody from thin air, is any crazier than anything else I've experienced recently."

"The way songs come to us is as great a mystery as any mystery there is. They're gifts and I'm always grateful. Maybe later we can work on fleshing that one out."

"I'd like that."

"It'd be my pleasure. I love music."

Emme nodded at Aidan.

"I love music, too. I used to sing all the time with my family. Being back in Kentucky seems to bring it out of me."

Then they ate. After the potato soup, which had salty pieces of bacon in it and bitter kale bits to balance it out, and the molasses bread Aileen fixed for lunch, Emme was suddenly exhausted. Aileen could see it on Emme's face, so she told Aidan to get back to work and suggested Emme go upstairs and take a rest. Neither of them argued. Emme slept the entire afternoon and all the way through supper. She didn't even dream.

CHAPTER 15

WHEN EMME woke up from her nap, it was dark outside, and no one was in the house. She found Aileen and Aidan sitting around a small fire in the backyard. Aidan had his guitar and Aileen was singing "Tam Lim." It was one of Emme's favorites. She loved the line, "And they will turn me in your arms to a lion bold." Emme thought it was magnificent when she was a child and loved that it had knights, fairies, and newts all in one song.

Emme wasn't surprised that Aileen, despite being barely five feet tall, could belt lyrics so fiercely. It was as if Aileen were pushing out a huge baby, birthing the song. But Aileen stopped when she saw Emme.

"Oh, please don't stop because of me. I love that one," Emme insisted.

"I need to be fixing you some supper. You slept right through it. I didn't wake you because I could see how tired you were."

"Honestly, that potato soup you fixed earlier was one of the best things ever. And I had two slices of molasses bread. I'm still full."

"Could I at least get you a drink?"

"No, ma'am. I drank a glass of water before I came out here."

Aidan got up and handed Emme an aqua-colored Ball jar. It was her favorite shade of blue. She realized right then that she loved it even more than cerulean.

"I saved some 'shine for you. This is the basic kind, not my special brew. It's sweet as summer tea, but with a zing like the finest bourbon, so be careful."

Emme had never drunk much alcohol, even when her Georgetown friends went bar-hopping in college. But she was curious about Aidan's moonshine. And after all the insanity of her life, she knew she should relax a bit, at least for a night. She took one sip and there was never a bigger duality. It was sweet like Aidan said, but it burned, too. Not a bad burn. She didn't cough like she did the first time her father had given her a sip of his special whiskey that she eventually grew to love. But the moonshine was so warm that it thrummed in her deeper than her throat and stomach. She felt a timpani beating beyond her gut. It was one of the most soothing things Emme had ever felt, all luxuriant rhythm.

"If you be sure I can't get you nothing, I've gotta be getting on to bed. It's past this old bird's bedtime."

"Thank you."

"One last thing, Emme."

"Yes, ma'am?"

"You probably think I'm boasting something awful, but I swear it true that Aidan is an honorable boy. He will help you any way he can since I know you came here looking for some answers."

Emme loved that Aileen had said "swear it true" like her family did. It comforted her. And Emme believed Aileen when she said Aidan was an honorable boy.

"Thank you. From the bottom of my heart I mean that. I'll see you in the morning."

Aileen kissed Emme on each cheek, like everyone did when Emme spent a semester abroad in Italy, and then she walked back in the house. Aidan was still standing up as his grandmother left.

When Aidan sat back down, he said, "I can be shy, but I know you drove out here for a reason."

"Yes."

"Then be direct with me and I'll be direct with you, too. I'll do what I can to help, including getting you another glass of 'shine."

Emme immediately felt more relaxed. She didn't know if it was the fact that she'd already finished off the first Ball jar of moonshine, the fire, or being with Aidan, but she started laughing.

"Another glass would be great, thanks."

Emme lifted up her jar and Aidan brought over a big jug to fill it up again.

As Aidan poured, he said, "Be careful with this stuff."

Emme laughed at Aidan's warning and then he laughed with her.

"I gotta keep my wits about me. And I do have some questions."

"Ask away."

"I'm just gonna come out with it and that's not normally my way. I'm usually way too polite. Or way too afraid."

"Afraid of what?" Aidan had walked back over to his spot by the fire, but was still holding the jug. He gestured with it as he talked to Emme.

"It's not just that Kelly has been arrested for a murder she couldn't possibly have committed. Or even that half the town, including my Aunt Deirdre, seems to be haunted by ghosts. That's not the worst of it."

"What is?" As Aidan asked Emme the question, he put his moonshine jug down very carefully. He watched his own hands as he moved it, but as soon as the bottle was on the ground, his eyes immediately went to Emme.

"That's why I'm here." Fueled by the moonshine, Emme felt a tsunami of words about to come out, and it didn't bother her at all. She somehow knew Aidan wouldn't mind. "I'm afraid of myself. Afraid that everything I learned in DC might not be true. Afraid what I fought to forget is stronger than what I learned. Afraid I have abilities that can't be explained by science or investigative journalism articles or college degrees."

Emme paused. Aidan lifted his Ball jar at her and simply said, "It's okay. You can go on. I'll listen."

"I've been seeing things." Emme then stopped, waiting for Aidan to look at her like she was crazy. When he simply nodded as if she had told him the most basic information in the world, she continued.

"Like so many people in my family see things. Before, though, I wrote it off as crazy nonsense, just family myths. Especially when I found out there's a medical explanation and it's called synesthesia."

"Synesthesia?" Aidan had been about to take a sip of his 'shine, but stopped to think about what Emme was saying. Emme could see his face suddenly shift from one of empathy to that of deep contemplation, complete with serious eyebrow furrow.

"There's more to it than that, though. But I can't make sense of any of it."

"Try me, maybe I can help."

"I remember your family seemed more open about your gifts than even my own. That's why I'm here. I need the truth."

"I tell the truth."

"I believe you. But I also need to save Kelly. And a friend of mine, or the mother of a friend of mine. I need to save her, too, because she's dying . . ."

"Emme, I'm so sorry . . ." Aidan and Emme looked at each other for several seconds. Emme could see how hurt he was for her.

"And maybe I need to save myself. But there just doesn't seem to be enough time for saving all of us at once."

Emme started to cry. Aidan didn't move to comfort her, but his body folded into itself in deep emotion and leaned closer to her in true empathy.

"There's not a timetable to figure out how to help folks."

"I hope not."

"You feel pressure because of Kelly and all the people you wanna help. That's a lot of pressure."

"Yes." When Emme said, "Yes," she had to fight herself. She didn't want to start sobbing.

"You also don't have to figure out who you are all at once, either."

"It sure feels like it, though. At least to me."

"It's not just you." As Aidan talked, he'd pause every sentence or two to look into his Ball jar. As he gazed down, Emme could see the length of his eyelashes more clearly, illuminated by the fire. When he looked back up at her, every time, Emme felt a wave of light wash over her body from her toes all the way to her head. She knew she shouldn't be able to feel the light as a tangible thing, but she did, just like all of her other senses got jumbled together during her mountain gift times. She wondered if Aidan could see the light wash over her.

"It's not?"

"When I went off to college, even though there were lots of other farm boys from small towns like me there, there weren't any others from Traveling families. At least not like me."

"No, I doubt there were boys like you." Emme knew Aidan thought she meant his abilities, but she meant all of him. Aidan was special.

"Some folks see only the bad things about us, so we keep it to ourselves. I especially didn't tell folks about my abilities."

"And what are your abilities like?"

"I can see things, probably like you do, or that I'm suspecting you can. It's rare enough for somebody to get glimpses of the future, rare for our grandmothers and aunts. It seems like every generation our ability gets weaker, though." Aidan sighed, and Emme realized that the words he'd spoken echoed Aunt Della's. "But it's really rare for a guy, at least that's what Meemaw and my mama say. They say I'm the only man they've ever met with some kind of second sight."

"I never . . ." Emme realized that was not true. She did know. So she started her sentence over. "I think I've always known, since we were little, that you had it, too."

"I don't even know what it is or if it's true, not completely." Emme was both relieved and sad to hear Aidan's uncertainty, but she quickly took another drink, trying not to show it on her face.

"What's it like for you?"

"Sometimes I dream things. Sometimes those things come true. That makes me feel . . ." Aidan couldn't finish.

"I know that feeling." Emme and Aidan looked at each other again and suddenly the fire wasn't the brightest thing between them. It was the feeling, a feeling that became light, and it moved inside their chests, on their faces, hovering around them both.

"Maybe it's my imagination. Maybe even when I'm sleeping I'm still making up stories. Maybe sometimes those stories come true. Luck of the draw."

"Maybe." After all the years she'd fought believing in her own abilities, Emme found herself wanting to believe that Aidan's were real. She didn't want to keep guzzling the 'shine and get flat-out drunk, though, so she didn't take another sip right away. She started rubbing the outside of the Ball jar absentmindedly, letting its cool smoothness soothe her.

"And maybe my magic moonshine isn't magic. Maybe we all just get so drunk on it that it makes it easier to believe what we wanna believe."

"So you have no answers, either." Emme realized that she should've been disappointed by Aidan not having the answers. That meant her trip to Marrowbone was futile. And, yet, Emme felt connected to Aidan in a way that made her realize she was exactly where she was supposed to be.

"Not exactly. Sometimes I still choose to believe in all of this. Why not?"

"I can think of a dozen reasons to not believe."

Although Emme wanted to believe in Aidan's gifts, the reality of what was happening in Red River, the reality of her whole life, prompted her to maintain some skepticism. She put the Ball jar on the ground in front of her and hugged herself as if she had become extremely cold.

"Me, too," Aidan said, "but there's some logic to it, too."

"That's where we disagree."

"But every religion and culture throughout the world has some kind of shaman, some mystical qualities. And they all believe in things that seem impossible. I can't disprove it. I can't prove it, either."

"Exactly."

"But when I'm not being cynical, I like to believe it's possible."

"I guess anything's possible."

"Of course I want to use it for good, too. I just can't always control it. It comes and goes. That's part of why I haven't been able to fully trust that it's real."

"Me, too."

"But for some reason, with you here, I want to believe more than ever that what I see is real, even if what I see scares me."

"Really? You get scared by it?"

"I'm a man, but I'm not afraid to admit that I get scared, too. We can be scared together tonight. Please, tell me more of your fears."

Emme looked down at the Ball jar. She uncrossed her arms, picked it up, and took the biggest swig of alcohol she ever had. And then she unleashed all her fears. Every time she took a sip of 'shine, she told Aidan more. She told him all about Kelly and Cy. She told him about Everett describing Cy with his head smashed against the wall. She told him about Kelly thinking something was in the room when it happened. She told him about everything Deirdre had said, how she was frightened by the banshees. She told him about all the women who'd gone mad. She told him about her trip down the Red River to the Bell Witch Cave. She told him how afraid she was that she couldn't forgive herself for Evan. She told him she was afraid for

Mattie, especially since Mrs. Maddox was dying. She told him she was afraid that her town would never learn from its mistakes, that the powers that be would go on letting women get assaulted and the town would still stay segregated. Emme told Aidan she was most afraid of not being able to save anyone, not even herself, and of not knowing what to do next. Emme was afraid that for the rest of her days death would follow her everywhere and that some of it was her fault, that she deserved it. Emme unloaded her fears until it was three in the morning.

"Emme, Emme, Emme." Aidan repeated her name, and it flowed out of his mouth as if it were an endless stream of soothing water.

"Emme, it's going to be all right. You have to believe me."

"I want to."

"You're so agitated."

Emme, her body agreeing with Aidan on its own, shuddered, and she found herself drawing her knees up to her chest to try to calm herself.

As Aidan continued to speak, Emme kept holding her knees to her chest. "I don't blame you. What a mess you and your family are in. What a mess for your whole town. You need to sleep, though."

When Aidan paused to let his words sink in, Emme found her body relaxing some. She pulled her knees from her chest and resumed sitting in a more natural position.

"You need to get some answers, too. My meemaw was right. I do have a stronger brew. I only bring it out at special times, when someone really needs it."

"And you think I do?"

"Yes, but it makes what you were drinking tonight look like watered down cat piss."

Emme couldn't help but laugh.

"Sorry for the language, but it's true. My meemaw says because I make this special brew, some of my ability seeps into it, so when you drink it, you get a little bit of my gift. If you already have a gift, too, it will get stronger when it mixes with mine. Then you can get answers."

"I could definitely use some answers."

"If there ever was a time for both of us to believe in mountain gifts and magic moonshine, then it's tonight. We'll both suspend our disbelief and I'll bring you some of the special brew. It'll make you dream deeply. It might even show you what to do next, if you're willing to try."

Emme grew succinct. "Yes."

Aidan got up and Emme followed him inside. He reached up to a high shelf in the kitchen and brought down an old brown jug. Nothing fancy except for a few vivid yellow streaks of color running top to bottom. Emme immediately recognized the jug from her vision of Kelly's painting. She was about to mention it, but was instead irresistibly drawn to Aidan's hands as he opened the lid. He poured a clear liquid into a plain white teacup that had been sitting out to dry on top of the sink and handed it to Emme.

"Go up to bed before you drink it. It'll knock you right out. I'll see you in the morning. And, Emme?"

"Yes?"

"I believe that this will do the trick."

"For tonight, I'll believe it, too.

CHAPTER 16

EMME DIDN'T dream about Kelly and Mrs. Maddox like she thought she would. Instead, she dreamed she was once again riding down the Red River in a canoe with Evan. Emme was in the front of the canoe paddling hard while Evan sat behind her. He was tapping out a Morse Code–like rhythm on the edge of the canoe. Emme stopped paddling to turn around and watch Evan's fingers. They were methodically tapping away. Emme counted as Evan repeated eight very particular taps.

"Is that Morse Code?"

"No. It is a code, though. It's the code of the universe. I'm repeating the number eight, the symbol for infinity. It's part of the math that's behind all that we see and all that we don't. It's the music used to create every single thing and the music that will save everything that's broken."

"What's broken?"

"Everything. Well, I'm not anymore. But I know everything is still hard for my mother, and Mattie, too. And for you, Kelly, and all of your family. Everything's still broken for everyone in Red River, isn't it?"

"Yes. It seems like every last thing is broken. Maybe me most of all."

"This code, it's the answer. Or it'll lead you to it. We're riding down the river to it right now."

"I'm so sorry, but I still don't understand. And I'm more than sorry. For before. For not having enough courage to really be with you."

"It's okay, it really is. There was a plan in all that happened, even the horrible parts. I know you'll see that soon."

"Do you promise it true, Evan?"

"I do. And you know the answer. You can feel this rhythm, the larger hum of the world. A hymn for everything. It's the same motif of the universe. Remember how I always rambled on about math, music, and the universe? How they were intertwined? About how I knew I could believe in something beyond myself because the math never lied?"

"Yes."

"Math is music, Emme. So is the whole universe. You're music, too. You're a song being written this very second."

"I understand you and I don't understand you at the same time. Like in high school, I guess."

"It's okay. It was always okay. But please stop looking at me now because I need you to turn around and face forward."

Emme spun around and saw that they were getting near the part of the river that was on Aunt Fi's property. Then Emme turned back to look at Evan again.

"We're almost home. I always wanted to bring you back here. You came once and it was one of the most amazing days of my life, to have you at the farm with my family. Even after that horrible time in the cave. With you there with us, you turned the worst day into the best. Now you'll be home with me again."

"No, it's not me who needs to go home with you. I'll still be with you, though. But only in my new way. Remember, no energy can be created or destroyed. I've just changed forms."

"The thermodynamic laws. You loved talking about them. So you'll never be gone, only changed?"

"Yes. Into something like the stars. We'll all be star stuff. Every atom in our bodies. In the universe. Singing star stuff."

"That's beautiful."

Evan stopped tapping the rhythm on the side of the canoe.

"There's someone else who will be with you. She'll be growing up on that wonderful farm of yours. Turn around and see the gift I have for you."

Before Emme turned, Evan started to change. He became millions of tiny stars growing brighter every second. The brighter he became, the more at peace Emme felt. So she turned around to see what Evan had been talking about, what his gift was. And right there on Fi's dock was Mattie.

CHAPTER 17

WHEN EMME walked into the kitchen after her moonshine-fueled night of dreaming, Aidan was already sitting there while Aileen bustled around. He didn't have a grin on his face as much as a half smirk, one side of his smile awake, the other asleep. Aidan didn't waste any time asking Emme how her night was.

"I see you survived my special brew. What'd you see? Do you have your answers about Kelly and Mrs. Maddox?"

Aileen gave Aidan a loving and gentle smack upside the head.

"Boy, you better stop pestering the poor gal with so many questions when she just woke up. She might've done got some good answers while she dreamed, but I'm pretty sure she's got a dang old headache, too, from your extra fine 'shine."

"You're so sweet, Aileen, but I'm doing well, all things considered."

"Glad to hear it, but surely I can get you something for breakfast?"

"I could use some coffee, please ma'am. And, Aidan, I did dream. It was a wonderful dream."

"So you found your answers."

"I'm sorry to say that I didn't dream of how to help Kelly. The dream didn't really make any sense, either, though it was sweeter than I could've imagined."

"Maybe it will still come true for you, even if it didn't answer your questions right now."

"I don't think there's any way that particular dream will come true, but I thank you for trying. And I really loved the 'shine of yours. Thank you for wanting to help."

The whole time Emme was denying that the dream was real, Aidan tried to not protest. He waited until she was done speaking and then said, "Emme, I'm sorry you don't believe it worked. I feel it in my gut that it did. I think if you give it time, you'll see there was more truth in that vision than you realize now."

"Vision?"

"Yes, I said vision. I think you saw the future, or a glimpse of it. I was up most of the night tossing and turning. I realized I can't keep going back and forth on what's plain to see. We have visions, Emme. We really do. I believe it even more today."

Just as Emme was about to argue with Aidan, she saw that sitting by his feet at the kitchen table were three packed bags.

"If it's okay, I'd love to ride back with you to Red River."

Emme was not expecting for him to say that and she was speechless again as Aidan continued to talk.

"I'd love to see your aunts again and to help you and them any way I can. I definitely want to help Kelly."

"That's kind, but . . ."

"I know you still don't believe that my moonshine works, but I want to promise you on my honor that I knew you were coming. I dreamed about Kelly a long time ago. I didn't quite know that these horrible things were going to happen to her, at least not like it's played out. But I dreamed about her, her name. I hardly even remembered that she was someone I'd met so long ago when I first dreamed her name. I saw it etched into a cave wall."

Emme sat stunned when Aidan said that, since it resembled what had happened to her at the Bell Witch Cave with Evan.

Aidan could see that Emme was upset. "I didn't mean to scare you."

"It's not you."

"I didn't know what it meant, or I would've tried to help sooner. But as soon as you showed up and started talking about it, I knew it all made sense. Like with your dream, at first I couldn't quite figure out all the puzzle pieces. You coming here and sharing your fears, what you said about Kelly. I understood my dream then."

"I wish I could understand my dream."

"Even if you don't think any of our dreams or visions are real, I'd still love to come back and try to help, if that's okay."

"Maybe . . ." Emme was actually shocked at how much she wanted Aidan to come back with her, but she tried not to show it.

"Also, I know it's time I get down to Nashville with some of my songs. They're ready. Your part of Kentucky is so close to Music Row. I can get a room somewhere in Red River, so you don't even have to put me up, but I'd surely appreciate a ride since you're heading back."

When Aidan mentioned Music Row, Emme regained her composure. Hearing him talk about Kelly's name on the cave wall had unsettled her, and the unexpected deep need she felt for him to return to Red River with her had unsettled her just as much. She believed Aidan's sincerity and knew that whether his dream was true or not, she could trust him.

"You and Aileen have been kind to me here. Of course you can ride with me back to Red River, but you should stay at least a night or so at the farm before going some place else."

"Thank you."

"I know my aunts would love to see you again first."

"I don't expect that, though."

"They'd insist you stay for a little while with us since you're practically kin, what with my cousin marrying your sister. I'm sure they'd also let you drive one of their many trucks when you need to, so you can visit Nashville. It seems there are more old trucks at Fi's farm than there are people to drive them."

"I appreciate it, I surely do."

After they'd both hugged Aileen for a good long time, Emme stayed to offer her some final words of gratitude while Aidan went outside and loaded their bags. When Emme left the house to join Aidan, the trunk was still open. She noticed a couple other things in addition to their bags. Emme was both a bit scared and incredibly grateful to spy two of the same kind of aged brown jugs with yellow streaks she'd seen Aidan pour his special brew out of the night before. The same kind as in her vision of Kelly's painting, too.

CHAPTER 18

IN THE car on the way back to Red River, Emme learned that Aidan was a talker. Emme, though tipsy the night before, remembered Aidan describing himself as shy when they'd been sitting around the fire. It wasn't that he was suddenly not shy anymore, it was more that Emme could tell he'd relaxed around her. Maybe her unburdening her worries to him for so long had made him trust her. Maybe just more time spent together made Aidan let down his own defenses.

Whatever it was, Emme liked it. While she desperately wanted to figure out how to help Kelly, her aunts, Mrs. Maddox, and everyone in Red River, Emme knew she also had to take in every bit of joy she could to combat the fear that still plagued her. Emme needed Aidan's endless enthusiasm to be a kind of talisman for her as she steadied herself to fight what she knew was going to be a deluge of emotions once she was back home.

"Please tell me more. I've loved everything you've told me so far about your Traveller family. And I remember bits and pieces from meeting you and some of them when we were younger, like I was telling you last night. But I'd love to know everything."

"I think one of my favorite things is our language. I'm not really supposed to tell what I know about it even though I'm not actively a Traveller anymore, but I know I can trust you. We speak Cant."

"Cant? I know Deirdre mentioned something about your language, but I don't know if she mentioned the name."

"It's really a hodgepodge, I believe, from Irish influences and even some of our fellow Gypsy nomads, the Romani. We share words in common, and certainly many of our ways, since we're both sojourners."

"I love the word *sojourner*. No wonder you're a writer and song-writer. You like words like I do. I always used to think of myself as a sojourner when I left home for DC and as I lived abroad in Italy. A sojourning Kentucky girl."

"I have a song titled that, Emme. It's called 'Sojourner Blues.'"

"Blues. I love some good blues tunes, though they're usually so mournful. Were you unhappy traveling?"

"No, it's just that I knew I had to settle down some place specific. Not at Aileen's, either. I was on a path. I am on a path. I have to be getting to some very particular place. I loved to see the world, I really did, though. But . . . well, this may sound corny."

"Corny is fine by me. I'll take corny over mean, cynical, hateful, scary, or prejudiced any day. Give me corny all day long."

Aidan chuckled at Emme's ardor for corniness.

"You'll love this, then. It does kind of sound corny no matter how sincere I am, so you'll get your wish."

"Good."

"I longed for something and somewhere specific. But I didn't know where it was. I just knew it wasn't where I was during those times traveling. So, however much I soaked in everything and appreciated everything and everyone I saw on my way, I was being drawn somewhere else. Somewhere permanent."

"Like Nashville?"

"I think that's closer to it than I've been before. And something else. You mentioned liking corny over prejudice."

"It's true."

"This may sound defensive and I certainly don't mean to imply that you've been anything other than open to hearing about my Tinker family, but some people have real prejudices against us."

"In what way?"

"Like so many things, I guess, it's complicated. But a few bad eggs have given all of us a bad name. Outsiders sometimes think every single one of us is a thief. That we're going around traveling from place to place scamming people. That's not the truth, even though I'm not saying that all of us are perfect, either"

"Trust me, I know no one's perfect, most of all me."

"In any group of people you're gonna have some bad folks. But I know, and I mean I really know this on a personal level, that my relatives are hardworking and honest. They learn trades. Then they share their skills out in the towns as they move from place to place. But they're not conning anybody, ever. I certainly haven't."

"I believe you."

"I did work roofing for a while right after college. Not all of us go to college. We're close-knit and like to stay together with all our traditions, which I love. But when I felt I had to go, they supported me. I worked back with the family for a little while, though, before settling with Meemaw."

"Aileen reminds me of my own family."

"She doesn't want to admit it, but she really needed the help. I want her to live forever, but she's getting on up there in years, so I definitely had to help. I also needed to stay still long enough to get some more songs done. But I never ripped off anybody."

"I see this everywhere, not just in rural Kentucky. Weird prejudices in DC. Everyone lumping someone into one group or another and judging whatever group's not their group."

"Yeah, I suspect it'd be bad up there, too."

"In DC it comes down to a zoo."

"A zoo?"

"One group sees the other with a donkey symbol attached to them and they think they're evil. The other group sees someone with an elephant symbol and they think they're evil."

"A zoo. Hadn't thought of it like that."

"Sure, they're bad folks who've done bad things in both groups, politics being what it is. But I choose to decide on an individual basis, I really do."

"I'm happy to hear that. Did you ever feel people in DC had preconceived ideas about you being from Kentucky? Did they make fun of your accent?"

"Oh, heavens yes. In DC, some folks think a southern accent equals stupid. My own editor, whom I'm ashamed to say I dated for a while, made fun of my accent. And he can't get past his own subjectivity about what's happening in Red River, either."

"In what way?"

"He doesn't want to look more deeply. He just wants the scandals. I don't know if he ever saw me for more than a hick. I even had people in DC ask me if I'd grown up without shoes, too. Not many, thankfully, but a few."

"I believe it. I've experienced it, too."

"Some people there wanted to know if I had relatives who were on meth or in trailers. Yes, a few in trailers. No to the meth. I had friends who had family members who were addicts. But it was never as black-and-white as simply plopping them or anyone in some preconceived box all neat and tidy."

"No, definitely not."

"Wherever I've lived, I see people want to judge the people who aren't from there. It works the other way, too. So many southern people think everyone's evil up North. I guess people just hate what they don't know."

"I should write a song about that."

"Of course I met amazing people in DC, too. And amazing people in New York and all over the world. But then there are those I call the lost causes. The mean ones who want to poke fun and look down their noses at people who are different from them. Those folks don't know what they were missing."

Emme stuck her chin out defiantly and then laughed. Aidan loved the sound of it. He'd heard some people describe laughter as a twinkling sound. Emme's wasn't twinkling, though. It was smoother and richer. Aidan loved Emme's sense of humor, how she tried to see the bright side of everything despite all the sadness and fear he knew she had to be feeling.

"When I get fed up with mean people, I know I can't do anything else but sing. Or at least listen to music or write a song."

"Me, too. Well, for a while I didn't sing. For a good long while I was silent, but that's a whole other story for another day."

"You not singing?" Emme got scared for a second that Aidan might drive off the side of the road because he turned to look at her for so long.

"But I still listened to music. And I spent so much of my life singing with my family and singing in a band in high school. And in many choirs and theatre productions in college. I've always met some of my best friends that way."

"Me, too."

"One of the true gifts of coming back home to help Kelly, even despite all the difficulty, has been that I've started singing again. Singing with my aunts makes my heart flutter. Maybe even my soul flutters."

"Emme, I'm not lying when I say I feel the exact same way."

"Let's sing something, then. Whatever you want."

"Do you remember 'Tell Me Ma'?"

Emme could feel her pink cheeks betraying her as she vividly recalled the night she met Aidan as a child. And what happened while that very song played. But Aidan seemed oblivious to it, so she forged ahead.

"That's one of my favorites."

"Let's start with that one, then. I can't think of a better song to keep our spirits lifted. Especially yours. I know you're carrying so much right now. And we're getting closer to your home."

When they started the song, they both sang melody. But after they'd sung several lines, their voices seemed to be climbing up a mountain. Not that they were tired, but their voices sounded as if they were anticipating something. They kept moving up the mountain until they crested the top on the lines, "She is handsome, she is pretty, she is the belle of Belfast City," where they broke into harmony. It made the sound soar even higher. There was a beautiful burgeoning of their voices during the rest of the song and the many others they sang that carried them into Red River.

CHAPTER 19

WHEN THEY got back to the farm, Emme brought Aidan inside and reintroduced him to Fi and Deirdre. Emme was flabbergasted that her aunts didn't seem a bit surprised she'd come home with him.

"You done known by now, or you should, that I seen this. I knew Aidan was coming, probably before you did."

Emme never ceased to be tickled by her aunts.

"Of course you did, Aunt Deirdre. I seem to be the only one in the family who doesn't know who's coming and going beforehand."

"If you trusted your mountain gift, I bet you'd know a helluva lot more, now wouldn't you?" Aunt Deirdre smiled as she teased Emme.

"I think you have a new ally in Aidan, because he seems to think my mountain gift's real, too. That I should use it more often. But, I suppose you knew that, right?"

Emme couldn't help thinking how preposterous, but sweet, it all seemed. All these family members and now Aidan, too, thinking she had special abilities.

Fi ushered them into the living room.

"Emme and Aidan, too, I'd be so pleased to offer you something to drink if you're parched from your trip. Supper's a few hours away, but I can scrounge up something if you'd like."

"Thank you, but Aidan's grandmother, Aileen, she's just like you. She couldn't possibly let us leave her house without some sandwiches and a thermos of coffee. So we ate lunch on the road. I'm still full, but Aidan might need something."

"No, ma'am, I'm fine, too. But I thank you kindly for the offer."

"Aunt Fi, I know Aunt Deirdre claims to know that Aidan was coming, but are you prepared for him, too? I knew once he got here that you'd want him to stay a few nights before he headed off to the boarding house in town, but I don't want to presume anything."

"Presume away. Mama told me Aidan was coming and that he needed to stay a bit here with us, so I've made up the guest room. But you never need to ask me, Emme. This is your home, too. You might've been gone a long time, but it's still your home. Aidan is welcome here as long as he sees fit to stay."

Aidan and Emme both said, "Thank you, ma'am," at exactly the same time and in exactly the same way, as if they were singing together again. There was an intimacy to it that made Emme want to bolt, but Fi distracted her with updates.

"I have some good news about Kelly. But before I get to that, I want you to know that Pastor Willard came by again and he was so sorry he keeps missing you."

"I'm sorry I keep missing him, too. What a lovely man. And still making the rounds checking on people after all these years. He's almost as old as Aunt Deirdre, isn't he?"

"There now, Emmeretta McLean." Aunt Deirdre laughed as she gently admonished her niece. "He's not quite as decrepit as me, but he's getting on up there in the years."

"He's wonderful. The way he helped me when Mama and Daddy were sick. And after Evan died. I would love to see him again, even if he finds out I never go to church in DC."

Fi and Deirdre exploded with a loud "Emme!"

Emme didn't know how to respond and simply stood there until Fi spoke again.

"Mama and I don't want to shame you. You're a grown-up now, hard as that is to believe. You can make your own choices. Just trust us when we say that Pastor Willard would love to see you."

"I'd love to see him, too."

"I was thinking, for someone who was supposed to be locked up tight and not allowed any visitors, Kelly certainly gets a lot. Rowdy snuck Pastor Willard in more than a few times, too. Love that Rowdy."

"He's something. I think everybody loves him."

"There's more news than that, though. Peter Rafferty, he's been working hard as Kelly's attorney. He came out here and talked for a good long time with me. No talking down, either."

"I respect him, too, Aunt Fi."

"He got me back in to see Kelly again and brought her a dress and other things for her arraignment, which is in just a couple days. Kelly's gonna enter a not guilty plea. Thankfully Peter talked her into that. She stopped that confession nonsense."

"That's fantastic news."

"She's doing so much better. They're gonna release her from the hospital to go to the arraignment. She's doing so fine she can walk a little bit now."

"I think she's tougher than any of us gave her credit for."

"Rowdy or one of them still has to be in the room with her when they uncuff her from the bed, though, for her walks."

"I tried hard to change the handcuffs part."

"I know you did. One of the saddest things I ever seen. Then afterward, they locked her right back up. But there's hope. I believe Peter's gonna find a way to prove she didn't do it. He's gonna make a motion for a . . . what's that word?"

"A dismissal?"

"A dismissal, yep. Once the judge sees everything, Peter thinks there won't be no trial at all. He says he can absolutely get the confession part thrown out because she was beat half to death and not in her right mind. I believe him."

While Fi had been talking about Kelly, Emme had started pacing. Since Aidan's special moonshine hadn't helped her dream of how to fix things for Kelly, she'd been worrying about what to do next. The fact that Peter had gotten Kelly to plead not guilty didn't fix everything, but it was a step in the right direction. Emme was still worried, though.

Fi showed Aidan his room and then went to fix supper. Everybody helped, even Aidan, in the kitchen.

Deirdre bragged on him. "You are gonna make a fine husband someday, you here willing to help us in the kitchen."

"Thank you, Mrs. Deirdre. For all the old things I love, I'm a modern man."

Emme pointedly asked, "How modern are you?"

"I believe there is no distinction between men's work and women's work. Everybody works hard on a farm. Or they should. That means everyone works in the field and in the kitchen. And the laundry room, too."

Fi and Deirdre both shouted, "Amen!"

Aidan had gone outside to the garden and picked some of the winter kale that was already coming in. It was a little stronger than the summer collards, so he'd put it in a pot on the stove and started cooking it down with oil, vinegar, and Tabasco sauce, too. He was about to ask if they had any ham pieces or bacon to add for a little flavor when Fi popped in some crumbled-up bacon pieces while he stirred. Deirdre then made more cornbread and Fi checked on the chicken she had baking in the oven while Emme set the table.

After supper, Aidan brought out his guitar. Emme was thrilled when she saw Fi and Deirdre get out two different-sized copper pots, each with its own timbre, and create a rhythm section for

Aidan. Emme remembered Evan on his drums, how much he loved matching the bass guitar tempo that Porter played. The memory didn't sting, for which Emme was grateful.

Emme's chest clanged brightly to the beat that her aunts were banging, and she started to sing. She closed her eyes while she offered forth song after song. She closed her eyes because she was in love with the music and wanted to focus on it. She also closed her eyes because she was afraid of looking directly at Aidan. It had been easy to sing with him in the car because she had to look straight ahead as she drove. But there in her own house, in the intimacy of it, an intimacy that wrapped itself around both her and Aidan, she couldn't bring herself to keep her eyes open.

Usually when Emme sang with her family, she switched between the many genres she adored. But in that moment, Emme wanted to concentrate on the Child Ballads. She sang one right after the other, "The Fause Knight Upon the Road," "The Elfin Knight," "Willie's Lady," "The Twa Sisters," "The Cruel Brother," "Sheath and Knife," "The Bonnie Banks o' Fordie," and "The Three Ravens."

The Child Ballads were notorious for having many verses, all of them long, but Emme knew every word of every verse of every song by heart, even though it'd been many years since she'd sung most of them. She sang all of them that night and went to bed exhausted, but more hopeful than she'd been in a long time.

CHAPTER 20

ON HER way into Red River, Emme left Aidan to help Fi and Deirdre with chores around the farm. Her first stop was the police station, but Everett was still gone, so she walked on over to the library to see if Mrs. Maddox was there. She was walking out the door just as Emme got to the building.

"I tried to call you at the farm, but the phone was disconnected."

"Aunt Fi did that. She got rid of it a while ago when Kelly moved back in. Cy called there too much and no one could handle all his swearing."

"That sounds horrible. I'd have gotten rid of mine, too."

"Here we are so close to the new millennium, but we have no phone. I kind of like the silence, though. In the newsroom in DC, we were all in one huge space together and phones were constantly ringing. Sometimes I liked the energy of it, but some days it drove me a little crazy."

Right after Mrs. Maddox came out, Emme saw Reverend Jones come out, too. He'd waited patiently while Emme finished talking.

"Emmeretta, it's always a delight to see you."

Gratitude overcame Emme as she saw Reverend Jones. Long before he'd performed an exquisitely heartfelt funeral service for

Evan, Emme had adored him. Lochlan High was so small that they didn't have enough money to hire professional sports coaches for the various athletic teams. But Reverend Jones had volunteered to coach track when both Emme and Evan had been running, even though his own kids had graduated years before.

Everybody called him "Reverend." Never Mr. Jones or Reverend Jones, just "Reverend." He had been a track star at Lochlan High before he went on to win college running titles when he attended Vanderbilt. He officially gave up competing when he went to seminary in Louisville, but he still remembered everything he'd learned and had generously shared his wisdom with everyone on both the girls' and boys' teams.

"Reverend, it's always wonderful to see you. Are you still running several miles a day?"

"You know me well, you know me well, indeed."

"Emme, I asked Reverend to come with me today."

Mrs. Maddox was finding it hard to talk, so there was a long pause between each phrase, longer than the last time Emme had spoken with her.

"Dr. Branham called me about my latest blood tests, and I wanted Reverend with me. I'd love for you to join us, if you don't have something you need to do for Kelly."

"Things seem to be moving in the right direction with Kelly, Mrs. Maddox, so I'm able to go with you."

They walked slowly over to the hospital. It wasn't far from the library, but Mrs. Maddox had to stop often to catch her breath. Reverend Jones helped steady her and let her lean on him. Emme tried to help her, too. When they reached the oncology floor and told the nurse that Dr. Branham had called Mrs. Maddox, she let them go back.

Dr. Branham smiled, but it was brief. Then he adjusted and re-adjusted his glasses, which Emme knew from experience was not a good thing.

"Mrs. Maddox, I'm pleased you brought such tremendous supporters. I'm afraid this is not good. I've learned to never delay telling people the truth. I know you like me to tell it straight anyway and I respect you and your wishes."

"Thank you. I'm ready for whatever you have to tell me."

"You can probably tell by how much more tired you are the past week that the latest test results are not what we hoped for."

"I had an inkling."

"The leukemia has advanced rapidly, faster in fact, than I'd anticipated. We could admit you right now for more chemo in an attempt to grant you additional time."

"Truthfully, how much longer would that give me?"

"I want you to know it will likely add only a few more weeks to your life and it will be brutal, worse than before. And let me clarify. The chemo is only palliative, not curative. The choice is up to you. Some of my patients endure the chemo for a few more weeks. Some don't."

"How long do I have without the chemo?"

"Without chemo, it's approximately six weeks. With it, maybe ten weeks, but a decidedly difficult ten weeks. Despite years as a physician, I must also state clearly that I'm proffering only an estimate, as every case is highly variable. And, Emme, I can see the wheels turning in your brain right now. I've already called in every favor and looked into every clinical trial for the specific kind of leukemia Mrs. Maddox has. There's nothing new at this time. Just the standard chemo to which I referred earlier. I'm so very sorry, Mrs. Maddox. But whatever you choose, I will ensure that you are as pain-free as I possibly can. You have my word."

Mrs. Maddox didn't cry. She didn't even sigh. She simply said, "I believe you Dr. Branham. I know you'll help me. You've already helped me. I do have a question, for you, please. Which would you choose if it was you?"

"Honestly, I'd choose not to do the chemo. I've met your

brilliant Mattie. That young lady is the smartest child I've ever met. If you try the chemo, you'll be even sicker and more fatigued than you are now and the few weeks it'll buy you will keep you very ill. You're immensely fatigued now, but at least you're not throwing up."

"I'm grateful for that. I detest being so tired, but am thankful I'm not constantly feeling sick to my stomach."

"If it were me, I'd spend the next several weeks with Mattie preparing her for you being gone. Spend it doing joyful things."

"I like the sound of that."

"We can give you some more infusions, but they won't help that much. Tomorrow we'll see about supplemental oxygen, too, and a wheelchair. But I still personally would choose quality over quantity at this point, if for no other reason than to maximize time, vital time, with Mattie. But the choice is yours. I will support whatever you want and need."

"Thank you. Reverend, Emme, I don't have to think about this. I know the answer is no chemo. I want every last minute with Mattie to be a minute of joy. I may be tired, but at least I won't be stuck with my head in a toilet. Sorry for the crude image. But you know what I mean." Mrs. Maddox was taking longer pauses between each sentence the longer she spoke.

Dr. Branham cleared his throat. "Mrs. Maddox, I think it only proper that I inquire, to make sure. Have you thought thus far about longterm plans for Mattie? If not, this would be the time to do it, while you're still strong enough."

"I've thought about it ever since you told me I have leukemia. I'm trying to get in contact with a distant cousin to see if she can take Mattie. Her name's Doris. I haven't seen her in twenty years, but it's worth a try. She's the closest blood relation, other than Mattie, that I have left."

Reverend Jones had tears running down his face. Emme knew it wasn't the first time he'd sat in a hospital room with someone dying. She was touched that he could still be moved by one of his parishioner's plights.

"You know Dee Dee and I, and everyone in your fellowship circle, will help you. You were just in here seeing Sissy Blankenship. She's getting out soon and I know she will return the favor. Everyone else will supply you with food and clean your house. Anything and everything so you can maximize your time with Mattie."

"Thank you, Reverend."

Emme had stayed silent since she walked into Dr. Branham's office. When she finally spoke, her voice sounded terribly hoarse.

"Mrs. Maddox, I promise that I will do everything I can to help you, too."

"Emeretta, that means a lot to me."

"You know Evan and I were close, but it's not only because of him. You were always wonderful with me all those times I practically lived in the library. You are loved by everyone in this town. We're all going to help."

"I never would want Kelly to have suffered, but I'm certainly glad you're here now."

"I am, too. And I want to help you and Mattie do fun things, like taking you both to get ice cream. Or drive you two out to the river. I know you think it's as beautiful as I do."

When Mrs. Maddox and Reverend Jones started to leave, Mrs. Maddox spoke softly, "Emme, you always cheer me up. No wonder Evan thought so highly of you. I'd love for Mattie to get to know you better, too."

"I'd like that."

"She's tired of hearing the same old stories about her father. She could use some new ones from you. Her preschool's over at lunch, then she'll rest a bit. So how about three this afternoon? I'm mighty tired and could use a little break, too."

"Of course. It's beautiful and sometimes sad how much she looks and talks like Evan. But the beautiful part outweighs the sad part."

Mrs. Maddox was still taking rests between phrases, but there was no doubt that she fully believed what she was saying, even as tired as she was. The earnestness in her voice sounded like a bassoon to Emme, and it made her see the color turquoise. "Emme, I understand about Mattie, how she reminds you of Evan. But the more time you spend with her, the more joy it is. Like no other. Far more joy than grief."

Dr. Branham reiterated his commitment to help Mrs. Maddox. As they walked out the door, he asked Emme to stay a minute.

"You know I believe in doctor-patient confidentiality, so I'm not going to say anything about any specific person. But, since you'd been wanting to know about the CDC earlier and all the women who came in right before Cy died, I wanted to update you. Everyone already knows this around here anyway, so I'm not betraying anyone."

"I know you're the kind of doctor with everyone's best interests at heart."

"Thankfully all the CDC people have gone for good and there isn't a single reporter left here, either. I don't know if you saw the latest reports, though?"

"No, sir, I was out in Marrowbone."

"The CDC got back their lengthier tests and reported that there were still no anomalies here. No airborne or waterborne illness. Nothing contagious. All of the women are back home now, too, completely better. Still frightened, but otherwise normal."

"Normal. The test results may be normal, but it doesn't feel normal to me. Certainly not to Kelly."

"I would suspect not. It really is the strangest thing. No one knows what to make of it."

"I don't, either."

"We've had some of the best epidemiologists in the world testing the blood samples and checking on the women who became ill. And psychiatrists came down from New York. Everybody's recovered, but no one knows what the cause was for the fevers, vomiting, and psychotic breaks."

"Psychotic breaks? All of them?"

"That's what the psychiatrists continue to call it, acute psychotic breaks. But they didn't believe it was mass hysteria because none of the women knew about the others. Since they're better now, it's over. So, that's the end of it."

"Let's hope so. This town has been through so much, I don't know how much more it can take. So much good here, but so much still to fix."

"I concur. I've tried to never get in the middle of the things that are wrong, but I do see them. I just don't do anything about them. It's not that I don't care, but I believe I have a gift for healing cancer patients, so I spend much time on that. I have always wished I'd known how to heal the old wounds, to bring everyone together better, though, in the larger community."

"I do, too. That's probably the biggest reason I left. There are far more good people in this town than bad, but the old wounds are still open."

"Yes, yes, I see that all the time."

"The old ways, some of them are good and some of them are bad. It's like we have our own Tower of Babel. Something's happened and we don't know how to talk to each other anymore, let alone treat each other well."

"The Tower of Babel. Fascinating analogy and applicable, too."

"Everyone speaks a different language now and no one can understand the other. Prejudices of all kinds. White against black. Men against women. Baptists against Methodists. Pro-wet county versus pro-dry county. Some of the worst wars have been about whether our county will legally sell alcohol. That's crazy. So much seems crazy here, though, and way before what happened to all the women."

"I have contemplated similar things. When all those distinguished women in our town became so ill on the same night, I realized that that wasn't even the most heartbreaking thing I'd seen in Red River. If I knew how to assist more effectively, you know I would do it. All I know indubitably is that I need to keep on with my patients."

"We're grateful for that, too."

CHAPTER 21

AIDAN WAS waiting for Emme outside the hospital's front door. He held the picnic basket that had belonged to her mother and father, and had Emme's camera slung over his shoulder. She realized that yet again she'd forgotten it. She'd been incredibly busy. Out to Black Mountain, then back to Red River, then on to Marrowbone, and then back to Red River. She'd neglected to take her camera the entire time. Emme was glad that she'd started singing again, but she still loved photography and was thrilled to see Aidan with the picnic basket and her camera, too. Emme would have been happy to see Aidan even if he'd come empty-handed.

"Your aunts are stubborn. Mrs. Deirdre even called herself a 'stubborn old mule.' I wouldn't go that far, but when those women make up their minds, there's no fighting them, is there?"

"I should've warned you. Nope, there's no fighting my aunts. Usually that's a good thing, though."

"I had a huge list of what all I wanted to help them with, but they insisted I take this lunch to you. They said it was the warmest October day they've ever seen, practically summer again, so they made me come here and take you outside for a picnic."

"I'm not sure I should go for a picnic right now."

"They said you'd know all the best spots in Red River. They also said you had to take a rest. That if you kept going at the rate you've been going that you'd pass out on us. They said you could use a break from worrying about Kelly and everything else."

"So they sent you to convince me?"

"At your service! Fi gave me the keys to her truck. She said I could choose the Ford or the Chevy. In the end, I let her pick, so here I am in the Chevy ready to drive you anywhere."

Emme had a fight with herself in a split second. She thought both her aunts, not just Deirdre with her talk of banshees, had gone completely mad. Emme couldn't possibly allow herself to go out for a picnic in the middle of the day when Kelly was still in the hospital, accused of murder. Not while Mrs. Maddox was dying, either. But . . . what good was she to any of the people she loved if she ran herself completely into the ground? It was getting close to lunchtime and she hadn't brought anything to eat, hadn't thought of anywhere to go. Emme knew she had a few hours before she'd promised to be at Mrs. Maddox's to visit with Mattie. She also knew that she shouldn't try to sneak in to see Kelly again. Not so close to the arraignment. Everett was still gone. Dr. Branham had already talked with her. So . . ."I guess I could use a break and I have some time before I see Mrs. Maddox. And I know, no matter how much I want to, that I shouldn't try to visit Kelly any more before the arraignment. That might be pushing my luck too far." Emme sighed a resigned sigh before she was energized with an idea.

"One of the things I've wanted to do for a long time was turn back to art photography."

"Sounds wonderful."

"I enjoy being a journalist and helping people, telling their stories with my camera. But there's still a part of me that would love to make real art out of my photos. Or at least try."

"What do you want to photograph?"

"One of the things I missed most in DC was all the barns

around here. Some are all jaunty and new, standing up straight and dignified."

"Dignified?"

"I love the dignified ones. They're colossal. They deserve respect. I also love the dilapidated ones, the merely used ones as well as the completely abandoned ones on the verge of collapse."

"Kentucky has some amazing barns."

"They all tell a story about our people in these parts, how we're tied to the land. I'd love to do a collection of photos of nothing but old barns."

"That would be perfect."

"I'd also love to photograph my family's musical instruments. Maybe even drive down to Nashville to get someone like Emmylou Harris, Bill Monroe, Dolly Parton, Ricky Skaggs, The Judds, Johnny Cash, Marty Stuart . . . oh my heavens I could keep naming so many folks I love. I'd love to photograph all of them with their instruments."

Aidan tried not to flat-out stare at Emme. In a very short time, though, he'd grown to respect her. He could see how powerful her hope was. Even after everything Emme had endured, her intrinsic positivity kept winning out. Little images of what could be would still push their way past the anguish she constantly carried. Aidan saw it and admired it.

"I didn't think you could top the barn idea . . . but musical instruments? Count me in."

"The stories those guitars and mandolins could tell. But the instruments can wait for a colder day. With this gorgeous weather, we need to be in the great wide open. So barns it is."

"Barns, indeed."

"Just for an hour or two. Then I need to go see Mattie. I promised Mrs. Maddox."

Emme took the keys from Aidan and drove since she knew all the back roads that led to the best barns. When they got to the Frogue

Farm, she parked near their red barn. She told Aidan they were long-time family friends of hers and they wouldn't mind them taking photos and having lunch there.

It didn't surprise Emme one bit that her aunts had gone all out with the picnic lunch. The basket itself had every utensil they'd need and the perfect plaid napkins and plastic cups with the same plaid pattern on the outside. The food was divine. Fried chicken that Emme loved as much cold as she did right out of the skillet. Cold bean salad with three kinds of beans—green, pinto, and white—as well as onions and apple-cider vinegar that Emme loved for its tanginess. As if that wasn't enough, her aunts had packed some biscuits already buttered and little individual Tupperware containers of the spicy red pepper jelly that Emme adored. There was a thermos of lemonade for them to drink. And there were even blueberry muffins for dessert.

After they finished their lunch, they went around the barn several times so they could walk off a bit of the meal. And so Emme could decide exactly what kind of photographs she wanted to take. She called it "getting acquainted with the subject" and reiterated to Aidan how much she loved barns.

"I love barns, too. We have a pretty decent-sized one, but I'm telling you, this one is massive."

Aidan peeked in and saw the beams that had held the tobacco as it cured. He said the complicated wood structures in the upper part of the barn reminded him of magnificent cathedrals in Europe. Emme agreed.

Emme was relentless. She took photo after photo. She even got down on the ground, lying flat on her back, so she could get shots of the rafters from a new angle. Aidan got down on the ground with her so he, too, could see from the new perspective.

"See how the sun pours through the cracks and then bounces off the rafters? It makes fantastic lines of light."

"That's amazing, Emme."

"It's not really refraction, but it's fascinating. My friend, Evan, would've been able to explain the geometry of it all. It's wonderful, isn't it?"

Aidan had spent more time looking at Emme as she photographed the barn than he had looking at the light. But he could easily see what she meant.

"It is. I don't think, even after all the time I've spent in barns, I've ever been lying on the ground looking up at one like this. I've never seen it this way. Thank you."

Emme stopped taking photos, put the camera down, and looked up at the splintered light in the barn. Aidan knew not to disturb her. Emme's mountain gift was back. The sun, the way it showered the old barn wood with its warmth, created a song for her. It wasn't one she'd ever sung or even heard. It was a simple fiddle and it sounded like it was skipping, the notes jumping around playfully. Much the same way the light jumped from rafter to rafter in the barn.

When Emme finally spoke, she was surprised by what she said because she hadn't thought it out beforehand.

"This is probably a vast understatement, but life is bizarre."

"What do you mean?"

"All that's wrong. Obviously everything that's happened with Kelly, the other women in Red River, Mrs. Maddox, Evan and his wife before. My parents. But not just here. There's so much suffering everywhere in the world."

"Unfortunately, you're right. Life can be challenging in brutal ways."

"But then there's all this beauty. There are still kind people. Really good people. Like Dr. Branham and Reverend Jones. My aunts who gladly took me in and raised me as their own when my parents died. And you, Aidan. You're good."

"I'm not perfect, but I try very hard to be good."

"I could tell that immediately about you. Call it intuition; I don't know. But I could tell."

"I think that's why I write music. It's not so someone can be looking at me and go, 'That Aidan sure is talented.' Nope. I wanna help people with my music. Tell their stories. Give them a place to go when they listen that's a kind of . . . well, I don't know the word for it."

Emme smiled. She knew the word Aidan was searching for.

"A refuge?"

"Yes, exactly. A refuge."

Emme and Aidan stayed lying on the ground in the barn for several more minutes. Emme didn't take any more pictures and neither she nor Aidan spoke. Even though there were several inches between them, they both could feel the other's heat, and it felt not only soothing, but rich, almost luxurious to them as they listened to the music in their own heads. They watched the sun continue to caress the rafters until Emme said she had many more places she wanted Aidan to see.

Emme next drove Aidan out to a twenty-acre parcel of land that belonged to Dr. Branham's family. In Lochlan County, even if they had a day job, many folks like Dr. Branham were still gentleman farmers. Dr. Branham had purposefully let one of his barns fall into disrepair. It'd already started crumbling when he'd bought the property back when Emme was still in grade school and he hadn't had the heart to tear it down. He thought it was beautiful, the slant of it, the weathered gray wood. In places you could still see patches of white paint from many years before. Emme had been a little frightened of it when she was younger because it had seemed ghost-like with those patches of white. But as she grew older, and as the barn grew older, too, she'd fallen in love with it and all the layers of paint. And the grainy, weather-pocked wood seemed even more glorious to Emme.

After Emme was done photographing Dr. Branham's barn, she told Aidan that she couldn't make up her mind. Should the final photos be black-and-white or color? She knew some of the reds of the barns would be lost, but she loved the old-time feel of the black and white, the way it made the contrast of light and dark starker.

Emme still loved her outdated cameras with real film she had to develop in darkrooms, but the camera she'd brought with her from DC was her work camera and it was digital. Emme shocked herself when a few years earlier she, too, had jumped on the digital bandwagon as it made editing photos so much easier for the paper. It was simply cheaper. She could take more shots and delete what she didn't want to use. She knew she could keep the photos of the barns in color, or easily change them to black-and-white, or even sepia, later. The options were endless.

"How can I ever choose between black-and-white or color?" she repeated.

"I'm not saying this to get on your good side or sweet-talk you, but I believe whatever you choose will be wonderful."

"Really?"

"Seeing how you see things today, I know you see them in a way most folks don't. I can't wait to look at all these photographs together. You should do a book."

"Thank you. I'd love to take more shots and put all of them together as a book and try to publish it. But I don't have time before I have to get back to DC."

"DC?"

"I keep hoping I can get things fixed for Kelly soon so I can get back to DC and find a new job."

"Have you ever thought about sticking around Red River longer?"

"But I enjoy journalism."

"I know you have a life in DC. But I also know, even if everything goes well for Kelly, that your aunts would love for you to be back home. Then you could do more of the artistic photos you want to, really take your time to complete those series and maybe even a book or two. Are you sure you couldn't stay?"

"I have no simple answers for you, or for myself."

"I don't think anything worth anything is ever simple."

"I didn't leave Red River because I wanted to, but because I felt I had no choice. I love much of it here and I obviously love my family. But this has always been difficult for me."

"Difficult isn't impossible."

"Difficult isn't impossible. Hmm . . . I like that."

"Good."

"Maybe that will help me overcome some of my fears, some of what we were talking about before, how I unloaded to you in Marrowbone. It's a lot to contend with, so let me just say that I'm trying to figure it all out."

"Now that I'm gonna be staying in Red River for a while, I'm always here to lend an ear and be a sounding board."

"Thank you. I really mean that."

Aidan drove back downtown and dropped Emme off to pick up her car before she headed to see Mrs. Maddox. On the way back, Emme told Aidan more about the history of Red River.

"I always love thinking about the story of places, how they got to be called what they're called. Some are great stories, and some are not so great. Our area has a little bit of both."

"I'd certainly believe that."

"Lochlan County is named after the huge lakes we have up in the northern part of the county. I'd love to take you up there if we ever have time. So many of my ancestors, like yours, are Scots-Irish and the big lakes reminded them of the lochs back in Scotland. So they paid homage to their homeland by naming the county Lochlan."

"Same reason Kentucky has a Glasgow."

"The Red River part is a bit harsher. Our town used to be named Lochlan, too. But during the Civil War, many of the families here fought, sometimes brother against brother, some on the Union side and some on the Rebel side."

"Being a border state meant hard times for Kentucky families going to either side."

"Exactly. Hard times burying all the dead. So much bloodshed. They claimed the river, which was named Keegan's River back then for some man, had run red."

"Hence the name."

"Hence the name. Not a happy story, but it's ours nonetheless."

"Sadly, that's a story that belongs to lots of folks."

"I can't help but sense echoes of that history still happening even now, of families split apart, of the town itself split apart. People are still fighting and dying."

"I'm sorry, Emme."

"But this has been such an amazing day, even with the bad news I received about Mrs. Maddox, that I'm going to focus on the beauty. At least for a few more minutes until you drop me off."

"Not to be getting all philosophical on you, but when I studied literature at Berea, we kept talking about metaphors."

"I love me a good metaphor."

"I think everything is a metaphor for everything else sometimes. Things echo each other like in the hollers. One person's actions affect someone else. I think we all forget that what we do can be affecting so many others. Sometimes generations in the future. I try my hardest to remember it."

"I haven't known you long, but everything I've seen from you so far is good. All your actions are kindhearted. They'll have positive echoes. Thank you."

"You're welcome. Anytime."

Aidan waved goodbye as Emme opened her car door. When she saw him smile, the way his face became a light, she heard more music. It was a full Irish band playing "I'll Tell Me Ma," the song that Emme had begun to think of as belonging to her and Aidan. And Emme started to sing.

CHAPTER 22

EMME ADORED Mrs. Maddox's house. It was one of the older ones, not as fancy as a Victorian, but highly detailed, and it was painted a pale peach color. It was only two blocks from downtown on the east side of Red River. Emme knew where Mrs. Maddox lived because everyone knew where everyone else lived, even though she'd never been to her house. Not with Evan. Not after he died. Not ever. Emme rued the stark separation between where different races lived. Back in DC, in some areas people of all ethnicities lived side by side. Many were even in the same houses and apartments.

Red River's unofficial segregation wasn't happening because of actual laws making it so, but because that was the way it had always been. Most people never even thought about it. Emme didn't have a clue how to make it better, so she pushed all her frustration down to concentrate on being positive for Mrs. Maddox.

Emme knocked once and Mattie opened the door.

"I'm so happy you're here."

Emme remembered her dream in Marrowbone. The dream that still didn't make sense. But as she stood at the door staring at Mattie, Emme saw Evan, too, and instantly heard the Ramones.

Evan had loved all kinds of music—just as Emme did—and their band had been a hybrid of genres. But Evan, being the mathematician he was, loved to play drums, banging out intricate rhythms. Some of the punk-rock bands from the seventies and eighties were particular favorites of his because of their drum parts. He called their rhythm *the zenith*. He'd introduced Emme to the Ramones's antic style, all pulsing verve.

The Ramones continued to thrash as they talked.

"How are you?" Mattie grabbed Emme by the hand and led her inside.

"I'm fine, thank you, Mattie. How are you?"

"I've loved the sunshine today."

"Me, too."

"I've got to be thankful for every single sunny day. That's what Grammy says, and I believe it, too. I've learned so much from her."

"I learned so much from her, too. She was my librarian growing up. Before I even knew what the word *fantasy* meant, I told her that I'd loved *A Wrinkle in Time* and asked if there were any more books with marvelous things in them. She gave me *The Secret Garden*, *The Wizard of Oz*, *The Hobbit*, *The Lord of the Rings*, *The Lion, The Witch, and the Wardrobe*, *Bridge to Terabithia*, and many others. Those books are still some of my favorites. I think your grandmother raised me almost as much as my family did because I spent so much time at the library."

Mrs. Maddox was napping on the couch in the living room. As Emme and Mattie sat down in nearby chairs, Mrs. Maddox opened her eyes and tried to sit up but was having trouble.

"You're here. Good." Mrs. Maddox kept trying to pull herself up, but couldn't.

"Please don't get up on my account."

Mrs. Maddox relaxed back into the couch. "It's comfy here, so I might stay snuggled up a little while longer. But after all these years, you should really call me Dorothy. You're a grown-up now, been living in DC and everything. It's Dorothy."

"Yes, ma'am, I'll do my best. Dorothy."

Emme emphasized the *Dorothy* so much that Mrs. Maddox started laughing, though it was more of a hoarse hacking than a laugh. Emme could tell she didn't have enough air to push out a full laugh, and it worried her.

"Can I get you anything, Mrs. Maddox. Umm . . . Dorothy?"

"No, no. I'll be fine."

"Technically yes and no, Grammy. About the being fine. I know you're sick and you're going to get sicker and pass away. But that's not the end of the story. Nope."

Despite her blatant fatigue, Mrs. Maddox whipped her head around to look at Mattie. Emme did the same.

Mrs. Maddox and Emme were both shocked and yet not surprised that Mattie already knew what was happening to Mrs. Maddox, even though Mrs. Maddox had just received word of the worst prognosis that morning and hadn't explained to her granddaughter yet.

"Mattheson Jubilee Evelyn Maddox. You are something, aren't you, Miss Priss? And I mean Miss Priss as a compliment, Emme. She's only a Miss Priss in a fun way, never in a snotty way. She knows better than to be snotty. But I can't keep anything from this child for long."

"Mattie, out with it. I know you want to tell us what you know and what you think. The cat's out of the bag, as they say, about my illness. But are there any questions? I don't want you to be frightened."

Mattie jumped out of her chair, ran over to her grandmother, and kissed her on the forehead.

"I'm only a little frightened. I've known you were sick for a while. It all comes down to math."

"Math?"

"The math of your breathing changed, Grammy. You kept breathing faster and faster even when you shouldn't have needed to. I knew that was trouble. I also knew every time we went to the hospital wasn't just to visit your sick friends. But you want to know what else I know, Grammy?"

"Yes, I do."

"Like I was saying before, this isn't all of it. The thermodynamic laws state that no energy can be destroyed or created. What's here now is going to always be here, even if it's in a new form. When you pass away, you may not still exist the way we see you now, but you're going to exist. It's like magic, and it's around us all the time."

Emme nearly fell out of her chair. Not because Mattie was once again speaking in a genius way anomalous for four-year-olds, but because Emme had heard Evan say those very same things when he'd talked about his father and grandparents dying. Della and Fi had talked about the same thing, too, when they remembered Evan. Most stymying, what Mattie had said matched Emme's dream in Marrowbone.

"Mattie, from the first moment I met you I knew you were like your father. You look like him and you speak like him, too. Do you know that he used to say the same things to me when we were in high school?"

"I know that he loved math, science, and music like me. Grammy's told me that much. But the other things I know? I just know them. I hope that's not too strange."

Mattie had left her grandmother's side and had come right up to Emme and sat in her lap as she was talking. Emme only had to look down a bit to see Mattie's face close-up. The little girl was even more beautiful than she'd realized.

"That's not strange. Everyone in my family knows things that seem impossible to know, but they do. I'm not sure I understand it, but it's the truth."

Mattie pivoted to where, as she sat on Emme's lap, she was looking across the room at her grandmother.

"Grammy, of course I wish you didn't have to pass away so soon.

It's just going to be a few weeks. I know you're already tired and you're going to be more tired. Your breathing has been so fast and it's going to get much faster. The rhythm is going to increase. But then it's going to slow down. I won't like that part. It'll make me very sad."

Mrs. Maddox's voice wavered in and out, thinning and thinning and thinning. "Oh Mattie, I love you so much, so very much that I can barely describe it."

"But the slowing down won't last long, Grammy. Then you'll change forms and then your rhythm, your true rhythm, will go on forever. And I'll be happy for you because you won't be so tired anymore. The math says that it will be okay. The math doesn't lie."

Emme knew she had cried more since she'd come back to Red River than she had in all the other days of her life put together. She didn't want to cry yet again in Mrs. Maddox's living room, but she couldn't help it.

"Oh, my lovely granddaughter. Sometimes I worry that for all your intelligence, it's not enough. It's not fair. You've lost both your parents and now you're gonna lose me."

"But you know that's not true, Grammy. You talked all the time about heaven before you even got sick. I haven't completely lost anyone and I'm not going to completely lose you, either. So please don't worry about me."

"You're right about that, Mattie. I misspoke. I do believe in heaven. But it's my job to worry about who's going to take care of you when I'm no longer physically here. So, I've been trying to find my cousin. Someone you'd love and who would love you, too."

"I think I'll be okay, Grammy. Sad at first, but then fine."

"Yes. I'll see to it. Dr. Branham says I have time, a little more time anyway, to get my house in order. That means making sure there's a plan for you. You're smart, missy, but you can't raise yourself all alone." Mrs. Maddox got tickled as she teased Mattie.

Emme couldn't believe after such a conversation that Mrs. Maddox could still laugh. This time the laugh sounded less labored.

"Mrs. Maddox . . . Dorothy . . . I'll do whatever I can with locating any relatives of yours. I've often done research at the paper. I mostly take photos now, but I was trained in all the writing and researching, too. And I've got great resources back there, should you need them. We can hunt down just about anybody."

"Thank you."

Mattie turned in Emme's lap to look at Emme's face.

"While Grammy is finding relatives, I'd love some help from you, please."

Emme didn't quite know what to expect from Mattie. She felt her own breathing quicken. She wondered if Mattie could tell that she made Emme nervous. Emme recalled when Evan had proposed to her and she hadn't said yes right away. Emme definitely didn't want to mess up again with his daughter, so she replied as positively as she could.

"Absolutely, anything you need."

"I'd love for you to please tell me more stories about my father. Every story you know. I've memorized every detail of everything Grammy has told me, but I bet you know even more."

Over Mattie's head, Emme saw Mrs. Maddox nodding adamantly. Emme would've told Mattie yes even if she hadn't seen Mrs. Maddox's approval, but it added to her sense of urgency.

"That would be amazing. When I leave here, I'm headed back to the farm to prepare for my cousin's arraignment tomorrow. But after that, since I'll already be in town at the courthouse, I'll stop by here. Would that work for you, Mrs. Maddox? I'm sorry . . . I mean Dorothy."

"That would be wonderful. After today's news and how tired I am, I won't be at the library anymore."

Emme felt a wallop to her stomach as she thought of the library without Mrs. Maddox.

"I can't imagine that."

"I might make it back once to visit, but not for work. I'm glad I saved my pennies all these years so I don't have to worry about taking this time off to spend with Mattie. I don't have to worry financially about Mattie at all. Not with my pennies . . . my pennies . . ."

Mrs. Maddox took a deep breath, then resumed.

"Not with my pennies saved and Evan's money that's in a trust for Mattie. All that to say, tomorrow afternoon we'd love to have you back. Maybe, if you're willing to stay with Mattie, I can make more phone calls to track folks down."

"That sounds like a great plan."

Mattie jumped out of Emme's lap and took her by the hand to Mrs. Maddox. Emme leaned over to hug the exhausted woman on the couch.

"I'm truly sorry for all that's happened to Kelly. I know she's gonna go free. I just know it."

"Thank you . . . Dorothy. See, I finally got it right. I may slip up and call you Mrs. Maddox occasionally, though. I hope you don't mind."

"Oh, I don't mind. You're a gift."

Mattie walked Emme the rest of the way to the front door.

"Emme, I think you're beautiful."

"Thank you. But, honestly, in comparison to you, I'm a Plain Jane, as they say. You're stunning. And with that amazing brain of yours, you can do anything."

Emme hugged Mattie goodbye, and as she did, she felt Mattie's hair brush up against her cheek. She could so clearly see the red tint in Mattie's otherwise dark curls and instantly heard a flute. It was a single flute with a perfectly clear tone. It played a sweet melody that bounced up and down, a butterfly effortlessly darting from flower to flower.

CHAPTER 23

WHEN EMME arrived at the farm, she saw that Aidan had outdone himself. He'd cooked a feast for supper. The weather was so warm that he'd grilled the chicken breasts outside. The smell made Emme feel starved. He'd grilled onions and corn, too. All of it from the farm. He'd made his own mess of greens from their winter kale, but he'd added a Louisiana hot sauce. He admitted to putting a bit of his moonshine in both the marinade for the chicken and the greens, too. He'd also set the table after insisting that Fi and Deirdre take the evening off.

Emme didn't know how to respond. What kind of man did all that? Fi let Emme know not too subtly that the right kind of man did that, the marrying kind of man made a feast, cleaned it up, and let the women rest.

"Surely your fixing this feast for all of us while we lolled about like Queens of Sheba makes you the best man ever." Deirdre spoke to Aidan, but Emme knew the words were meant for her, too.

"You're too kind, but I'm definitely not the best man ever."

"But you're definitely the kind of man some gal ought to snatch right up and marry fast before someone else gets you. Fi and I can't thank you enough. I bet Emme's mighty grateful, too, ain't you?"

Emme tried not to make eye contact with any of them. She just said, "Yes, ma'am."

As if Aidan's gallantry while preparing supper wasn't enough, he cleaned every single dish. And he cleaned out the grill, too. Then he asked Emme to go for a walk.

"I'd be honored if you'd stroll with me. This night's almost as warm as it was today and the moon's dancing out there. A big, jolly yellow thing smiling down on all of us. I bet we don't even need flashlights."

"After everything you've done for us tonight, cooking supper and all, absolutely. To say thank you." What Emme thought, though, was that it didn't matter that Aidan cooked. She would've wanted to walk with him anyway, big dancing moon or not. She wanted to be next to him, to feel his warmth near her again.

"You're the one doing me the favor of letting me stay here. It's the least I can do to repay you and your aunts, to cook a meal or two."

"There aren't many men out there who cook and clean like you. Not around here. I bet you wouldn't even be afraid to change diapers if you had a baby."

The word *baby* jumped out of Emma's mouth naturally because she always felt comfortable with Aidan. But with that one word she suddenly felt shier than ever. She wished her mountain gift was back, that seeing the huge moon created a song that would take her mind off of her embarrassment. But the gift was as ephemeral as always. It happened when it happened, and it didn't happen then. She was left with the weight of her words.

Aidan was either oblivious to the implications or it didn't bother him. And he was seeming less and less shy, too, as more words poured out of him.

"No, I wouldn't be afraid of diapers. I think any man worth his salt, especially any father, would gladly help with diapers. Babies.

Kids. They're magic, Emme. They haven't been around enough yet to be really afraid of the world that they start hiding their true selves. I love to see small ones free in who they are. Makes me want to keep being that way, too."

Emme stopped walking and Aidan stopped, too. She tried not to glance at him, but she couldn't help it. She had to see him, even if only briefly. As she looked at him in that moment, he looked at her, too, and they looked at each other deeply, until the deepness was too much, something that became weighted to the point that they could touch it. Then they had to look away.

"Sometimes I think I'm imagining you. You say the most splendid things."

"I hope you like what I'm fixing to say now."

"I'm sure I will."

"Good, because I definitely believe I gotta stay in Red River for a long time. I'll move to the boarding house, which I should do no matter what your aunts say, because I need to support myself. I appreciate their kindness, though."

"They adore you."

"Once I move, I hope it's only temporary at the boarding house. I want to find a place of my own. A little land. I've got some money saved up and I'll do any job I have to in order to pay all my bills until my songs sell. I'll muck stalls at anyone's barn."

"I'm sure you'd find plenty of takers around these parts."

"I love Marrowbone. But Red River? After what I saw today? I know it's the perfect place for me. So I gotta stay. Even after Kelly goes free, I gotta stay."

"You mean if Kelly goes free."

"You gotta know I believe she's gonna go free. Tomorrow. It's gonna be tomorrow. Just you wait. You'll see. I've already seen it."

"I know you came out here to help with Kelly after you dreamed about her and you wanted to spend a little time to see about your songs down in Nashville. But now, you really want to stay? For the songs?"

Emme, who started walking again, didn't want to flat-out ask if he also might be staying because of her. And Aidan, following Emme, didn't say it, either.

"I see so many things. Like you, I don't always understand them at first. I trust I will in time, just as you will. Here lately, it's been getting easier to trust what I see, to be grateful for the gift. It makes me believe it's real now."

Aidan and Emme had found their way to the edge of the Red River. The moon was so vivid that its light shot down through the trees and lit up everything, even the heavily wooded parts. It seemed as if the moon's shards were dancing in the trees along the water's edge and even more so in the water itself, everything illuminated. Emme wasn't afraid of the river anymore, not with Aidan there with her. She didn't think of the frightening canoe trip with Evan at all.

"Emme, I love water. It's . . . it's primal." They stood for a good long while, watching the moonlight embrace the river, until they finally turned in tandem to head back to the house.

Aidan didn't grab Emme's hand, but he placed his fingers on her elbow as they walked. Emme had never known that an elbow could be so sensitive. It wasn't like there was suddenly more heat in her elbow. Instead, it was as if it were more alive. Awake. As if she was noticing for the first time that she had an elbow and she thought it was magnificent, every pore conscious, humming.

Despite the festive feeling from earlier in the evening, there was a somber quality to the house as Emme and Aidan joined Fi and Deirdre in the living room. They were all afraid to talk about the arraignment. Afraid to hope that Kelly would somehow be set free and able to finally come home. Fi suggested they sit by the fireplace, even though it was too warm for it to be lit. They didn't sing, either.

Fi finally worked up the courage to ask what was most on her heart.

"Emme, I know you've talked to Everett. Do you think they'll let Kelly go tomorrow?"

"You probably know more about Kelly's odds after talking with her attorney. I spoke to Everett a couple of times, but then he ran off to Louisville and I haven't been able to get a hold of him since. When he left, he did tell me he was hoping to go up there to get some information to help Kelly, though."

"I've hoped all day. Hell, I've hoped for a long time now." Deirdre sounded almost sullen when she said it, as if she was getting tired of hoping with no answers.

"Mama, we've all been hoping, and fretting, and dropping to our knees praying, too."

Despite their anxiety about going to the courthouse, being in one room together was reassuring. Fi and Emme on the couch, Deirdre in the recliner, and Aidan sitting on the floor with his back up against the sofa near Emme. No one wanted to sing. But there was unplanned humming. One of their favorite Scottish tunes, "Dark Lochnagar."

What happened next was odd for Emme. Usually her mountain gift made a different sense come to life. But as they hummed, she didn't see anything. Instead, Emme's gift expanded the music they were humming. She heard bagpipes, but as celestial as they were, they were just as full of lamentations. Eventually, though, everyone stopped making sound. The bagpipes quieted for Emme, too.

As on Emme's first night back, they all fell asleep in Fi's living room, then Emme woke up briefly. She quietly climbed off the couch because she wanted to make sure Fi and Deirdre were covered up as it had started to cool down after the surprisingly scorching fall day. Aidan was sprawled out on the rug in front of the sofa. She delicately stepped over him and snuck upstairs to get one of the bigger blankets off the bed. One long enough to cover Aidan's tall frame. As she tried to ever-so-gently lay it over him, he looked up at her with one of the kindest expressions Emme had ever seen.

"You're so wonderful it seems impossible. You have my heart, Emme."

As soon as he'd said it, he went back to sleep. Emme climbed back onto her half of the couch and put her feet up next to Fi's. And she, too, went back to sleep. But not before she had a chance to replay Aidan's expression and words in her mind. She thought that was the perfect thing to think about as she drifted off, instead of letting her fear about Kelly take over. She was more thankful for Aidan than she had words to describe.

CHAPTER 24

EMME DROVE out to the courthouse alone since she'd promised to stop by and see Mattie afterward. Fi, Deirdre, and Aidan were right behind her and kept waving. Emme could see the repeated hand motions as she glanced up in the rearview mirror. She'd wave real big, so they'd see her waving back. Emme liked having to keep the waving up because it helped work off some of the nervous energy she felt.

All of them had dressed up. That wasn't surprising. What surprised Emme was the suit that Aidan wore. She hadn't assumed that because he was a farm boy he had no suit. No, Emme knew better than to make such assumptions. It was only that Aidan in his jeans and old button-up shirts seemed perfect. When she saw him in his suit, though, that was perfect, too.

When they walked into the courthouse, half the town was there. Even as sick as Mrs. Maddox was, she'd come. Reverend Jones was sitting with her and Emme noticed she was propped up against him. Pastor Willard was right in the front row. He waved and smiled broadly at her. It was as if they were running into each other at the store or football game, not Kelly's arraignment.

She loved him for that. It also looked as if he'd saved spots for them on the bench up front. Emme walked with Fi, Deirdre, and Aidan, aware that everyone was watching. But she didn't feel any judgment from any of them, except for a slight purse of the lips from Mrs. Drury.

All of Emme's cousins were there, of course. Some were the ones she knew had gone half-mad right before Cy was killed. They looked perfectly fine now. All of her teachers in high school, middle school, and all the way back to grade school, were there. The bridge club that her mother had been a part of. Her father's fishing pals. Cecil must've gotten one of his boys to mind the store, because he was there, too. Emme could've used one of his duck calls at that moment.

Even Clancy Bleeker was there. He'd held a grudge against Emme's father for years after he'd lost a spot on the city council to him. His face showed nothing but compassion now. So many people from Red River had come, and even a few from up in Cloverdale in the northwestern part of Lochlan County, too. Rowdy and Porter were there, but she didn't see Everett.

Just as Emme sat down next to Pastor Willard, Terry Dossett brought Kelly in. Emme was thrilled that her cousin was up and walking. Her face had healed some, too, even in the few days since Emme had last seen her. As Kelly caught Emme's eye before she had to sit and face forward, she smiled. The swelling had gone down and Kelly could smile with both sides of her mouth again. Her face had many green and yellow bruises, but they were much better than the red and purple that had been there before. And she was outfitted in the dress that her lawyer had picked up from Fi. She was still hand-cuffed, though.

Soon after Kelly sat down next to her attorney, one of the Thompson boys said, "All rise for the honorable Judge O'Connor."

Judge O'Connor had just started to talk when the door at the back of the room opened. Everett came walking in with a man Emme had never seen before. Everett was still dressed in his sheriff's uniform, but the man had a suit on. A three-piece suit complete with vest, bow tie, and matching pocket square.

Everett took off his hat and asked if he could approach the bench with the district attorney and Kelly's attorney, Peter Rafferty. Emme didn't know the district attorney, a tall woman in a navy suit. She thought she knew everyone in Red River, but sometimes new people moved in. After Judge O'Connor said they could approach, Everett walked up with her and Peter Rafferty. Emme could see Everett talking to the judge and gesturing to the gentleman he'd brought with him.

After several minutes, including when Everett pulled out a folder Emme hadn't noticed he was holding, the judge asked Dr. Eddings Schubert to approach the bench. Dr. Schubert had a leather portfolio out of which he pulled numerous papers and photographs. The DA and Peter Rafferty both nodded yes. Then the judge nodded yes. Everyone shook hands. Then Everett and Dr. Schubert came and sat next to Emme, the DA took her seat, and Peter Rafferty sat down next to Kelly again.

The judge then spoke some of the best words Emme had ever heard.

"The DA has agreed to drop the case against Kelly Spruill after seeing overwhelming evidence from Dr. Eddings Schubert, sworn affidavits from numerous other expert witnesses, as well as the summarized testimony of Sheriff Everett Harper, who states that he now believes that Mrs. Spruill's own confession is not admissible. The expert witnesses, the sheriff, and the DA agree that there are too many factors here, all of them provable and documented, to consider Mrs. Spruill as a possible murder suspect in the death of one Mr. Cyrus Spruill. There is no need for further deliberation of any kind since the DA has now dropped all charges. Mrs. Spruill, you are free to go home. As are you all."

Judge O'Connor banged the gavel once and Peter Rafferty hugged

Kelly. Terry Dossett came right over and uncuffed her. Kelly then slowly stood up and turned around. Kelly still looked more exhausted than happy to be free, but she didn't look frightened, either, and that made Emme thankful. She knew that Kelly would rest more easily after she got home. Kelly was going home. Emme could barely wrap her mind around it and kept saying it softly to herself. It must've finally dawned on Kelly, too, because when Emme next glanced at her, her mouth was open.

Emme half-expected Deirdre to yell out, "Girl, shut that mouth before a hundred flies get in." But Deirdre's own mouth was wide open. Fi was dancing a little jig right there in the courtroom. She ran over to Kelly and very gently hugged her. Everybody commenced hugging everybody. After Fi and Dierdre hugged Kelly, Emme, who could still see her swollen arm in a sling, grabbed her good hand and said, "I'll hug you when you get that stupid sling off, Kelly. I love you so much."

Kelly still looked shocked. It happened so quickly. She hardly had time to process it. She was still on painkillers, too, and that slowed her thoughts down.

"I know you had something to do with this, Emme. Thank you. I know you went after Everett and set a fire under him to finally make things right. I bet Aunt Della had something to do with it, too, even all the way up there on Black Mountain."

Emme knew Kelly was right. Somehow Aunt Della had played a part in getting Kelly set free.

"Aunt Della knows right this second that you're free. I bet she knew this was gonna happen eons ago."

Fi told Kelly that she was going to take her home, where she belonged, right then and there. No more time in hospitals or courtrooms. She yelled out for Aidan to come on with them if he wanted a ride back to the farm.

"Kelly, I'm so sorry I can't go home with you right now. But I promised I'd help someone. I bet you need some rest, though. By the time I get back, you will have had a fine nap in your own home again and then we can catch up, if that's okay?"

"As excited as I am, I just wanna go home and rest. The pain meds make me sleepy. I wanted so much just to get home when I was in the hospital. You go do what you have to. I wouldn't be good company right yet anyhow."

Emme kissed Kelly on the cheek and turned to leave when Aidan came up to her and started whispering in her ear.

"I promise you I don't like to gloat, but this is a good thing. I knew she was gonna go free."

"Gloat away. I'm too thankful to mind."

"I'm thrilled for Kelly and for you and your aunts, too."

He pulled away from Emme so he could look right at her. Then he winked at her, an old-fashioned wink, so charming that Emme almost winked back though she'd never been a winker. Instead, she smiled.

"Yes, you were right. I've never been happier to be wrong. I thought this thing might go on forever and they'd take her to jail. I want to go home and celebrate with everyone, but I promised a little girl I'd come see her. So I'll have to tell you how right you were later, okay?"

"I'm just teasing you. I'll go back with your aunts and Kelly, though heaven knows how we're all gonna fit in Fi's pickup truck now. They weren't expecting Kelly and I didn't want to shoot off my mouth and promise that she'd be free, even though I saw it. You know what I see doesn't always happen exactly like I think. I didn't want to get their hopes up."

"That was probably a good idea."

"Luckily, the weather's as nice as it was yesterday. Actually, I think it's warmer, the warmest day in October I've ever felt, so I'll just ride in the back. I love that feeling riding in the back of a truck on a beautiful day. I'll see you soon."

Emme didn't need her mountain gift to picture Aidan grinning in the back of a pickup truck. It seemed exactly like the sort of thing he would do.

"I'll see you later tonight. Just promise not to gloat too much."

Aidan gave her a silly, smirky grin and Emme watched him walk off with Fi and Deirdre. And with Kelly. What a miraculous thing to watch Kelly walking away, even if she was limping. She was free.

Emme didn't have to look far to find Mrs. Maddox. She was still sitting on the bench next to Reverend Jones. She looked exhausted.

"Mrs. Maddox? Are you sure you should've come to this? I appreciate it, but . . ."

"It's Dorothy and I'm just resting a few minutes more. Can you and Reverend Jones please help this old woman to the car so we can pick up Mattie?"

"Yes . . . Dorothy. I knew I wouldn't remember to call you that for long."

"I'm surprised I'm this tired. The arraignment was the shortest in history. I'm still shocked, but pleasantly so."

"Me, too. Where's Mattie now?"

"Still in preschool. But she'll get out any second. Juanita, the mother of one of Mattie's little friends, won't have to pick her up if we can get over there in a jiffy."

"In a jiffy. We can make that happen."

"I may be tired from this dreadful leukemia, but I can still feel excitement, Emme. And I'm excited for you to . . . to . . . whew! Gotta stop."

"Can I get you something?"

Mrs. Maddox slowly took several deep breaths.

"Just needed a little more air. I'm excited for you to spend more time with Mattie. Every time you two are together, something wonderful happens. It warms my heart to see it and I need the warmth. I need it so much because I've been mighty cold lately."

"I'm so sorry. Would you like to borrow my blazer? It feels almost like summer out there now and I don't need it at all."

"No, this kind of cold doesn't go completely away no matter what I put on. It's okay. Once I see Mattie, I'll get a little warmer. It's as if that child is carrying around a thousand suns in her. Not just the warmth of her body, but of her. I know that sounds crazy."

"I've heard and seen plenty of crazy things lately, but that's not one of them. I know exactly what you mean. Mattie's light is special."

CHAPTER 25

EMME TOOK Mrs. Maddox to Mattie's preschool at St. Paul's Methodist, Reverend Jones's church. Reverend Jones, who arrived first, helped her in. Emme had pulled right up under the overhang the congregation used when there was bad weather. Even though there was no rain, Emme wanted to get as close to the church as possible for Mrs. Maddox.

Emme and Reverend Jones helped Mrs. Maddox walk slowly down a small hallway that led to Mattie's preschool. Emme loved seeing the preschool room's Dutch door, where the bottom half was closed to keep any small children from wandering out, but the top half was open so grown-ups could easily peer in and out.

As Mrs. Maddox and Reverend Jones talked with Susannah, Mattie's teacher, Emme peeked inside and saw ten children. Four were in one corner sitting on the floor with large, brightly colored building blocks. Two were sitting at a little table coloring. The last four were sitting in the other corner on top of a red mat, the same kind Emme remembered from her own childhood school days. Mattie was in the middle of the other three and was reading them a book. She was a tiny teacher. Emme thought it was the cutest thing she'd ever seen.

Mrs. Maddox, even though visibly tired, thanked Susannah profusely for all that she did for Mattie and the other kids.

"You are a marvel. I see you getting down on the floor with those kids and playing with them every day. You help them with their manners, sing with them, and take them outside to play. You even help them with their alphabets and prereading skills as well as their numbers. Thank you."

"I don't have to tell you, Mattie doesn't need my help with reading. She practically teaches me how to read. Phenomenal. The other children seem to have no problem with Mattie being so far ahead. They adore her reading to them."

"That's wonderful to hear, Susannah, thank you."

"You're very welcome. Mattie reads with such expression. I've never seen anything like it. My older sister, Gracie, who teaches down at Russellville Elementary, well, I told her about Mattie. Gracie said she's met a few early readers, but none like Mattie. I don't think any of the teachers I know have ever seen anyone as bright."

"Your compliments are generous and dearly appreciated."

"Mattie sings even better than she reads. She pours her heart into every song and it's so obvious it brings her joy. We feel it right along with her."

Mattie, hearing her name, looked up from reading to smile at Mrs. Maddox, Reverend Jones, and Emme.

"I'm so sorry everybody, but I really need to go home with my Grammy."

All the children started saying goodbye to Mattie, and the room grew into a medley of young voices.

"I'll see you soon, though, and promise to finish the story later."

Mattie got up off the mat and turned around to blow kisses to her little friends.

Susannah opened the bottom part of the door and let Mattie through, but not before giving her a big hug. Then Susannah addressed Mrs. Maddox.

"I'm so sorry to hear that you've been sick. Mattie was telling me about it today and said that she wasn't going to be at preschool very much for a while. Is that true? Is there anything I can do?"

Mrs. Maddox made the *tsk, tsk, tsk* sound. She might've been dying, but she still had her way of letting Mattie know that no matter how smart she was, Mrs. Maddox was in charge.

"Mattheson Jubilee Evelyn Maddox. You have no business telling everyone my business. I know you meant well, but I need to make those decisions of who to tell and when." But she smiled right after.

"I'm sorry, Grammy. I was just trying to think ahead and help."

"I know you were. Just next time please check with me first."

Mrs. Maddox took Susannah's hand.

"Thank you again, Susannah. Mattie should've let me speak with you, but she's correct. I'm sick and may want to spend some more time with her these next few weeks while I'm still well enough. I'll call you tonight and work out the details with you."

"Anything you need at all, I promise to help. Bye, Mattie. Be good for your grandmother."

"Yes, ma'am."

After Reverend Jones helped Mrs. Maddox and Mattie back into Emme's car, he said goodbye. "Dorothy, you call on me for anything, any time, night or day."

"I will."

Mrs. Maddox sighed.

"Are you okay?"

"Heavens to Betsy, I know I'm sick, but I can't believe that I didn't think of Mattie's car seat. I'm going to have to start carrying a little notebook everywhere with reminders. I'm not only tired in my body, but in my brain. I can't forget things like car seats, though. I know we're just going two blocks, Emme, but can you make extra sure Mattie's safely belted in?"

"Of course."

Emme clicked and reclicked the seatbelt five times to make sure it was securely fastened around Mattie. As she did it the last time, Mattie lifted up to kiss Emme on the cheek.

"Thank you. You're the sweetest thing."

"Yes, she is. Mattie, I'm proud of you. I already know the caliber of human being you are, so much like your daddy and your mama, too."

"I've seen how nice you are to me and how nice you are to everybody, not just at the library, but everywhere."

Emme thought she should be used to the wise-beyond-her-years words that came out of Mattie's mouth, but she wasn't. It was as if Mattie was four going on thirty-four. Such wisdom was housed in such a tiny body.

When they arrived at Mrs. Maddox's house, she politely requested that Emme and Mattie help her get situated in bed. She said she needed to make some calls and that she wanted Mattie and Emme to have more time together. It was obvious she was exhausted, too.

"You two have fun now. Mattie, you can take Emme into the kitchen and show her where the drinks and cookies are."

"Do you want any, Grammy?"

"Thank you, dear, not now. I just need to rest. I have some water right here and that's fine."

Emme noticed that Mrs. Maddox had already lost weight since she'd first seen her in the hospital parking lot less than a week ago. Emme knew the wasting away part well, having watched her own mother wither quickly at the end.

"Come on, Emme, you'll love the kitchen. It's one of my favorite rooms in the house. Well, that, my room and the library. The library not only has all the amazing books, but the piano is in there, too. That's where I write my songs."

"Of course you write songs, just as your father did. And I did, too. Sometimes we wrote them together. Well, we and the rest of the band we were in."

"Please tell me about it."

Mattie giggled at everything while they were in the kitchen

getting snacks. Then Mattie took Emme to the library. Emme could tell right away why it was one of Mattie's favorite rooms. Emme loved it, too. It was painted a warm hunter green and there were built-in bookshelves everywhere along all the walls, except for a bay window, in which the brown piano sat. It was a very old baby grand and it nestled in the space perfectly.

"Grammy said this room was a dining room, but we have one table right in the kitchen that we use. You saw it. This room is perfect for the piano and I love to sit in one of these chairs and put my feet up on the coffee table. Grammy says I can do that while I read."

There were also two wine-colored wing chairs with a simple wooden coffee table between them. The coffee table was covered in books, including the *The Pillars of the Earth* by Ken Follet, one that Emme had read and adored. All about building a magnificent cathedral. She remembered Aidan when he described the barn as if it were a cathedral. There was also a very worn copy of *To Kill A Mockingbird*, *Stuart Little*, and a very tiny copy of Emily Dickinson poems. Emme loved every single one of those books.

Emme and Mattie sat in the two wing chairs and started talking about books and music.

"Do you like *Mary Poppins*, Emme? Not just the movie. I've read every book about her by P. L. Travers. I want to go to London some day."

"Ooh, I love that one, too."

"How about *Alice in Wonderland*?"

Emme laughed. "Yes, I love that one as well. It's a classic."

"I'm not trying to judge anybody, as Grammy tells me that's definitely not good behavior, but not everybody reads. I don't understand that, though, because every book takes me somewhere, somewhere new and . . ."

Mattie paused.

"Magical," Emme said.

"Yes. Magical. Music does that, too. At least to me."

"I feel exactly the same way. So did your dad."

"How long did you play music together?"

"We sang in choirs together all throughout middle and high school. But the band we had with a few other friends, that was just a couple of years."

"My dad played drums, right? We still have his old drum kit out in the garage."

Emme knew talking with Mattie wasn't anything like talking to a regular four-year-old. Emme loved kids of all ages, but talking with Mattie was akin to talking with the best adult and the best child at the same time. All the articulate insights of an adult and all the wide-eyed enthusiasm of a child.

"Yes, Evan played drums. He could play anything, though. I guess he practiced piano on that piano right there."

"Yes. Grammy showed me photos of him at this piano and at the piano at church. He took lessons there with Mr. Markson. He's the choir director. When my father got older, he would play piano for the whole church sometimes on Sundays."

"I didn't know that. And here I thought I was going to be telling you things about your dad that you didn't know."

"Grammy told me lots and I've looked at all the photos. I've seen some of you in them. You're so pretty now, just like you were then."

"That's so kind, thank you."

"Why did you join a band with all boys in it? How'd they let you in? Sometimes at preschool or at church the boys want to play by themselves and don't let girls in. That's sad."

"I agree. Quite sad. I did kind of have to prove it to them at first. But I had taken so much piano and I'd been singing with my family practically all my life. And I could play a little bit of any instrument, really, because I learned guitar and mandolin from my father, fiddle from my grandfather and uncles, and more piano and some dulcimer from my mom, aunts, and grandmother. The only things I never learned to play were woodwinds."

"Oh, like flutes and piccolos. I love every instrument in the orchestra."

"I do, too. I used to think I'd major in music, but when I went off to Georgetown, I fell in love with the history of Washington, DC. I took art classes that turned into photography classes and lots of history and journalism classes. And then I became a journalist, which kind of combined all those things. Sometimes I still write stories, but mostly I take photos for other people's stories. But the music never left me. I kind of left it for a while, which I'm sad to say, but it's back ever since I came home. I find myself singing all the time again."

"Since you could play all those instruments, is that why they let you in?"

"Kind of. Also because I'd listened to and loved every genre of music. The band I had with your dad and our friends Porter, Todd, and Mikey, well, we were really a mix of genres. The old Child Ballads I grew up singing are still my favorites. I took some of the themes of those songs and mixed it up with some of the blues, jazz, and country I love, too, and even added in a touch of rock."

"I bet they loved that."

"Yes. Your dad and the other guys loved that I thought that way, that I could create something new with them. They also loved that any time we'd come up with a song, whether it was a new one we'd written, or a cover, that I could play any instrument they needed. Your dad played drums, Todd played lead guitar, Mikey was on rhythm guitar, and Porter played bass. Porter was so good that he played professionally for a long time. I played mostly keyboards, but if we needed a mandolin part, or a little fiddle, I could do that, too. And I tell you, Mattie, I play a mean tambourine."

Mattie and Emme started laughing together and Emme could see Mrs. Maddox looking at them through the doorway. Emme and Mattie had been so busy talking and enjoying each other's company that neither had noticed Mrs. Maddox watching them. Mrs. Maddox smiled at both of them. She still looked exhausted and thin, but Emme saw contentment on her face, too. Then she walked slowly back to her bedroom.

"Your dad was fantastic on the drums. He loved math so much and he was like a computer, though those were pretty new to all of us back then. He knew about them, though, and was always talking about binary things, all those zeroes and ones. He kept perfect time on the drums. He and Porter on the bass worked well together, the real timekeepers. Phenomenal."

"What was the band's name? Somehow I don't think Grammy has ever told me."

Emme started laughing again when Mattie asked about the band name.

"There are different interpretations of the name. We were called "Hawking."

"Hawking?"

"Your father loved the astrophysicist Stephen Hawking. He'd come up with amazing insights into cosmology, the 'whys' behind the universe. Your dad didn't agree with all of his theories, but he loved the way he thought. And Porter wanted to learn falconry or to work with some kind of bird like a hawk. I, of course, went all Robert Penn Warren on the boys. Do you know Todd County, just west of us?"

"We go out there sometimes. Grammy has friends at the library there and they always meet up."

"One of my favorite poets was Robert Penn Warren. He was born in Guthrie, just a few miles from Red River over the county line in Todd County. He had a poem called 'Evening Hawk' that I read and reread when I moved to DC and missed Kentucky."

"You must've loved that poem to make it the band name."

"I was obsessed with the idea of making hawk into a verb and thinking about music as *hawking*. They're majestic. But your dad kept insisting the name was really for Stephen Hawking and math.

He said music was really just math. Beautiful math, but still math at its core. The other guy, Todd, he didn't care one way or the other. But your dad? He never gave up on that one, claiming the name was for math all through high school."

"I love math, too. I love reading also, but music's my favorite. Because it's the perfect blend of math and reading, at least when I write my songs."

"You really write songs?"

"Sometimes. When I feel things that I can't get out any other way. Would you like to hear something I've written?"

Emme wanted to hear and she didn't want to hear. She was hesitant because she had the feeling that when Mattie played, her own mountain gift would come back and show her something frightening. Of course Emme knew she could never predict when it was going to come. And it was silly to expect anything negative, especially not with Kelly free. And definitely not in the room with the magnificent Mattie. Still, Emme was leery.

Mattie sensed Emme's hesitancy.

"I won't if you don't want me to."

"Oh, honey. Please play. I'm sorry. Even though today was such a great day with my cousin Kelly able to come home, I think I've been on edge all week. It's lingering. Please. Play me something."

When Mattie got up and walked over to the piano, Emme was reminded again that she was a little girl, her tiny body in such contrast to the big piano. Sometimes with the way Mattie spoke, so insightfully and sincerely, Emme forgot she was only four. But Mattie looked very small as she climbed up on the bench. Her feet couldn't reach the pedals.

When she started to play, the first song Emme thought of was "Moonlight Sonata" because Mattie's song was both beautiful and haunting, with minor key chords. Emme didn't know how the little girl could create such a fluid legato sound without the sustain pedal, but she did.

Emme's fear of seeing something frightening while Mattie played was for nothing. Emme didn't see anything except what was right before her eyes, a wunderkind who was the most fascinating child that she had ever seen. Emme herself had been described as "playing with her soul," but Mattie truly did. Emme didn't even notice the tears that rolled down her face until Mattie stopped playing and turned to her.

"I'm so sorry. Are you terribly sad?"

"Have you ever heard of happy tears? I loved your song so much that all the happiness bubbled up inside of me and had to come out, and it came out in tears."

"That was my heart."

"Oh, I know. I could tell."

Mattie came over to Emme in the chair and looked her right in the eyes.

"I think I'm a little tired now. I normally take a nap when I come home. Could you please put me to sleep so we don't have to bother Grammy?"

"Absolutely."

Emme followed Mattie up the stairs to one of the two small bedrooms. It was painted a shade of pale sky blue that perfectly set off the reddish tint in Mattie's hair. Seeming to fly around the room were dozens of colorful birds and butterflies, all suspended from the ceiling by clear fishing wire.

"Your room. All the birds and butterflies. It's splendid."

"Grammy did it. It's like I'm living up in the sky and flying with the birds and the butterflies. It makes me feel very triumphant."

"I'd feel triumphant flying with these splendid creatures, too. And the colors are fantastic. Who painted them?"

"That's the best part. My Grammy put together this display at the library. She asked a lot of different painters, the art professors at Western Kentucky University, if they'd like to paint some of them for the library and they did."

"That's one of the best ideas I've ever heard."

"They did more than Grammy ever imagined they'd do and when it was over she asked them if she could take them home to me. Every one of them said yes. I get to fly with them every day. But now I'm going to sleep a little in my nest so I can fly with them more later. Thank you."

"You are very welcome. Thank you for playing me your song and showing me your room."

Emme closed the door and went downstairs to Mrs. Maddox's room. Mrs. Maddox was asleep, but when Emme turned to go back out, she heard her call her name.

"Please don't go. I just rested for a bit. I need to talk to you."

"Mattie and I ate cookies. Can I get you one?"

"No, thank you. I'm not on any chemo anymore, but I'm still not very hungry. Later on I promise I'll make myself eat some soup that one of my friends from the library brought by, though, to keep my strength up as much as I can. What I really want right now is to talk seriously with you. Is Mattie asleep?"

"Yes, ma'am. She asked me to walk her upstairs. I forget sometimes, with how articulate she is, that she's still a very young child. She needed a nap. But she let me know. Her room is glorious."

"All those artists who donated those birds and butterflies. My, my. What a gift for the library and now for Mattie."

"She seemed truly grateful."

"Do you know what else would be a gift to Mattie, Emmeretta?"

"No, ma'am."

"You."

"What do you mean, Mrs. Maddox? Forgive me. Dorothy."

"There's no time to skirt around things. I don't want to be blunt, but I have to be."

"All right."

"I couldn't find my cousin and even if I had, I don't think I'd want her with Mattie. I know you've only been with her a few times, but you girls are like two peas in a pod. I know Evan loved you for a reason. For many reasons. You are a loving and gifted young woman."

"Thank you, but . . ."

"I want Mattie to go with you after I pass on. I talked it over with Reverend and my sewing circle, too. All of them offered to take and raise her, but I know it's you. It's like I can hear Evan whispering it to me, too. It has to be you. I know you probably want to go back to DC now that Kelly's free, but maybe you'd consider staying."

Emme was stunned more than she'd ever been stunned.

"Dorothy. I'm . . . I'm . . . I really thank you for the honor. I adore Mattie. I may love her already even though I've only been with her a couple of times. You know I loved Evan. I didn't do right by him. I let my fear overwhelm me, but I loved him."

"I know you did."

"But I don't know if I can do this."

"Do you feel called back to DC?"

"No, ma'am. Not really. I was just yesterday thinking about staying for a whole bunch of reasons. I've always wanted to try to do more art photography and I could do that better here. I still feel guilty that I stayed away so long from Red River and look what happened to Kelly. Maybe I could've prevented that if I'd stayed."

"That didn't happen because you weren't here."

"Maybe. But I still wonder about it."

"If you don't feel called to move back to DC and there are so many reasons you'd want to stay in Red River, and now Mattie needs you, why would you not stay? I don't understand."

"Because some things are still the same."

"What things?"

"Please, I don't want to have to say it out loud. You know. You have to know. Better than anyone."

Emme saw Mrs. Maddox smooth down the quilt in which she was wrapped. Emme could also see the fierce determination on Mrs. Maddox's face. Emme knew she was dying, but hadn't lost her sheer tenacity and immense intelligence. Those came out in Mrs. Maddox's every word, even though it took her a long time to speak.

"Ah, yes. The subtle but persistent racism. The 'we're integrated but we're really not.'"

"Yes, ma'am. All that and more. It's why I stayed away. You know it grieved me because you also know I love Red River."

"Yes, I do."

"I love everyone here and in all of Lochlan County. I know at the end of the day there's more good than bad. But the bad breaks me, it breaks me again and again. The stuff with Kelly? There's more to it than you know. It's not just problems with whites versus blacks. Women aren't always valued, either. Not like they should be."

"Oh, don't I know it, don't I know it. But . . ."

The sigh that came out of Mrs. Maddox then was intense and vast for someone who couldn't quite get enough air into her lungs.

"How can you help change any of those things if you're not here? Don't you become part of the problem if you keep running away?"

"I've been thinking that, too. Porter. You remember Porter, right, from the band?

"Oh, I still see Porter all the time. He stops by regularly. Not many white boys come out to our street, but he does. And I love him for it."

"See, right there. That's what I'm talking about. We're supposed to be integrated, but we're really not. How could I raise Mattie like that? I don't worry for me, but I worry about her. How could I possibly be sure that I could protect Mattie?"

"I know you mean well. You think if you don't have the answers, if you can't fix everything right away, then you've failed."

"Yes, that's it."

"That's not the way it is. You're almost the same age as Evan is. Or Evan would be. He'd have been twenty-eight. You're twenty-eight?"

"Yes, ma'am."

"Twenty-eight is barely old enough to even know who you are, let alone to know how to fix all the problems in the world, though I give you credit for trying. But there's no way you can fix it all."

"But I want to."

"You couldn't fix your mama or your daddy. You can't fix me. All you can do is try your very best. Stick around and fight the good fight. Hold on to the joy while you can. Trust that the answers will come when they come."

Emme felt like punching the wall. She really didn't have a mean bone in her body, and certainly not a violent one, but she was so frustrated. With herself. She wanted to be the person that Mrs. Maddox wanted her to be. That Mattie needed her to be. But she felt inferior to the task.

"What do I do now?"

"You try. Really, that's all. Just try, Emme. Please promise me that you'll just try."

Emme sat down on Mrs. Maddox's bed and grabbed her hand. She couldn't look at her for a minute and they just sat there with Emme holding Mrs. Maddox's hand. Finally Emme worked up the courage to speak.

"I'll think about it. I can't assure you that I'll say yes, but I'll consider it with everything in me. I promise it true."

"I believe you. For you to even consider it, you've given this dying woman more peace than you could imagine. Remember, all you have to do is try."

CHAPTER 26

IT TOOK Emme a while to make her way to the house. She'd had to park down near the barn and walk the rest of the way up the long driveway because there were many cars and trucks parked along it and even out past the pond. Emme knew half the town was there to welcome Kelly back. When she finally reached the house and started to walk up the steps, Aidan came out the front door.

"Kelly's resting upstairs now. She promised she'd come back down and sing with us afterward."

"Thank you for letting me know."

"I came out here to figure out what songs to play. There are so many people in the house right now it's hard to think. How'd your visit go?"

"It was sad and wonderful at the same time."

"I guess that pretty much sums up life."

"You're right."

Emme and Aidan sat down on the porch swing, though at first they didn't swing.

"Your aunts sure got this celebration put together awful fast."

"If there's one thing for you to learn about Aunt Fiona, it's that she's always ready for a celebration. And no better reason than Kelly."

Emme and Aidan swang slowly, until they settled into a comfortable rhythm. Emme felt the swaying through her whole body, and it seemed to move the most inside her chest. It shook back and forth in her heart and it took everything in her not to reach over and touch Aidan. The swinging porch rhythm wanted that, she wanted that, she wanted to touch Aidan.

"Even with no phone they somehow got word to a ton of folks. All the people from the courthouse are here and a lot more, too."

"Everybody knows everybody's business in Red River lightning quick. I'm sure within fifteen minutes of Kelly going free everyone in the whole county knew and now most of them are here."

Emme was surprised, given that her whole body was shaking in tandem with the porch swing, her voice didn't shake, too, when she spoke.

"I thought about asking your aunts if maybe they'd been using some of their special sight, if they saw Kelly going free last night like I did and had more time to prepare for today, but decided against it."

Emme realized that Aidan was kicking his feet like a metronome, keeping the porch swing moving in the exact same rhythm as she was. It was perfect, their tandem rhythm.

"Why?" As Emme and Aidan continued to swing, and as the rhythmic power of that swinging also built inside her chest, Emme realized that she anticipated every word Aidan said as if she was waiting for him to make some grand pronouncement. It made Emme's anticipation grow to a tangible thing she believed she could hold in her own hands. She looked down to see if she could see it being grasped between her fingers.

"The more I thought about it, I remembered how much anxiety was flying around the house last night. They were afraid she wouldn't come home. No one but me really knew Kelly was gonna go free today. I saw the surprise on your aunts' faces when that expert came in and then the judge released her."

Aidan tripped a little then. One foot caught on the porch and the swing lurched forward. Both he and Emme stopped swinging. They turned to look at each other, then looked down as they simultaneously planted their feet and kicked off at the same time to start the porch swing swinging again.

"It was the best kind of surprise. We were all shocked that it could happen so quickly, but I'm sure it didn't take long for my family to get used to the idea and start fixing everything up for a grand party."

"As amazing as your aunts are, I still don't see how they got everything out in such a short time. They barely asked me for help, but every chair from the whole house, even some from the barn and the attic, is now crammed into the living room and kitchen."

As Aidan talked of Fi and Deirdre's many chairs, he let his arms swoop around, cutting large circles in the air. When Emme started to speak, he finally lowered them.

"The chairs around here are like the trucks. I lose count. They're kept in every shed and barn. More than we could ever possibly use, until now. Kelly wanted to get married and have her reception out here and I think Fi got a few extra at yard sales. Until Cy put a stop to that and they went up to a big hotel in Louisville instead."

"They definitely could've had a wedding here. That's the biggest punch bowl I've ever seen. Those glasses that go with it are something, too. I think you could serve the entire town."

"The etched-glass punch bowl?"

"They have more than one?" Emme chuckled because she was charmed by the incredulity in Aidan's voice.

"Yes, they have three. I bet if you look closely around the house, you'll see the others. But the etched glass one is the biggest and it's a beauty. I always teased Kelly and told her that I'm sure Fiona bathed her in that ginormous punch bowl until she was six."

"All those extra chairs, tons of food they whipped up out of nowhere, and lots of platters to put it on, forks, plates and napkins, and not one, but three punch bowls ready for a party. I swear they called some brùnaidhs out of the woods to help get it all set up."

As Aidan started to laugh at the tiny miracle of Emme's aunts and their busy ways, Emme's mountain gift came to life. She saw an orange grove with rows and rows of trees, each one dotted with plump fruit that not only boasted the vivid sunshine hue, but smelled of Christmas, of the spiced cider that had orange slices in it. Her mountain gift only stayed for a few seconds, but it was one of the most powerful mélanges of sensations Emme had experienced.

"They're likely to tell you the same thing, at length, so don't get them started. Or we could be hearing brùnaidh stories the entire night."

And then Emme cried. She unconsciously pushed both of her feet down flat on the ground and the swing stopped. Tears crowded the outer edge of her eyes at first, then flew down Emme's face. Aidan used his thumbs to gently brush some of them away.

"I'm sorry to bring up the brùnaidhs." Aidan's voice suddenly held shadows in it. Emme could hear that he was confused by and worried about her crying.

Aidan reached over and offered his hand to Emme and she took it. Emme didn't feel heat at that point with their hands touching, just a sense of completion, of rightness. Her hand being with Aidan's hand was right.

"It's not the brùnaidhs. It's that we're sitting out here on the porch and laughing about all of this. My aunts have created a massive celebration. And they should, they really should."

"But?"

"It doesn't seem real yet. Even though I know seeing the punch bowl will make me smile, Kelly's still upstairs exhausted. No matter how much we try, we can't erase this past week for her. Or the past years with Cy. And Mrs. Maddox is still dying. It's a lot for me to process. So many things to still worry about."

Emme squeezed Aidan's hand, but then let it go. As much as she'd wanted to touch him minutes before, and as right as it felt for them to hold hands, her sadness was stronger.

"I know you're concerned about them."

Emme started to rub her head, as if a migraine was coming on.

"As heartbreaking as Mrs. Maddox's cancer is, what happened to Kelly is also heartbreaking, and it's not going to completely go away, no matter how big a party we throw."

"What makes you say that?"

Emme continued to massage her temples.

"There are more wounds she has to heal from, much worse than the ones we can see. And however good it is that Cy won't terrorize her anymore, in many ways it's as if she's starting everything over. It makes my head pound trying to figure out how to help her move forward."

"I'm sorry about your head. But as for Kelly? The idea of a clean slate is used too much by everyone, but I like the idea of it for her. It fits."

"I don't know if a clean slate is likely, though."

"You honestly don't think it's possible?"

"It's possible. But sometimes . . . things . . . it's . . ."

"You don't have to talk about this if you don't want to."

"I'm having a hard time saying the words because they're horrible. I guess in the end I just don't know."

Emme made a small anguished sound. Aidan heard it though she tried to muffle it. It was guttural. It was fear.

"Know what?"

"How can someone get beyond what she's been through? Technically she survived it, but is that enough?"

"I honestly can't answer that and guarantee that Kelly will be completely healed with one hundred percent certainty. But I believe your cousin is like you and your aunts, isn't she?"

"Yes, in many ways."

"I've seen nothing but strength and honor from your family. And true joy on top of that. That goes way back from my family knowing yours back even when we were kids." As Aidan spoke, Emme relished the memory of meeting Aidan as a child at the wedding where they were lassoed together.

"So what I can say with certainty is that I believe Kelly will fight with everything in her to move forward. I'm not denying what she's been through or saying it'll be easy or fast, but I believe she'll do more than survive."

Aidan's voice held not authority, but wisdom. It soothed Emme. She believed him. She found herself nodding her head along when he spoke. Yes, she thought as he talked, Yes.

"What do you mean by *more*, though?"

"I think, after getting on with life here on the farm, surrounded by the people who love her, that's how she'll do it. That's how she'll eventually do more than merely exist. She'll thrive."

"I believe what you're telling me, but there's all this other mess. I still don't understand what all's been going on in this town. The stuff beyond just Kelly. And if I don't fully understand it, how can I fix it?"

"I'm not saying you shouldn't be worried about all of that. But maybe you could rest just a bit more easily tonight knowing that at least one of your problems has been solved. Kelly's home."

"Then I really should feel more joy right now. Maybe I'm ungrateful?"

Aidan whipped his head back in disbelief. "I don't think anyone would call you ungrateful. I just wish you'd allow yourself a little peace for one night. You and your entire family deserve that."

Emme was about to thank Aidan for helping her feel better when Pastor Willard came out. But Aidan didn't need to hear Emme say the words for him to know that she was already feeling less anxious. He could see it in her smile.

"Emmeretta, I am overjoyed to see you, especially on such a festive day when we get to celebrate Kelly's release."

Emme and Aidan both got up from the swing. Emme hugged Pastor Willard before introducing him to Aidan.

"Thank you, but I already met this wonderful young man inside when we were having a lively discussion about musical instruments. I think Aidan far surpasses me with his expertise, but he was too humble to stop my rambling."

"No, sir, you didn't ramble. I think you definitely qualify as an expert on musical instruments. Speaking of instruments, I'm going to get my guitar."

Emme and Pastor Willard barely had time to sit down on the swing when Aidan popped back out with his guitar.

"Your aunt said Kelly was waking back up and wouldn't mind if I played a little. I think I'll get warmed up. I've had some requests for this evening. Emme, do you want to sing with me?"

Pastor Willard got up quickly, even in his old age, and offered his hand to Emme as he spoke to Aidan.

"Would you play us a fine dancing tune? I think a bit of spinning around, even with an old fart like me, is what Emme might like right now."

"Pastor Willard, do my ears deceive me? Did you just say *fart*?"

Emme enjoyed Pastor Willard's banter and jumped up to dance with him on the porch.

"Yes, my dear. I honestly don't believe it's the end of the world to say the word *fart*. Perhaps that's blasphemous, but I doubt it."

Aidan started playing "Cotton Eyed Joe." It made Emme wish she could keep dancing with Pastor Willard and run up and grab her fiddle, too. She knew Aidan was right. Emme needed to allow herself to rest in the fact that at least one of her concerns had been assuaged. Kelly was home and a celebration was long overdue.

Emme could hardly keep up with Pastor Willard and she loved that. They swung each other to-and-fro and do-si-doed on the front porch just like they were back at the square dances and barn parties Emme attended while growing up. She almost forgot all the nagging questions that needed answering. Almost. She was surprised her mountain gift didn't manifest, but she was used to it coming and going as it pleased. Still, she loved Aidan's playing so much she expected to see some phenomenal vision any second.

Despite his burst of energy, eventually Pastor Willard had to stop dancing. Emme walked him inside for a drink, where he immediately downed two cups of punch.

"I'm parched. This is divine. I could guzzle down the entire thing, Fiona."

"I appreciate it, Pastor."

Aunt Fi was flitting around in her usual energized way, perhaps even more energized than Emme had ever seen her. Pure jubilation on her face at Kelly's release. Emme went over to Kelly, who was sitting on the couch with a cup of coffee in her hand and her feet propped up on the coffee table. People from Red River were milling around the house, all chattering away.

"I heard some fine guitar-playing out there. That Aidan is something."

"Can I get you anything?"

"I'm still waking up from my nap and this coffee's just what I need. That was the best nap I ever had, though. Even so drugged, I couldn't sleep well in the hospital. I still have healing to do from the surgery, but I know I can do it faster here. It'll certainly be happier here, too."

"You sound like yourself again. A lot of the swelling has gone down and the weight of, well, of all that horrible stuff. So much of it's gone now that you're free. You're home and I couldn't be happier."

"I guess you'll be leaving soon now, though, now that I'm free. I surely wish you'd stay, though."

"You're not the only one."

"You mean Mama and Grandmama?"

"But I'm just gonna have to figure it out for myself."

"Would you consider it?"

"Yes. But no influencing me, pretty cousin. I have to think it through."

"I won't try to talk you into it. What I will do is suggest you bring that handsome Aidan a cup of punch. I saw him walk back outside and he must be sitting on the front porch all by himself, poor thing."

"That sounds like a good idea, if you don't need anything else."

"Nope, I'm perfectly fine. Later, I know Mama will bring out a cake—or probably three—and I'm excited for everyone to sing and dance. I don't know if I can quite belt out anything yet, but I sure would love to sit and listen to it. To you especially. But I need to keep waking up. Just promise you'll come back in and sing more later."

"Sounds like a plan."

Emme grabbed two glasses of punch, one for her and an extra one for Aidan, and headed back outside.

"Would you like some of Fi's famous punch? It's not spiked yet, so it might be too tame for you without a touch of 'shine in it, but it's still wonderful."

Aidan looked up at Emme with a sense of a wonder on his face. Then he smiled and took the glass, immediately downing the entire thing in one gulp.

"Pardon me if that was rude. I can't believe how warm it still is. Today really has been hotter than yesterday. I bet this is setting some kind of record."

"I can get you more, if you'd like."

"No, thank you. But that's kind of you to offer. It was tasty."

Emme noticed that Aidan was having a hard time maintaining eye contact with her. He'd look at her for a second, then he'd look above her or to the side of her. It made Emme want to turn around and see if something or someone was hovering.

"I suppose it'd come as no surprise that I'd probably like to add 'shine to everything, though, even when it's this good."

Emme adored how Aidan said *everything* like *everythang*. Even though she knew it was good for her work in DC that she'd lost most of her accent, she missed hearing others speak with the special Kentucky twang she loved so much.

"Fi probably wouldn't mind if you spiked it, just as long as it's the milder kind and not your special brew."

"No, I won't be spiking it. Promise." Aidan again looked at Emme directly for a second before his eyes darted around. Emme was perplexed.

"Both your 'shines pack a wallop, but the special brew made me have the most bizarre dream. I think it might turn our poor town upside down all over again if everyone here got some of the harder stuff and started dreaming like I did."

"I wouldn't want that."

"Though I loved all of your moonshine, I did." Emme realized that it was her, too, who was having difficulty making eye contact with Aidan. She didn't want to be rude, so she forced herself to look directly at him.

"Emme." Finally Aidan looked directly at her, too, and gasped in air.

It worried Emme. Whenever someone took that much air in, she knew they were preparing for something. Usually something bad. Emme had too much bad already. She couldn't take any from Aidan, so she braced herself.

"Yes?" Emme squinted one eye, and most of her face, as if she were preparing for a blow to the head.

Aidan laughed, hard, but continued to maintain eye contact.

"You look like I'm gonna tell you your favorite horse is dead. I know I sound serious. This is serious. But it's not bad, I promise. At least it's not bad to me. I'm hoping it won't be bad to you, either, so please don't be fretting so."

Emme relaxed her face, but still sounded tentative. "Okay." She drew out the *okay* until it had five syllables instead of two.

"You mentioned the 'shine in your dream." Aidan still held her gaze, but he'd started fidgeting. He adjusted his shirt collar, his belt, his collar again that had been perfect all along, and then he rubbed his chin stubble.

"Yes?" Emme could hear it in her own voice, how her *yes* held anticipation in it.

"I know I told you about the dream. With Kelly and her name in the cave and that's how I knew I was supposed to come back with you."

Aidan put both his hands in his pockets, which Emme found so attractive that she immediately felt a warmth spread up from her stomach to her chest to her face.

"Yes." This time Emme drew out the *yes*.

"Don't think I lied to you, because that's not true. I told the truth. I just didn't tell everything." Aidan looked down at his feet when he said his last sentence.

"I'm sorry. I don't understand." Emme's gaze had become a searchlight, switched on and looking intently at every part of Aidan's face, trying to discern what he was thinking and feeling.

Aidan stood up, hands in his pockets, and walked back and forth. He moved across the full length of the porch, then sat back down next to Emme on the swing. He took his hands out of his pockets, and even though he rested them on his thighs, and they appeared to be motionless, Emme thought they looked tight with the potential for movement, as if they could leap up and start gesturing wildly, an animal holding still until it bounds like raw energy itself across a field.

"I did dream about Kelly. Just like I told you. But I also dreamed about you."

"And?"

Emme didn't know exactly what she wanted Aidan to say, but she knew she wanted him to say something about her. Something hopeful. Because there was a new fluttering in her chest. It flew up to her throat and made it difficult to talk. It wasn't a bad sensation, only that the fluttery feeling competed with the words she wanted to say.

"It's not that I wanted to hold anything back to hurt you. Just the opposite. I heard you that night by the fire. I mean I really, really heard you. You've been so afraid."

"That's true."

"I wanted to help, not make things more difficult for you. So I didn't tell you that I dreamed about you. I knew it would confuse and maybe frighten you, too." Aidan was not able to keep his hands still. Nor was he able to even sit. He stood up and paced again.

"Why would it frighten me? You didn't see my name on the cave wall, too, did you?" Emme placed her hands palm down on the swing. She felt as if touching the swing's smooth wood surface could somehow ground her, somehow decrease her growing fear. Emme desperately hoped Aidan hadn't dreamed about her and Evan at the Bell Witch Cave.

"I didn't see you or your name in the cave. But I have dreamed of you many times. Sometimes I just saw your name. Often I saw your name with another word, though."

Aidan had maintained eye contact with Emme nearly the entire time they spoke, even as he'd moved around. But right then he turned his back to her. He finally stood still, too.

"It's okay. You can tell me." Emme raised her hands from the porch swing and brought them together, palms touching, as if in prayer.

"I promise it true that I saw it. I saw it many times. Please don't feel pressure or any kind of fear. But I need to tell you." Aidan remained standing with his back to Emme.

Emme sat still with her hands still pressed together as she waited to hear what Aidan saw in his dream. She felt every second as if it was a heavy weight.

Aidan finally turned back around. His arms hung by his side, and his face held a resolve that to Emme reminded her of the mountains.

"I saw your name with the word *wife*."

Emme's pressed-together hands came undone. She sat there with them in front of her, open hands suspended in midair, as she tried to figure out what to say.

"For years I've been waiting for you to come back. I've known since college that you would be my wife. I've dreamed about you ever since what happened to us when we were standing so still together as kids at the wedding."

The moment that Aidan mentioned them at the wedding, his hands jumped from his side and resumed their fervor for motion.

So Aidan had remembered Emme and the wedding, Emme thought! The fluttering in Emme's chest that had flown up to her throat was now in her head. Her thoughts were flying around, many birds frantically darting everywhere.

Emme couldn't say a single thing.

"Aw, now I've done it. You're upset." The idea of a silent McLean woman worried Aidan.

"It's just that I don't know what to say. I truly don't." Emme let her hands rest in her lap.

"I don't know how to make sense of it. I definitely didn't know how to make sense of it when I was growing up. I dreamed about you often, seeing you from the wedding. Then in college I started dreaming your name. Just your name at first, then the wife part. I thought the name matched you, the girl I met at the wedding, but later I kept seeing an older you, too, so I wasn't quite sure."

"And you dreamed of Kelly, too?"

"Yes, I also dreamed of Kelly's name. I didn't understand it until the day that you came out to Marrowbone and I saw you all grown up. Your beautiful face, Emme, and your beautiful heart worrying about your family so much. It was you. I think I started falling in love with you right then, that night by the fire as you shared your fears. Certainly being here on your farm with you and your family has convinced me."

Emme had to close her eyes. She sat on the porch with Aidan with her eyes tightly shut, trying to take in everything he said.

Aidan seemed almost bashful as he stuck his hands back in his pockets. "I'd love to seriously start seeing you. I know all of this is fast and you might need to go back to DC. But if you do, I'll visit. I hope you stay here, though."

Emme opened her eyes. "I've been trying to figure that out."

Aidan came over again and sat down next to Emme on the swing. "This doesn't have to happen overnight. We can take our time."

"Thank you for that." Emme, even though part of her wanted to turn and kiss Aidan, or even more so, look into his eyes more than she'd done before, forced herself to face forward on the swing.

Aidan nervously tapped his foot in rhythm on the porch floor.

"But please, I'd at least like one chance to take you out on a proper date now that Kelly's free and you're not so worried anymore. I didn't talk to you about this before because I knew you were carrying the weight of the world on your shoulders. I know you're still worried about Mrs. Maddox, but I can try to help you with that, too."

"Aidan, this is all so much."

"I'm sorry. I know I keep saying that, but it's true. But I didn't want to wait any longer to tell you. I felt like I was betraying you by not telling you about the dreams. But I don't want to pressure you, either."

"I'd love to go out on a date with you. But things have gotten even more complicated." Emme turned to look at Aidan.

"What do you mean? I thought Kelly was free."

"She is. It's not that. It's Mrs. Maddox. It's more than Mrs. Maddox. I know I told you she was dying and that's still true. But she wants me to take Mattie, her little granddaughter. Evan's daughter." Emme forced herself to keep looking at Aidan as she told him about Mattie.

Aidan never dropped eye contact. He didn't flinch. "I know that must be a ton to take in. But that makes me fall a little more in love with you, right this second."

Hearing Aidan say again that he was in love with her made Emme flush deeply and look straight ahead again. "Really? I thought that'd scare you away."

"Are you kidding me? When a woman wants to give you her child? That's probably the finest compliment any human being could give another one."

"You think?" Aidan couldn't see Emme's smile as she faced forward, but he could hear it in her voice.

"I have no doubt that's because you're so huge hearted. I knew it when we were children, even though I was just a stupid boy back then. Probably still a stupid boy right now."

"Aidan . . ."

"But a stupid boy smart enough to know that Mrs. Maddox wanting you to take Mattie is one of the most wonderful things I've ever heard."

Emme was incredulous. Instead of making Aidan flee, the idea of Emme becoming an instant mother seemed to make him respect her more.

"It seems as if I'm always thanking you. And I'm sincere every time. Thank you. Those words mean the world to me. I just wish I knew how I could do it. Take Mattie."

Emme felt her leg shift itself closer to Aidan's leg. She knew she was in charge of her leg, yet she believed she wasn't in that moment. It had truly moved itself closer to Aidan. As their legs touched, Emme's mountain gift started up. She couldn't hear a specific musical instrument, only a deep thrumming instead that mesmerized her. How odd, she thought. "I didn't even really see anything first, I just felt Aidan's leg."

"Don't you want to? You told me she was amazing." Aidan's question drew Emme away from the thrumming sound.

"Yes, she is. That's a vast understatement if ever I've heard an understatement. But I'm worried about all the problems that have plagued our town. That plagued Mattie's father."

"I remember you spoke a lot about all that that night by the fire."

"Those problems still exist. I don't know how to fix them. I've never known how to fix them. I'd hate to have them hurt Mattie. What would happen to her if she started living with me? Would someone burn a cross in the yard? Just for her being in a white family? What if I got her killed, Aidan? I couldn't live with myself!"

"Emme . . ." Aidan placed his hand behind Emme's head, and gently rubbed her hair.

"There are other grave things beyond that, but I'm afraid to put them into words."

"You can tell me."

"I feel this responsibility for her. More than simply I'm the parent and she's the child. Much more." As Aidan continue to rub Emme's hair, and as their legs still touched, Emme realized it was the closest the two of them had ever been physically, and that tension made Emme both nervous and exhilarated, even as she still thought of Mattie.

"What else makes you worried for Mattie?"

"She's a girl. Because of what all that's happened to Kelly. So much more than you know. And what I guarantee you has happened to many other women. I don't believe this town, however much I love it, respects women enough. And please know that I'm being very polite in describing it that way. The reality is much worse."

Emma bounced both of her legs on the porch, breaking their contact with Aidan, as she described her fears.

"That's horrible."

"Yes, and it means Mattie has two battles to fight, battles that I'll have to take on for her, too. One as an African American and another as a female. I so desperately want to do right by her, but I don't know if I can protect her. I'm sitting here with all this joy around me, but many of my thoughts have been trying to figure out how to protect her. I don't have all the answers."

"But you don't have to have all the answers now. You just have to try." Aidan rested his hand on her shoulder. The warmth of his hand spread through her entire torso.

Emme realized that Aidan's words echoed Della's and Mrs. Maddox's. She sat quietly for a long time, and Aidan didn't say anything, either. Emme's thoughts tumbled around, bumping into each other as she tried to figure it all out until she finally realized the truth that Della, Mrs. Maddox, and now Aidan, had been trying to get her to see.

"You're right. I don't know why I keep thinking I have to figure everything out right away. I don't understand why I'm just seeing it now, but my thinking has been skewed. No one figures everything out at once. No one's life is perfect with all the answers lined up right before them. And I'm not doing this by myself, either."

"No, you aren't."

"Perhaps my deepest self is a pessimist, though I thought giving up on things when I couldn't fix everything instantly was pragmatism."

"I wouldn't describe it either of those ways. I don't know what the right word is. I just know you shouldn't expect yourself to have all the answers right away."

Aidan removed his hand from Emme's shoulder, but Emme didn't feel it as a loss. She felt as if his hand were still touching her, as if it would always be touching her.

"That may be easier said than done for me, but I'm willing to try."

"So, are you going to take Mattie? Will you stay?"

Aidan smiled his half smile, one that made Emme desire him more every time.

"I think so. I'll try to help Mattie, even if I don't have perfect clarity right now as to how to do it."

"Hot damn!" Aidan clapped his hands together, and it startled Emme at first, but then she laughed.

"I'll adopt Mattie when Mrs. Maddox passes away. And I can

promise you at least a date or two. We have to see about everything after that. But, like with Mattie, I'll try, Aidan. I'll try with you."

"That's all anyone can ask for."

Aidan leaned over and touched Emme's cheek with his hand. And, even though it was the first time he'd done such a thing, Emme would've sworn that her face held the memory of Aidan's touch, that her skin somehow had been lonely for his fingers to return. Emme wondered if he felt the same way. She wanted to kiss him on the cheek, hoping that her lips felt like something Aidan needed to remember. So she leaned over and pressed her mouth to his face and her lips and his skin, oh her lips and his skin, they belonged together. They had needed to come back home with one another.

Emme felt an urge, a desire so intense it was as if a song from deep inside her needed to be sung for the whole world to hear. That's how much she needed to taste Aidan's lips. But Emme didn't dare make things more complicated than they already were. So she had to settle for that single kiss on the cheek and it, with all its power, became a living thing between them, so alive and such a force that it seemed to lift Emme and Aidan up. They felt as if they were floating up off the porch and out into the warm October night.

CHAPTER 27

THE FIDDLE music coming out of Fi's living room drew Emme and Aidan inside. Pastor Willard was playing, too. Emme had forgotten that he did it so well. Emme loved how the older generations, even those who didn't have money for lessons, had all learned to play musical instruments. Even though Emme's parents could afford for her to have piano lessons from a professor at the university in Bowling Green, they assured her they would've taught her to play themselves if they'd had to. It was their favorite form of entertainment. Like their parents before them.

"Come on, child, and join us before the night gets away." Deirdre grabbed Emme and Aidan and pulled them to the center of the room.

The McLeans had had a television, but rarely turned it on. Only on Sunday evenings. Both of Emme's parents and siblings had grown up without television or formal music lessons, but each could play multiple musical instruments. Emme adored the vast collection they'd built over the years. Pastor Willard was playing one of her father's favorite fiddles, the one with the scratch on it in the shape of an L. It'd been too long since it was played, at least in front of Emme.

It added to the sense of happiness she felt about Kelly's freedom and Aidan's words on the porch.

What cheered Emme the most, though, was seeing Kelly trying to sing along. She couldn't hear her voice, but she could see her cousin's lips moving and her face had color again.

It seemed as if the number of people in the house had more than doubled. There was so much whooping and hollering—what Emme's family had called square dancing. Pastor Willard was fiddling away with versions of some of Emme's favorite barn songs like "Turkey in the Straw," "Virginia Reel," and "The Barn Dance Medley." Kieran Ferguson had his guitar and was playing, too. There wasn't enough room for people to dance fully, but everyone was singing along and clapping or slapping their hands on their legs.

Emme noticed Aunt Fi had her big copper pot out again and was beating a fine rhythm. She could see her little cousins, Shannon and Siobhan, twirling around best they could with all the people crammed together in such a small house. There was Sylvie from the hair salon. Denise from the hospital. Porter wasn't playing, but he was there, too. How'd she missed him before? There were oodles of people in those rooms, celebrating together. Aidan wasn't playing his guitar, but he was clearly happy to sing with everyone else.

The only thing that bothered Emme was not a single African American was there. Emme was sure Fi would've welcomed anyone into her home. But Fi spent most of her time on the farm and at church, a church that was all white. She didn't regularly interact with the African American community, and vice versa.

Emme had loved Evan's daughter the first time she saw her. And of course she wanted to help Mrs. Maddox. But what would it be like for Mattie growing up on Fi's farm? How could Emme build a bridge between two races for her? For the town? And that fear was one more on top of what she had tried to describe to Aidan.

As horrified as Emme had been when she couldn't get Cy locked up to keep Kelly safe, at least her cousin was a grown woman. To think that someone could assault Mattie, who would become her daughter, was even worse. No wonder Kelly didn't tell Fiona what had happened to her. She knew it would shatter her mother. Emme had already started to think of herself as a mother and it changed how she saw everything.

Though thinking about Mattie stirred up Emme's worry again, the revelry surrounding her gave her some assurance that she would eventually figure out answers. But Emme noticed then that Aunt Deirdre's face had darkened. And as soon as she saw Deirdre, Pastor Willard hit a painfully sour note on the fiddle, and Emme immediately had one of her visions. It was even darker than Deirdre's expression.

Emme saw something that made her think she'd finally gone crazy, too, just like all the other women in Red River. What Emme could only describe as *hags* overwhelmed her vision. Hags with grayish, moss-colored hair flying from their heads. The same shade Deirdre had described to Emme when she'd first returned to Red River. And they had greenish-yellow skin. Emme would've sworn they were witches. Except they had wings. Brown wings, but the wings had a sheen as they shifted positions. Emme was mesmerized by the wings. Almost as if they belonged to filthy angels. Deirdre had sworn she'd seen the exact same thing, too.

Hags. Witches. Ghosts. Banshees. Angels. Emme had no idea exactly what they were. She instinctively knew, though, that they were good, despite the parts of them that frightened her. Emme realized to the outside world it would seem impossible, not only her seeing them, but her knowing they were good. Yet Emme knew without any doubt that they were both real and good.

But they were madder than hell. Emme sensed that, too. Just like Deirdre's words out on the porch Emme's first night home.

Emme then looked over at her great-aunt as Deirdre started yelling over the fiddle, guitar, and everyone singing and dancing.

"You're back. Please, oh please, no. What do you want?" Deirdre reached her hands out. Then she started screaming.

Emme saw that Shannon and Siobhan, who couldn't see Deirdre from where they were, fell to the ground holding their stomachs and crying. Shannon threw up. As Deirdre shouted more, all the music stopped.

Fi ran over to her mother. "Mama, what is it?"

Deirdre kept screaming in between her wild words. "They're back. Everything's gone to hell!"

Everyone flew into a blur then. Emme ran to Deirdre. She could see Pastor Willard and others rush to Shannon and Siobhan. She heard someone yelling to Porter to run next door to call an ambulance. And all the while Deirdre kept screaming, "It's happening again. It's back. They're back!" And then she fainted.

Dr. Branham rushed through the door next.

Everyone in the room immediately opened up a path for him. Two EMTs that Emme recognized as kin to the Frogues followed him. Emme knew Porter hadn't even made it out the door yet, let alone gone next door to call an ambulance. Emme didn't know how Dr. Branham knew to be there, but she was exceedingly thankful he came.

As Shannon and Siobhan were carried off in stretchers, both of them vomiting, Deirdre was trying to sit up. Her face had turned white. Dr. Branham was taking her pulse. Emme was just glad that she'd regained consciousness.

"Deirdre, it's going to be fine. I promise. Please calm down. Your heart is rushing too fast."

"I don't know if you'll believe me."

Dr. Branham looked up at Fi and Emme and told them that Deirdre's pulse was still fast, but it was slowing and that was good.

"Fi, please get your mother some cold compresses and water and ibuprofen. She's started running a high fever like everyone else tonight. I want to get her temperature down immediately if that's the case."

Emme asked, "Everyone else?"

Dr. Branham put his hand to Deirdre's forehead as he spoke.

"It started happening again. At first just one or two. Not as bad as before. No one seemed to be having as blatant of a psychotic break as before. But they were moaning, mentioning the witches, the Red River. All of it again. And they had the same spiking fevers and extreme nausea."

"Dr. Branham, this is horrible. I just saw it firsthand. It really is bad."

"We're going to fix this, no doubt, Emmeretta."

The reporter in Emme clicked in. She needed facts. "What other details can you give me?"

"After five women came in like before, I started trying to get a hold of people to drive out to see you, but everyone was already gone. Fi had invited me, so I knew the party was on. I'd planned to be here, but then I'd gotten calls for extra hands at the hospital. I knew many of the ones who'd come in the last time were going to be at your house, especially the young girls, Shannon and Siobhan. When more people came over from Logan County's hospital to help out, I knew I needed to get out to your farm as soon as possible and bring the ambulance up with me."

"I'm so glad you did, Dr. Branham."

Aidan had helped Fi get cold compresses and brought in a cup of crushed ice cubes. He was encouraging Deirdre to eat a few of them.

"Good thinking, young man."

Emme realized Dr. Branham hadn't met Aidan, but Emme didn't think it was the time for introductions.

As Deirdre's temperature started to cool from the compresses and ice, she felt well enough to sit on the couch. The room had cleared out as everyone wanted to either go help Shannon and

Siobhan at the hospital or simply to give Deirdre space. What had once been a room crowded with loudly celebrating people now seemed too quiet with just the few that were left.

Emme wondered where Kelly was. She looked around the room and saw her cousin sitting on the floor with her back to the wall that led to the kitchen. She was crying.

Emme went to her immediately. "Oh, honey, I'm here . . ."

"I felt it. Not as bad as the others, but I felt it, too. Or them. I felt them. I don't understand any of this. I thought after Cy died, no longer around to hurt me, and when I got to go home . . . I thought all the bad stuff was over."

"I did, too."

Aidan came over to help Emme get Kelly to the couch. They set her right next to Deirdre. Both women were calming down but were still visibly shaken. Emme was grief-stricken all over again seeing two people she loved so ill and upset.

Dr. Branham kept on helping Deirdre and Kelly, with Fi assisting him. Emme went to the kitchen and Aidan followed.

"I'm confused. Enraged, actually. I don't understand this one bit. I'm not so naïve as to think that I can understand everything, but I believed all of this . . . this . . . haunting or whatever you want to call it, would stop when Kelly came home."

"I believed that, too."

"That's what my gift, brain, or heart, any of those or all of those, told me. So why is everyone still haunted? Why is everyone still so sick? I don't get it, not at all."

Aidan paused, closed his eyes, and furrowed his brows. "What's left undone? When we were out on the porch, I saw you happy to have Kelly home. But you also knew there were still issues here in Red River. In your family and the whole town. Those things are still undone, right?"

"All that did feel undone to me."

Aidan opened his eyes, though his brows were still furrowed.

"Maybe you gotta retrace your steps. The thoughts you were thinking."

"I knew Kelly would have a hard road ahead. Not just to heal from surgery, but because all that bad stuff was allowed to happen to her in the first place. Everett saved the day with that expert witness, but he never fully admitted that he should've locked Cy up in the first place."

"Yes. That sounds like one important loose end that needs to be tied up. What else?"

"I agreed, at least I told you, that I was going to take Mattie. But I need to tell Mrs. Maddox, too."

"Anything else?"

"When everyone was singing and dancing, right before all the bad stuff started back up, I was worried about something."

"Right before everyone got sick again?"

"Yes, right before."

Aidan smiled. A confident smile. "What were you worried about? It couldn't be an accident that what you were worried about, enough to stop you from completely joining in that wonderful party, well, it's not an accident you were thinking it before everyone got sick again."

As soon as Aidan said it, Emme knew he was right. One hundred percent right.

"I was worried about Mattie. I was scared for her because at this big party for my cousin, there wasn't a single African American. There's still an unspoken segregation. I was petrified of Mattie not feeling truly welcomed. And I also worried that some day horrific things would happen to her like they did to Kelly. That I couldn't protect her."

"Maybe that's it?"

"Maybe."

"I know these things are far more complicated than I can possibly understand and no one, not even you, can fix all of it, certainly not by youself."

"No, definitely not me on my own."

"But figuring out how to make Red River a bit safer for a little girl, that'd be a step in the right direction. That'd be something powerful."

"Yes."

"That's the answer, or the start of it. If it's not the complete answer to these troubles your family and town have been having, at least it's worth considering."

"I hope so."

"Whether you can stop the haunting, I don't know. But it's the right thing to do, to try something no matter what."

"Now I have to figure out how to do it."

"Just try. That's all you have to do. Try."

Those words again. Emme was not only getting used to them, they were fueling her determination.

CHAPTER 28

EMME AND her family didn't sleep. All night they gave Deirdre ibuprofen and cold compresses. She moaned off and on for hours. Kelly wasn't as ill, but was still exhausted from her surgery. Too exhausted to sleep. The pain from all the activity, the arraignment, and coming home had caught up to her. And the pain from what had happened to everyone at her party. Her arm still hung in a sling, and Emme helped change the bandages. Kelly wanted to rest in the recliner. No sleeping. Just resting, eyes open, and darting around the room.

Deirdre didn't throw up anymore, but she didn't want to eat, either. Nor did Kelly. Their nausea was back, so Emme and Fi kept bringing them ginger ale and crackers. Fi, Aidan, and Emme weren't nauseous, but they didn't feel like eating anything, either. They just drank endless cups of coffee. The punch bowl was still out, as if it were mocking them.

Aidan manned the fire. For two days it had been in the nineties in Red River in October. It had, as Aidan predicted, set records. But much later in the night, after the women started getting sick again, it was as if it had never been hot. It didn't cool gradually, either. Winter came slamming through as though fall didn't exist at all. Overnight it went from being sweltering to the low twenties. It didn't snow, but gray frost appeared everywhere, the land dully pewtered.

As soon as Aidan felt the temperature dropping, he had started a fire, which he maintained all evening. He brought down the cots Fi told him about from the attic for Fi and Emme so they could be near Deirdre and Kelly. There was no hope of sleep, but at least they could stretch out and rest when they weren't helping. Aidan stayed sitting with his back to the side of the couch nearest the fire. He didn't doze off a single time. There was no singing and hardly even talking from him or anyone else. That one thing, far more than Deirdre and Kelly's physical ailments, frightened Emme most of all. No one in Emme's family was ever quiet for that long if they were awake.

The silence throughout the night did give Emme time to think. At first she wanted to ask Deirdre and Kelly more about what they'd experienced. She needed to hear specifics about the bizarre events from their perspective. But they were both too sick to answer, so Emme had to ponder everything alone. She thought of what had transpired as hauntings, though it wasn't clear, especially after her last vision, that that was what they were.

If they weren't hauntings, what were they? Perhaps there would never be an accurate description. Emme realized she would have to relinquish her desire for specificity. As the night progressed, she believed what had had happened in Red River could never be clearly defined. To herself she referred to the events as *the occurrences*, purposefully addressing them ambiguously. Even though Emme sensed no evil, what she and everyone else had felt wasn't pleasant, either. Far from it. More questions, less answers.

Everything had been and would probably remain nebulous. Emme didn't like nebulous. The reporter in her wanted concrete details. Specific definitions. All the who, what, when, where, and most importantly, the why behind what happened.

Even knowing she would get nowhere, Emme played over in her head everything she had heard and experienced about the occurrences since she learned of them back in DC. She recalled Deirdre's surreal actions when Emme first returned to the farm. She remembered Kelly's pained descriptions when she was in the hospital. Della's words on Black Mountain kept repeating themselves in Emme's head, too.

Emme reached far back in her memory to recall everything Evan had ever said about ghosts, the universe, and energy. Emme remembered her own experiences at the Bell Witch Cave and during Kelly's celebration. Almost as if she had moments of perfect recall tantamount to a photographic memory, Emme could see the words from books she'd read about the afterlife, inexplicable forces in the universe, science, and theology.

Emme spent a particularly long time from two until four in the morning silently repeating the lyrics to all the Scottish murder ballads she knew, the ones with hauntings, unusual creatures, the stories with myth and mystery. She let her mind become child-like again when she pretended the brùnaidhs were real. She pulled up and out of herself endless details about the Scots-Irish lore that had populated her entire life and that of every person in Red River. She knew the lore remained even more deeply ingrained in and alive to her Appalachian kin nestled in the hollers or up on the mountains like Aunt Della.

Emme thought of all the mountain gifts. She concentrated on the endless versions of the sight her family had, herself included, and wondered if she could ever fully give in and accept it. She realized that so many of the women in town affected by the occurrences were her own kin. That most could trace their family back to the same mountains in Eastern Kentucky, and even back to Scotland and Ireland.

For hours, a profusion of details, memories, and bits of history and information blended, then turned and formed new shapes, a kaleidoscopic array of thoughts for Emme. She knew without a doubt that some inexplicable thing had happened in Red River and she let its power envelop her. Emme tried to let its peculiarity seep into her until it felt more comfortable.

Near the end of her relentless contemplation and analysis, Emme also knew that the closest she could possibly get to defining the occurrences came down to what Aunt Della had said about balance. About how angry and frightening things weren't always evil. Nearly an impossible concept to accept, but truer than anything else Emme felt or believed.

When she looked at her watch and saw that it was nearly six, Emme realized again that for everything she could understand about the occurrences, there were many more things she couldn't understand. Every known thing led to five other unknown things. Emme was finally resigned to living with that kind of humbling ambiguity, but she also knew she had to follow through on seeing Everett, to make him take more responsibility for how he'd failed Kelly. He was inevitably tied to the occurrences, even if Emme had no idea how she could convince him of it.

By the time the sun came up, Deirdre was running a slight fever, which had created a mottled look on her face. Vivid red cheeks, but her mouth, lips, and everywhere else painfully pale. But Kelly, despite not resting, felt stronger, at least strong enough to try to eat. She said she still felt strange and sensed things, but she didn't elaborate on what those things were. Deirdre stopped moaning and asked Fi to go get her some fresh clothes. Emme helped her get to the downstairs half bath so she could wash up and change.

When Deirdre came back out, she didn't look good as new, but there was no screaming, no moaning, and even the color on her face looked closer to normal.

Emme marveled at Fi yet again, as always. With no sleep and, despite also tending to both her sick mother and her sick daughter, Fi's tenacious spirit overflowed. She fixed breakfast for everyone—scrambled eggs, toast, and coffee—though Deirdre only wanted a small piece of toast.

Emme ran upstairs to shower while Fi cooked. She quickly dressed and packed a few extra items, including her camera, into a small backpack before she ate. Emme was going to see Everett. Aidan had offered to accompany her into Red River, but Emme knew she had to go alone. She needed to talk about very personal things with Everett. It wasn't that she didn't trust Aidan. It was only that she knew Everett might not open up in front of someone he thought of as a total stranger. Also, Emme believed her meeting with Everett might very well end up with them screaming at each other, and she'd rather Aidan not see her like that.

CHAPTER 29

EMME HAD been driving her rental car all week, including her trips to Black Mountain and Marrowbone. But today she needed to use one of Fi's trucks, with its four-wheel drive, because of the frost and ice that had arrived so abruptly overnight. She chose the old red Ford and hummed to herself as she drove the few miles into town. She hummed no tune that she knew. But the melody called to her nonetheless. She kept repeating it. She didn't see any visions, just heavy fog from the massive temperature change. A gray film covered everything. Emme drove very slowly.

When she reached the square, Emme parked right outside the police station and tucked her head down. She didn't want anyone to notice her. Emme didn't want to chat. She was on a mission. A mission to get Everett to admit he should've done more. And better still, to promise that he'd never let anything like what happened to Kelly happen to anyone else again.

Once inside, the first person Emme saw was Porter, and she couldn't ignore him. Especially not since he'd been there last night when the insanity started. Porter, despite looking as exhausted as Emme felt, offered his giant grin.

"I didn't get to talk to you much after everybody started getting sick. I didn't even get to say goodbye. And, um, nice party, I guess? Do you think your Aunt Fi got distracted and maybe accidentally poisoned the punch?"

Ah, Porter. Emme loved him for trying to make light of a crazy situation. She whacked Porter with her backpack.

"Ow, Emme! I thought you only ran track in high school. That feels like you played baseball or football."

Porter cleared his throat, making a rumbling sound. He had such a deep voice, almost as deep as the bass guitar he played. A not-so-distant thunder since he was standing next to Emme.

"All jokes aside. How's everybody doing? I only left because, with Dr. Branham there along with you and Fi, I knew you three would be able to help Deirdre and Kelly. I wanted to ride behind the ambulance with your little cousins. Man, I should remember their names, but I didn't sleep much last night."

"Shannon and Siobhan. It's okay, they're much younger than us."

"Come on. This is Red River. They might be little, but of course I know who they are. I just couldn't for the life of me recall their names. I'm more tired than I thought."

"You look exhausted."

"I followed, let's see, I've got it straight now, Shannon and Siobhan to the hospital and then I came over to the station. I knew it was starting up like before and we'd be getting calls. With having only a few ambulances, some of us had to take the police cars out to help those that didn't have anyone able to drive them to the hospital."

"How many this time?"

"The grand tally would be exactly like last time. Twenty-seven. Same women and girls as last time, too. Spookiest thing ever."

Porter yawned.

"How much sleep did you get?"

"Ummm . . . about thirty minutes."

"Me, too. I don't know how I didn't drive off the road getting here. Adrenaline, I guess."

"Then what are you doing here? I'm about to go home to see my family and grab a few hours so I can be back this afternoon. All the ice makes the roads treacherous. There'll be some idiots out there driving way too fast."

"I think I passed a few of those on the way over here."

"Really, why are you here? Not that I'm not glad to see you. I always am. But you look wiped out. No offense."

"None taken. But I have to see Everett. Right now, if possible."

"He's here. He'd never say it flat out, but he's torn up by all this. He kept muttering to me all night about how it was his responsibility to keep Red River safe and he wasn't doing a good enough job. He said he'd helped Kelly and didn't know what else to do."

"He's not going to like what I have to say, but I'm going to go in there and tell him what to do."

"I wish you luck. Though he might be face down on his desk. By the way, you need to get Fi to get her phone turned back on. I surely would've loved being able to call y'all this morning and check on you."

"I was thinking the same thing."

Emme started to shake Porter's hand, but he grabbed her arm and pulled her into a hug.

Then Emme went into Everett's office. She didn't even knock.

Everett wasn't asleep, but he was resting his chin in both hands with his elbows on his desk. He was staring off into space and his eyes were bloodshot. Even though it was freezing, Emme could see sweat stains all over his shirt, and his face looked slick with perspiration, too.

"Emme."

"Everett."

Emme almost wanted to laugh because their single-name greeting made it sound as though they were facing off in a Western. Two gun-slingers about to fight.

"Look, I'll bottom-line it. I have no clue. That's my answer to everybody asking me what's going on in our town."

"I might have an answer, but you're not going to like it."

Everett sat up in his chair. He rubbed his face for a second and took a drink out of the olive-green Army coffee mug that sat on his desk.

"And why's that? But before you begin, I want to say that I tried to help Kelly and it worked. She's free now."

"I know, and we all appreciate what you did up in Louisville. But none of this should have happened in the first place. You and everyone in this town knew that Cy was beating Kelly. And you were one of the few that knew he was raping her, too."

"We've gone round and round about that. You know my hands were tied. Proving that a husband rapes his wife is nearly impossible."

"Nearly, Everett. But not impossible. At least you could've tried."

"Cy's dead and Kelly, while hurt, is gonna survive. The case against her was dropped. End of story."

"Really? What about last night makes you think it's the end of the story? Everything is still a mess."

"But what does that have to do with Kelly?"

"Everything. But you're going to have to take a leap of faith. Because it's Kelly. And it's other women. And it's the racial divide, too. Everything's part of everything else, all the stuff that's gone wrong. We're a small town, but we've got more than one problem. That's what happened last night."

"Even if I'd slept, honest to God I doubt that I'd know what the hell you were talking about."

"I don't know how to explain it and I may not always fully believe it myself, but today I do. All of this stuff is connected."

"Connected?"

Emme knew that, as tired as Everett was, she couldn't tell him every detail of what she'd thought all night about the occurrences. She had to give him the synopsized version and hope it would be enough.

"It was no coincidence that all the women first got sick right before Cy died."

"All the women keep saying it's ghosts or banshees being mad."

"Sort of. Not quite, though."

"Then what is it?"

"Everett, I know you have kin that come from the same places in Scotland and Ireland as mine."

"Yes."

"And you know a lot of them think they've got the sight."

"I don't know how much I believe that."

"I believe in my people, all these good women, even when I don't understand everything. Recently I've gotten better at accepting it, all the things I don't understand and can't explain fully. I trust my family. That's enough for me to think that there's something to all of this. That they can't all be lying. They're not all crazy or sick, either. They're tuned into something that's beyond us."

"Beyond us . . ."

"Or even part of us, but part of us in ways more ancient and deeply mysterious than we can comprehend with our conscious minds."

"What do you mean by ancient and mysterious? Emme, you're gonna make my head explode with all this hocus-pocus garbage, and after the night we had."

"Just hear me out. All the lore and myths that we sing about in our ballads, all the ghost stories and tales of brùnaidhs and every other strange occurrence, maybe it's partly true. Maybe it's largely true, but in this modern age we have a hard time accepting it."

"I'm having a hard time accepting it, right here and right now. Don't make a lick of sense."

"But don't you trust your family? Your family hasn't been making things up and neither has mine, not when they talk about the sight and everything else. Even if you can't believe in all the wild things all the other people say around here, surely you can believe in your own family. Believing in them doesn't mean you have to understand it all."

"I agree with that, the understanding part. I don't think I'll ever be able to get it all straight in my mind."

"My Great-Aunt Della explained it to me best. Helped me begin to figure it out, though just a bit. I'll never fully get it, but . . . it's about balance."

"Balance?"

"Yes. Evan used to talk about balance, the equation of the universe he said. Things always add up. No energy created or destroyed. But things have not been balanced around here."

"I can agree with that."

"I think maybe we've been visited here by something, not necessarily just banshees, ghosts, or witches, but then again, why not? Who am I to say? All I know is that it's something beyond the norm, an inexplicable force."

"What the hell?"

"Someone might say a type of spirit or angel. Or maybe even the universe trying to right itself, trying to bring back that balance. I honestly don't know for certain. I don't think we're supposed to figure it out definitively. But it's . . . they're fed up. That's what I know."

"Spirits or angels?"

"Yes."

"Or maybe the universe itself?"

"Yes again."

"Seeking balance?"

"Yes, yet again."

"That sounds crazier than the Bell Witch or banshees everyone's been gossiping about after folks got sick! And what are the ghosts and witches, or maybe the universe itself, fed up with exactly?"

"With everything wrong in Red River."

"Lots been going wrong here. I'll own that."

"They've been trying to get our attention."

"My attention was certainly got."

"What put them over the edge, I guess, to the point . . . well, to the point that all these unimaginable things happened, was Cy."

"Nobody was sad to see him gone."

"It's been building for years, if not decades or centuries. And if not spirits or angels, then some powerful energy rattling around, trying to keep what I said before, balance."

"Energy." Everett was so tired that he said the word *energy* with the least amount of energy possible, and Emme, despite the horror of the night before and the seriousness of the conversation, smiled.

"Like I said, the universe righting some of the wrongs, since you never did. Since nobody could see fit to fix any number of things wrong here."

"I'm sorry."

"I know, but you have to believe this. The universe consists of potent energy. Stars being born, supernovas when they die. Massive power when atoms split. Maybe our town split open, too, and the universe set out to fix it."

"The universe, eh? Atoms splitting and all of that . . . that would be enough energy to throw a big man clear up two stories and smear his brains across the wall, wouldn't it?"

"Yes, exactly."

"I'd given up trying to figure that part out."

"Me, too."

"We all know Kelly couldn't have done it, but nobody could've, no man, nobody, absolutely nobody could've done it."

"The reason your expert helped get Kelly released so easily is because everyone knew she couldn't have done that to Cy. The thing is, it's blatantly obvious that no human, not even ten of Red River's biggest guys, could have done that to Cy, either."

"You truly believe a kind of spirit or ghost, or angels, or some balancing power of the universe did that to him?"

"Yes, I do. I can't explain it all, the specifics of how. I can't identify one particular thing that it is, or they are, because what's happened is something beyond us, Everett. I know that much."

"Cy must've been more of a bastard than we knew."

"I think when Cy came after Kelly that last time, on top of everything else in Red River, it was the tipping point. Cy's last bit of hatefulness acting like a magnet, drawing the force here with no choice but to stop him. Maybe things like this happen all over the world, too, but no one ever guesses what's really behind it."

"Might explain a lot."

"I believe it definitely happened here. Maybe our mountain blood, and all the abilities that go with it, makes us able to sense it more. That could be why women from the same few families sensed it so strongly."

"But after Cy was killed and Kelly was free, why did it come back? Or why did *they* come back? So many women keep talking about *them* and you do, too."

"Because there's unfinished business. Probably just last night some woman was assaulted. The statistics say that's true, even in a small town like ours, and that's unconscionable. And don't even get me started on the continued racial issues, how we're basically still segregated, how . . . well, all of what I just mentioned is enough to make someone, or something, very mad."

"Some of that is both sides choosing to stick to themselves. No one's enforcing segregation, Emme. And there's only been one really bad incident this year."

"There shouldn't be any, Everett. Not in 1999. But I have an idea in mind to help with that. At least a little bit. I won't go into that now, though, because I want you to concentrate on the violence against the women."

"What exactly am I to do?"

"Believe the wives. Lock up the husbands or anyone else. Publicly shame them if you can't get them to trial. But try to get them to trial. Help the DA build stronger cases. No means no, even when it's a wife saying it to her husband."

"You know the 'he said, she said,' is difficult."

"Yes, it may end up 'he said, she said' in court, but so be it."

"So be it."

"You know you need to believe anyone who comes forward, married or not, young or old. You believing the women, just trying to make a case stick, will help heal more than you realize."

"Do you really think that?"

"Yes. Make the women, the girls, all of them . . . convince them that you'll do everything humanly possible to see that justice is done."

"That will honestly fix this?"

"I can't promise that. I'm just beginning to see how complicated everything is. That means there are no easy fixes. But you should try. Everyone wants to convince me to try things, too. We should both try harder. Even if we don't always have a clear path forward or know whether or not we'll succeed, we have to try."

"And then what?"

"Then more women and girls will speak out. It will domino forward in the best way. Men will be less inclined to hurt women if they know there are awful consequences. But you have to promise."

"I do."

"And Everett?"

"Yes?"

"Stop being a damn coward."

Everett got up and walked to Emme. She thought he might yell at her. Or, more likely, that he would fall over any second. From exhaustion, or from the blunt force of Emme's words.

Much to Emme's shock, though, Everett started to cry.

"Please forgive me. I wish Kelly was here. I'd ask her for forgiveness, too."

Emme fidgeted. Forgiveness was tough, but it was the right thing to do since she believed Everett was sincere. "Okay."

Everett continued crying, even as he kept apologizing.

"So much of this could've been prevented if I'd just done my job better. If I'd stood up for her more. I knew the right thing to do, but I didn't want to go against Cy and his family. I try hard to be a good man, a good sheriff. But sometimes I mess up."

"Yeah, you did."

"You're right. I'm a coward. Should've fought harder. Will from now on. I promise."

As Everett wept, Emme became more aware of the light in the room. It had been overcast all morning, and gray seemed to permeate everything, even inside. A ghostly membrane between Emme and the rest of the world. But as Everett broke down, the gray faded.

"Don't you feel better, admitting that what you did was wrong? Promising to make it better?"

Everett stood up straighter. His eyes appeared less bloodshot. Maybe it was just his expression. He was still obviously exhausted, but he seemed more peaceful, too.

"I do. I just couldn't take it anymore. Last night drove me over the edge."

"I felt the same way."

"I was thinking about these things anyway, even before you came in here. Well, not the spirits and universe stuff, but about helping more people. I'm glad you're here to talk me through it. I may have messed up, but when I give my word, I keep it."

"You could literally save lives by doing this."

"I'd like to help bring all the folks in our town together, too. I've met some real asses, prejudiced cops a few counties over. Even with all the bad that's happened here, there's not as much in Red River as in some places. Our cops are good guys. You know Porter."

"Definitely a good guy."

"Shouldn't be any bad cops anywhere, though."

"You're right."

"I don't know how to get either side to stop staying to themselves. I can't enforce that, can't force folks to live together."

"The thing is, you said either side, and I firmly believe there shouldn't be sides. Or separate parts of towns."

"But some of this, the social parts, that's not my jurisdiction. I can't make somebody live some place they don't feel comfortable living."

"Like I said before, I have a small plan for that. It won't change everything. It might not even change much at all, but I have to try."

"I wish you luck. Is there anything else I can do?"

"Keep your promise. And for heaven's sake, go home and get some rest."

"Yes, ma'am, Emmeretta McLean."

On the way out, Emme marveled that the gray film covering everything had been replaced by silver. Millions of pieces of frost shone across the road, the trees, and the buildings. Stardust suddenly glistened everywhere in Red River.

CHAPTER 30

EMME WAS nearly blinded by the luminescence of everything as she walked from the police station down South Main. More of the clouds had drifted away.

Despite her fatigue and the ice everywhere, Emme decided to run to Mrs. Maddox's house to tell her she'd adopt Mattie. She didn't mind it when the icy sidewalk caused her to slip and fall because being on the ground allowed her to view the ice crystals close-up.

From a distance, everything seemed to be a dazzling white or silver. But up close, Emme saw myriad colors. The lilac and lavender drew her in. Instead of her mountain gift creating a song in her mind, Emme felt as if the sound, a lively trombone doing a big-band number by Glenn Miller, was coming out of the ice.

Insanity, Emme thought, but the good kind. Not like half the town gone mad. Emme could've stared at the lavender ice crystals for much longer had she not been so eager to see Mrs. Maddox and Mattie.

When Emme reached Mrs. Maddox's house, Mattie was lifting a tree branch up to the window, holding it up high so Mrs. Maddox could see. It was covered in what appeared to Emme to be diamonds, though she knew it was just ice. Mrs. Maddox sat wrapped in a blanket in a big chair by the window. Mattie wore a lavender parka, very similar to the color that Emme had been marveling at on the sidewalk minutes before.

"That's a fantastic fairy wand you have there."

"Emme!" Mattie ran over to see her.

"Please be careful, sweetheart. It's warming up a little and I think things are starting to melt, but it's still pretty slippery out, even on the grass."

Mattie held the branch up to Emme.

"It's funny that you called it a fairy wand, because that's exactly what I thought it looked like. It's marvelous."

"And so are you."

"Why are you always so nice to me?"

"The better question would be why wouldn't I be so nice to you? You're remarkable."

"Thank you."

"You're very welcome. I bet your grandmother has the makings for hot chocolate in there. Why don't we go in and ask her?"

"Oh, I can tell you exactly what we have. I go shopping with Grammy. She's been so tired lately that her friends have gone with us, too. But I always make sure I get to help make the list. I also try to be a good helper while we shop and put everything away. We do have everything we need for hot cocoa. We even have tiny marshmallows."

Emme and Mattie walked up the steps and opened the door to Mrs. Maddox's house. The heat of the house was immediately soothing. As excited as Emme was to be there, she would have to fight falling asleep amidst the warmth. Being up all night had finally caught up with her.

"Emme, Constance Dennings called and told me that many of the town's women were back in the hospital. Word got around mighty fast. Is everything okay for you?"

"Things were rough for a while, but they're better now."

"I'm sorry I couldn't make it out to the party. Your aunt went over to her neighbor's and called up a bunch of folks to celebrate Kelly's release. I was touched that she'd invite me. I don't think I've ever been out to your farm, but I was too tuckered out to come. Reverend and his wife came over here last night to bring us supper. I was there with you in spirit."

Emme wished that Mrs. Maddox had been able to come to the party, mostly because it would mean that she was not so sick. Emme knew Mattie was mature beyond her years, but she also knew it would break the child's heart when her grandmother passed away. And Emme herself was going to miss Mrs. Maddox. But she had to focus on what she could do. And right then, she couldn't stop Mrs. Maddox's cancer, but she could bring her peace by letting her know that she'd adopt Mattie.

"I hope you don't mind, but I offered to make Mattie some cocoa. Would you like some, too?"

"Yes, dear, that'd be wonderful. I'm not hungry, but I love to drink warm things. I'm so cold all the time. It was blazing hot for a few days and I loved it, but now it's turned from summer to winter overnight."

"It's certainly the day for it with all this ice. What a bizarre week. Now the weather's been going berserk, too. I'll get some cocoa for all three of us, though Mattie seemed oblivious to the cold."

"Mattie was outside for almost an hour. Even in that parka and those mittens, I was about to call her in. But I knew she loved it out there. She was dazzled by everything once the sun came out."

"Yes, Grammy. I loved it."

"What were you trying to say to me? I could see you mouthing the same two words, but I couldn't quite make them out through the window."

"Crystal palace. Everything looked like a crystal palace outside."

"What a wonderful description, Mattie. I know I'm your grammy and I'm very biased. But I love how you see the world."

"I don't know why, but everything's magical to me."

"I love it that you think things like that. I believe you'll keep thinking that way your whole life."

Emme made hot chocolate for everyone with extra marshmallows for Mattie. When she was done, Mattie announced that she needed to go brush her teeth. She asked Emme if she would take her upstairs for her nap.

"I got so tired playing outside. But it was worth it to see the world sparkling like that."

"I can tell you're tired. And I agree with you about the sparkling part."

After Mattie had brushed her teeth and taken her socks and shoes off, Emme tucked her in bed. She sat next to her for a second and looked at her.

"Are you sure you're doing okay, now that you know about your grandmother? You can talk to me if you need to."

"Since Grammy's not here, I can say it."

"Yes, you can tell me anything."

"Part of me is very sad. I've tried not to talk about it much. I don't want to make things harder for her."

"Of course you're sad. I am, too. It's okay for you to say that, even to your grandmother."

"I believe everything I said before. I know I'll see Grammy again. But sometimes it's scary and I'm a little mad that she has to go just like my parents."

"That's normal. Just because you're so intelligent doesn't mean that you don't have feelings. You have a big brain, but you're still a little girl. And this is something that's very difficult."

"It is. I'd fix her if I could."

"I believe that."

"But at least there's something good coming from it."

"What's that?"

"And I think it's perfect!"

Emme chuckled every time she heard Mattie's enthusiasm.

"What's perfect?"

"Your name."

"I'm sorry. I'm really tired, too, and I don't understand. My name?"

"Emme. It's so close to Mommy. It's going to be very easy for me to say it when you adopt me after Grammy goes to Heaven."

Emme didn't know how to respond.

"Grammy told me I had a wonderful mother and father. Now she's going to see them again. I will miss them all. But I'm thankful I'll have you."

Emme wanted to ask Mattie if she didn't have a touch of the mountain gift, too. That red in her hair, like Evan's, came down from Scotland and Ireland on the same path her family's mountain gifts traveled. Mattie's intuition was too uncanny for it to simply be that she was analytical, able to comprehend better than most anyone else. Yes, she was a genius. But Emme had only decided to adopt Mattie the night before. That made Mattie's knowledge of it extraordinary. Some day she'd have that conversation with her. But right then, Emme finished tucking Mattie in for her nap.

"If your father were still alive, he'd tell us both that this was part of a very large and balanced equation. We've both lost family members, then gained new ones. But I don't want to talk of loss any more today. Soon we'll have no choice but to deal with that and you can talk about it as much as you need. We'll do it together. But today is a day of crystal palaces. So please close your eyes and remember the way the sun turned the ice into diamonds."

"I love you already, Emme."

Emme kissed Mattie on the forehead. "And I love you, too."

Emme walked slowly downstairs to talk to Mrs. Maddox, who was still sitting in the chair by the window. She was afraid that, despite Mrs. Maddox having come up with the idea, she might regret it now that she was getting sicker.

"Dorothy?"

"Yes, dear."

"Do you feel well enough to talk for a few minutes? I promise I won't be long."

"I'm quite tired, but I want to hear what you have to say."

"I think you're right. I believe I'm the person who needs to adopt Mattie. I'm scared, but I want to do it."

"I knew it. I knew this would be the case. If I've ever had a true epiphany, it was the one that you should adopt Mattie. Even before I had no luck tracking down my cousin, I thought of you."

"I'm more honored than I have words to convey."

"Before I officially knew I was dying, I knew the cancer was bad. When I saw you at the hospital that first time when Kelly was still there . . . well, when I saw you with Mattie, I knew this was the answer. Even then, I knew. But I needed to get you to know it was the answer."

"I've been told lately that I'm stubborn. Or too afraid. I'm probably both. I suppose it was a kind of epiphany for me, too. I dreamed of Mattie before I went with you to Dr. Branham's office. And before you asked me to adopt her."

"You did?"

"Yes, ma'am. When I went out to Marrowbone. I was shocked to dream about her. I figured I would dream about Kelly. But there Mattie was. Out at the farm waiting for me when I rode up the Red River in a canoe."

"My, my. That's something, Emmeretta."

"And Evan was there, too."

"Was he happy? Wait, what am I saying? Of course he was happy."

"Yes, he was extremely happy, able to use all his intelligence, to see everything in that way he always saw everything, in math, all of it connected. I believe he's at peace right now, too."

"I'll miss Mattie so very much, but I'll see Evan again. I believe it."

"I believe it, too, Mrs. Maddox. Dorothy. It's strange, in a way. I've pretty quickly gotten used to the idea of adopting Mattie as my daughter. But I still can't quite get used to calling you by your first name."

"You have good manners. That's how your parents raised you. I understand and think it's a good thing. But now, as much as I want to do something to celebrate this decision we've made together, the very best decision, I need to rest. Will you please walk me to my room?"

"Yes, ma'am."

It was becoming harder and harder for Mrs. Maddox to stand up without getting too dizzy. Emme helped her into bed and tucked her in, just as she had Mattie. She even kissed her on the forehead, too.

"As much as I'm grateful to you for taking Mattie, because I know you will make her happy, I want you to know that I'm doing this for you, too."

"For me?"

"I don't know if you've figured it out yet, but both you and Mattie are remarkable . . ."

Mrs. Maddox had grown winded merely from taking the few steps from the living room to her bed. Every word she spoke took more of her dwindling air. She took in a few extra breaths before she started speaking again.

"You've both suffered so much, yet you're still joyful most of the time. You two are going to make each other happy."

"I think I'm going to be even happier about having Mattie with me than Mattie will be, though. Thank you, Mrs. Maddox."

Mrs. Maddox had fallen asleep before Emme finished speaking.

CHAPTER 31

EMME WAS almost to Cecil's when a tree caught her eye. As exhausted as she was, Emme was compelled to take a few shots. The sun highlighted the icy branches and the melting drops falling from them so vividly that the entire tree seemed to have caught fire. White fire. Emme was incredibly glad she'd put her camera in her backpack so she could try to capture the wintry blaze.

Once outside the truck, Emme couldn't take a photograph. She only stared at the tree. She marveled at its luminosity. Emme's mountain gift began working in a circle. Sight to sound to sight again, round and round, a marvelous loop of senses morphing into each other. As she stared at the tree's brilliance, she heard singing. It sounded as if it could be Della. Or someone or something that sounded like her. Emme couldn't be sure. But what Emme was certain of, was that whomever or whatever it was, the song was one of the ancient Celtic tunes, though Emme couldn't make out the Gaelic words. But Emme felt the meaning of the song without needing to hear the lyrics. The song was light. Not just about light. Every note, every lyric, became pure light.

The canticle grew louder, too. The louder it became, the surer Emme was that it was Della, and her voice was as mighty as it had been when Emme was young and had spent many days up on Black Mountain. Back then, Della's voice would jump off the mountain, roll down a hollow, come back up again, hit another mountain, and bounce right back to them stronger than ever. Emme had been mesmerized on the mountain and she was again. She stood still, staring at the tree and listening to Della singing.

Then Emme heard the voice double. Della was singing with someone that Emme would swear was her mother, and they were blending again the way only kin can, each voice melding into the other. And then more voices, voices that Emme didn't recognize. But they seemed familiar somehow. There was a polyphony of ethereal voices, building and building, proliferating and then growing some more, and even more after that, and again more.

Until the burgeoning gave way to silence. The tree became once again only a tree with ice on it. Pretty, but only a tree. And Emme knew that Della had passed.

When Emme pulled into the driveway, Deirdre sat on the porch. She was wrapped in the quilt they'd covered her with the night before. Emme could tell from her face that she, too, knew Della was gone. But she wasn't crying.

"How did you do it? I'm so much better. They've gone. I was confused. They weren't bad. I understand it now. They came to help, didn't they?"

"I'm glad you're better."

"I'm still not exactly sure who or what they were, but when they went back up, they done took Della with them. I saw the tree."

"Really?"

"I saw it like I was there with you. That was them. Changing. No more anger."

Emme's face grew wistful.

"I'm ready for all the anger, mine especially, to be gone."

"They're all light now and so is Della. Or energy like your Evan used to describe. Maybe it's the same thing. I'll sure be missing my sister, but if she gets to spend forever singing with them like that and being light that dazzling, then I know she's much better off. Did you hear her and them singing, Emme?"

"Yes, I believe I did. I heard something. Something marvelous. Like everything else that's happened lately, I don't know quite what it was, though. But that's okay. I don't have to have all the answers."

Emme had finally stopped trying to deny or explain what she saw and heard. It didn't matter if it was synesthesia or a mountain gift. It was hers. And it connected her to her family.

Deirdre opened up the quilt, which was different shades of russets, browns, and golds except for the two white circles in the middle. It was her wedding quilt, and she wrapped Emme up in it and walked her inside Fi's house.

Emme knew that everyone else had experienced some sort of change, too. Not only was Deirdre up and walking around, healthy again, but Kelly was much better, too. Fi was back to bustling. They all knew Della had passed, but they all knew it was a beautiful thing, even though they would miss her.

Kelly seemed intensely animated.

"You did it, cousin. The last time Della sang to me, it was horrible. She was trying to help me, though. She needed you to get up on that mountain to save me, to save us all. But today when she sang, oh, Emme, it was beyond beautiful."

"You look like you're feeling so much better. But I didn't save anybody. There has been something in Red River far more powerful than me doing the saving."

"Whoever or whatever did the saving, it doesn't matter."

"Why so?"

"I don't feel sick hardly at all anymore. I think I can talk about some of this now, too. At first I didn't think I'd wanna talk about it ever again. I didn't wanna mention Cy's name. I was afraid to ask for anything or speak anything. I was almost afraid to breathe."

"That's understandable."

"I also didn't wanna speak of it because I realized today that it was partly my fault anyway, for going back over there that night to get some of my paintings."

"Oh, Kelly, that's not . . ."

"I should've stayed at Mama's. If I'd just left them there or sent someone else for my work, Cy and I wouldn't have started fighting again and none of what happened later would've happened."

"In a million years you should never blame yourself for what happened to that monster. Or to you. Definitely not to you."

"I tried to pretend I was okay at the party, but things still felt so unsettled. I know I have a long journey ahead of me. But just a few minutes ago, when I heard Della, that was the first time I really thought I could eventually heal."

"I believe you will."

"Some day. It'll take a while, but I'll get there. Thank you for what you did."

Kelly tried to hug Emme. But with one arm still in the sling, it was only a partial hug. Emme, though, was grateful for even that.

"I honestly didn't do much. I think it was so many things that I can't even describe or understand, and . . ."

"And?"

"You may not believe me, but partially it was Everett. He apologized to me and wanted me to get that message to you, too. He's incredibly sorry things had to get so bad for him to see. I suspect you'll be hearing directly from him, soon. I believe him, too."

"After he refused to help me before?"

"I think he feels so badly now precisely because he refused to help you before."

"That'd definitely be him changing his tune."

"I think he's not only sorry about you, but I think he sees he has to change for the future, too. For any other woman that comes to him."

"That'd be something. I'll just have to see if he follows through."

"Whether the man is wealthy and powerful or not, I don't think Everett is going to take any kind of spousal abuse or any other abuse lightly. He promised, and I think he's honest-to-goodness telling the truth."

"I hope, and I mean hope this with every ounce of who I am, that no woman has to go through what I went through."

"I hope that, too."

"But if she does, she needs to know someone will help her. Please tell me one more time. I can't hear it enough. Is Everett really sorry?"

"Yes. And if he doesn't keep his promise, I'm gonna have to kick his ass."

Fi yelled out, "Emme, language!"

Everyone erupted into laughter, but Fi would not be deterred.

"Mama, see what a bad influence you've been on her? You're the most cussing lady I ever did meet, you persnickety old woman. You gotta cut it out or you'll keep influencing these young gals something awful."

Deirdre definitely felt better. She harrumphed louder than ever.

"I without a doubt think Emme should kick his ass if he don't be keeping his word. I surely do. If I wasn't quite so old, I'd go kick his ass myself and I'd be kicking it good."

All the women had to wipe tears away from laughing so hard. Emme also heard a male voice laughing behind her. Aidan was standing in the kitchen. Emme had half a mind to jump up and kiss him, but figured the sleep deprivation was probably making her think of doing wild things.

"Deirdre, I think you could still kick anyone's ass if you wanted to. I'd pay big bucks to see it, too."

"Hush, boy. You be making this old woman's cheeks turn red from all the flattery. I thank you, though. I surely do."

Emme, partly out of utter exhaustion and partly because she

wanted to avoid looking at Aidan, started talking rapidly about everything that jumped into her head.

"Aunt Deirdre, I definitely don't doubt you. You could kick anyone's ass. Sorry, Fi, that I said *ass* again. And you're right, I probably did get a little of that from Deirdre. But you know, I heard every cuss word under the sun in DC. I'd just walk down the street and there'd be foul language flying around everywhere."

Emme spoke so rapidly that she could hardly be understood.

Fi went over and touched her on the arm.

"Slow down a bit, honey. Did you have five cups of coffee?"

Emme's words kept on racing out of her mouth.

"Once I was going down the escalator at Metro Center and someone was coming up the other escalator. We reached the same point, and right before I went past him on down and he went past me on up, he looked me right in the eye and said, 'To hell with you!' I mean, come on. Who does that? He was in a nice suit, handsome guy. And he looked me right in the eye as we passed on that escalator and he said, 'To hell with you!'"

Fi cleared her throat dramatically.

"Things like that don't happen here in Red River. For one thing, there are no metro stations and escalators."

Deirdre thought the idea of Fi discussing escalators was hysterical. She laughed even harder, but Fi wasn't finished speaking her mind to Emme.

"If someone spoke to you like that here, I suppose Mama would go kick him in the hindquarters."

Fi turned to look at her mother.

"Yes, Mama, that's what you should say. You should say hindquarters. I suppose you could say butt, even though that's kind of crude, too."

Fi went back to looking at Emme.

"All this to say, my dear, do you think you'll stay?"

Aidan and Emme said, "Actually . . ." at the same time, and the room was once again filled with laughter. Aidan was a gentleman and let Emme proceed.

"Actually, Aunt Fi, I think I will stay. I haven't had a chance to tell you. There's something really big I need to share with you. I . . ."

Emme had faced many fears recently, so talking to her aunts about Mattie shouldn't have been difficult, but it was.

"Go on."

"Please, I need to ask it. A favor, and a big one."

"Emmeretta, you know Mama, Kelly, and I love you. Anything. I don't even have to hear what it is to be knowing that I'll say yes. Especially if you're staying here in Red River."

"I know you say that now . . . but it might get kind of crowded for a while here at the farm since Kelly's back and then when I move back in."

Aidan lifted his hand as if he was still in school.

"Y'all have been mighty hospitable, thank you so much, but I'm high-tailing it out of here tomorrow to go to the boarding house."

Fi quickly addressed Aidan.

"You don't have to leave, either, young man. You've been a fine help here to all of us."

"I appreciate that, but I'd meant to tell everyone I was leaving after the party last night since Kelly got to come home, but then things . . . well, the night was something, wasn't it?"

Fi shook her head emphatically at Aidan. "No words to describe it."

"Eventually I'll buy a place of my own. I'm staying in Red River for good."

Aunt Deirdre got up off the couch and walked over to Aidan, who was still standing in the doorway to the kitchen, gave him a big smack on the lips, and said, "It's about damn time!"

"Mama!"

Fi acted disgruntled again, but Emme could tell she was pleased. So very pleased.

"Fi, a woman's gotta be allowed to speak her mind and I was just speaking mine. The plain old truth. Unvarnished, maybe, but the truth. So help me God."

Emme stood up, walked to the fireplace, then turned around so she could look at everyone. She opened her mouth, then closed it again.

"Oh my heavens, this one's gonna be big, ain't it? Hell. Let it out girl."

Kelly laughed so hard she snorted. "Grandma, you're gonna make Mama explode if you keep cussing like that."

Then everyone turned to look at Emme as she made her big pronouncement. She told them about everything that had transpired between her and Mrs. Maddox. About how she was going to adopt Mattie and stay in Red River. She asked if it would be okay if both she and Mattie could stay at Fi's for a while until they bought a place of their own.

Fi wasted no time telling what she thought. "I absolutely insist. This house will be completely full again. Full of amazing women. Well, women and one young girl."

Emme couldn't help but smile as she thought of Mattie.

"That's one of the most fabulous things I've ever heard, you adopting that child. I'm so very, very sorry about Mrs. Maddox, though, I truly am."

Deirdre added, "We all are."

"Mama's right, but how wonderful that Mrs. Maddox'd want you to take her child. That's a huge compliment to you, Emme girl."

Aidan shook his head hard in agreement. "That's exactly what I told her. It's probably the biggest compliment someone could give her."

Emme felt embarrassed. "All this talk about me like this. I'm not a saint. This is the right thing to do. And I'm the lucky one. Mattie is unlike any person, child or grown-up, that I've ever met."

Kelly looked pointedly at her cousin. "Does she remind you of Evan?"

"Definitely. He was a genius, too. But Mattie is beyond even Evan."

Kelly was intrigued. "In what way?"

"I've traveled the world. But not a single person comes anywhere close to being like Mattie. She's empathetic, brilliant, and musically gifted. And speaking of gifts . . . I think she might have some of our mountain gift."

CHAPTER 32

EMME, FI, Deirdre, and Kelly were busy preparing for Della's funeral, which finally convinced Fi that it was, indeed, time to turn the phone back on. One of Black Mountain's residents, Boyd Weathers, had had to go to an awful lot of trouble hunting down a cousin in Red River so they could drive out and tell Deirdre that Della had died. Of course, she already knew.

A long-time friend to Della from just down the mountain, Boyd had driven up the morning of her death to check on her. While Red River only received a relatively small amount of frost and ice, Black Mountain had been blanketed by inches of snow. No one expected it that early in October, so Boyd wanted to make sure Della was okay.

Della had sat down in the rocker after offering Boyd some coffee. The sun coming through the stained-glass window stunned him, like everyone who came into Della's living room.

"Boyd, I never get tired of looking at it, either."

Boyd and Della both stared at it for a full minute in silence before he spoke again.

"Are you sure you're okay? Can I do anything, anything at all for you, Mrs. Della?"

Della had a contented smile on her face as she kept looking at the stained-glass window when she answered Boyd.

"I was plenty warm through the night. But there was a slight draft, more than usual, coming through the bathroom this morning. I don't know if something is wrong. I'd appreciate it if you looked. Thank you, Boyd."

"I'll be glad to check it out. With this snow having come on so fast, and no telling how long it'll last even with the sun out now, I'd hate for you to have a big ol' hole in the roof or a wall somewhere letting the cold sneak in."

When Boyd came back after inspecting the bathroom, Della looked as if she was asleep. When he told Deirdre about it, and later everyone at the funeral, he said she was in the same position as he'd left her. Except her head was slightly resting to the side on the rocker, as if she was taking a nap. She had the same smile on her face as when he'd left. But he knew she was gone.

Boyd, who you never would have thought had a poet's heart by the look of him in his old overalls, which he wore even to the funeral, made everyone cry with his recollections.

"Della went to where there is more of the light that danced on the stained glass. I know she's dancing with that brightness right now, and always will be."

It was words like that, spoken by so many, that made Della's funeral a celebration. As much as they'd all miss her, they also knew they were lucky that they got so many years with her. She was the oldest of three girls, with Pearl, Emme's grandmother, in the middle, and Deirdre the baby, though it was tough for anyone to imagine Deirdre as a baby.

They had the funeral in a little church at the bottom of the mountain. At the end of the service, everyone drove back up the mountain, which had quickly thawed out when the temperature warmed up again. They had lunch and a party at Della's house. It was a real Irish wake, even though Della's family was no longer Catholic. Lots of Aidan's Traveller kin who had known Della were there too. And all of Della's friends on the mountain, whether they went to church or not, many of them naturalists and self-proclaimed hippies. Della had always said she admired her hippie friends since they grew the best herbs.

Emme spent time with Boyd by the stained-glass window, trying to figure out how to describe it.

"You could say it's an old-fashioned disco ball in the middle of Della's house. The way the midday sun hits it, sending dozens of colors darting across the room."

Emme's mountain gift didn't come out. There was already so much music. It seemed that every single relative and neighbor had brought an instrument. Emme saw dulcimers, fiddles, guitars, flutes, and mandolins. People would play solos, then join in together. There was nearly an entire orchestra in that one small room.

And that's what Deirdre called it, except in her blunt Deirdre way.

"Y'all, this here is the best hillbilly orchestra I ever done seen. Hillbillies always make the best music when we be playing together. Hot damn!"

And Fi responded in her normal fashion to her mother's cursing.

"Mama, hush now. There are babies running around here. This is a funeral."

Aidan had come with Emme and brought some of his 'shine. He said 'shine was the great equalizer. It worked as well at funerals as it did for weddings. Even the Baptists partook.

Because Aidan and many of the rest of them had driven several hours to get there, they pounded the drinks down for only thirty minutes, then stopped, and drank strong black coffee so they could make it home safely. When everybody finally said goodbye, they were all sober, but only a bit sad. Not because they wouldn't miss Della, but because they were grateful to have known her at all. That gratitude was forefront in everyone's minds as they parted.

On the way up, Emme had regretted that they'd taken two separate vehicles, but the trucks could only hold three people, and they really needed the trucks' four-wheel drive. On the way back, Emme was glad to be alone with Aidan.

"I surely wish I'd been able to get to know Della. I met her once or twice at those weddings way back when, but that wasn't enough. It sounds like she was as much of a character as your other aunts."

"The stories I could tell you."

"Tell me as many as you can. We have a couple more hours to go. What do you remember most about her?"

"That's tough. I remember so much. We often went up to visit for little stays with her. But sometimes during the summers, Kelly and I would spend a couple of weeks up there with her and our cousins. We never went to some fancy place on vacation. The mountain was our summer camp. We never needed an air conditioner. It was much cooler up there. Mountain breezes really are heavenly. I think, though, if I had to pick one detail out of everything I remember, it'd be the silence."

"The silence? Maybe I misinterpreted something that all those folks were saying, but it doesn't seem like your Aunt Della was much for silence."

"That's the thing, though. Normally she wasn't. She was used to getting in everyone's business, telling everybody what to do in the most loving way, like Deirdre. And she was almost always right, and she knew it."

"My Aileen would've gotten along well with your Della. What else can you tell me about her?"

"Also like Deirdre, she had many stories. Stories of our kin coming from Scotland and Ireland. She was born here, but her parents, my great-great grandparents, weren't. But she was the oldest and she remembers more of the stories from them than Pearl or Deirdre. We loved to hear her talk about the brùnaidhs most of all."

"Oh, I got lots of the brùnaidh stories, too. Mischief makers. I tried once to blame them when the blueberry cobbler went missing, but nobody believed me."

"I tried that, too. Just once. I had to go pull weeds in the garden for an hour straight when I fibbed like that, so I only did it that one time."

"That sounds like something my grandmother or aunts would've done."

"Della had the most amazing songs, too. I loved to hear her sing, especially up on that mountain. I learned more Child Ballads from her than from anyone, though all my aunts and my grandmother knew them. But she knew every word perfectly. So when she wasn't bossing us around, she was singing. Those rare times when she was silent, it was a big deal."

"And when was that?"

"It was when she'd take us to the place not too far from the house where the trees cleared. You could see down our mountain, see the holler below, and see all the mountains in the distance. Black Mountain is the tallest in all of Kentucky, so we could see and see and see."

"I want to go back there with you when the weather's better."

"When we were getting close, almost ready to come out of the trees to the clearing, she'd just tell us, 'Sshhhh.' Really softly. Even when we were small we knew to be quiet. When we reached the clearing, we'd just plop down. Half the time, as mesmerizing as the view was, I'd be watching Aunt Della. The look on her face as she looked out over the Appalachians. I know this sounds crazy, but the look on her face was ferocious."

"Sounds like a wild animal."

"Not like a wild animal. But close. I never quite figured it out. Maybe she was saying to the mountain, which could be cruel and hard as it was beautiful, that she was as strong as it was. That it couldn't defeat her."

"I know so much of my family has a love-hate relationship with the mountains, too."

"Sometimes I think she looked that ferocious because she knew some folks were threatening her mountain, the strip mining and all. I think she was daring them, when she set her jaw like that and grew so quiet."

"Daring them to what?"

"Daring the outsiders to take her on. To take her mountain on. I think Della's silence was a combination of her fear of and reverence for that mountain. But that probably makes no sense."

"I think it makes sense. You make perfect sense to me, Emme."

And that's when Emme asked Aidan to pull the truck over.

"I'm sorry it took me so long, but I can't wait another second."

Emme and Aidan didn't so much kiss then as they touched in a way that was profoundly inevitable. It was dark, but Emme had the sensation that if she opened her eyes she'd see light darting all around the truck, in between their lips, all over their faces, coming off their eyelashes, and in the tiniest fraction of space separating their bodies that were pressed up so hard against each other. Emme kept kissing Aidan with her eyes closed and imagined that the light moving inside the truck jumped out the windows, through the places in the door cracks that weren't tightly sealed, through the exhaust pipe, endlessly flickering streaks of light moving beyond Emme and Aidan, beyond the truck, and up to join the night sky.

CHAPTER 33

EMME DIDN'T know how to interpret the mood at Fi's the day after the funeral. Lingering sadness over Della merged with a sense of expectancy as everyone anticipated what would happen next. After her conversation with Everett, Emme had held onto her sense of hope that things in Red River would improve. As she helped Kelly get her nightgown off and her clothes on over her cast, Emme wondered aloud about the future.

"Do you think it could really happen?"

"Which part? The way I'm looking at life right now, not just being on pain meds, but how fast everything keeps on changing . . . you could mean anything."

"I guess I mean all of it. Everett keeping his promise. You healing, really healing, and painting again. Me adopting Mattie. Aidan staying. And all the crazy things stopping."

"I wish I could tell you. At breakfast this morning I was thinking everything through. With me still recovering, I've had a lot of time to think. I know, and you do, too, that nothing in this life stays on solid ground for long. I'm just trying to get better. Right now, if I can only get out of this cast and paint again, I'll be happy."

"More than you know, I hope you paint again. Here you are a lefty, and of course that's the arm that would get broken. Have you tried doing things with your right arm?"

"I think I'm getting fairly good, but not enough to paint with yet, which is what I want. Maybe I want too much too fast."

"Of course you want to paint again. I don't think that's rushed. I think it's me who wants too much too fast."

"Like what?"

After Emme helped Kelly finish dressing, they walked downstairs and sat on the living room couch to finish their conversation.

"Everything I said and more. I definitely want whatever got messed up, like your arm, to be made right. And now. Yesterday."

"Maybe we just need to go on no matter what happens."

"Wise words. I know I need to be more realistic about our town."

"As much as you and I both wanna make everything perfect, that's not gonna happen and you know it."

"But surely things can improve."

"I think they can. Not everyone will come around to seeing things the same way as you, but what you're about to do is leading by example. Some folks will support it and some won't. But you can't stop."

"I've given up too easily in the past."

"If I've learned anything from this mess I've been in, it's that we need to trust our instincts. I should never have married Cy in the first place. My gut said that, but I ignored it. Your instincts say to adopt Mattie. They also say to worry some about the town getting behind it. You know not everybody wants to do the right thing, but you can't fix everything at once."

"You're right. There's no way that everybody in this town will change. If a few more people did, though, that would be a move in the right direction. I'll be grateful for any improvement."

"Me, too."

"Sometimes I realize I'm nearly delusional to expect so much. And with worrying about Mattie, I haven't even really thought about how the town will react to Aidan."

"Aidan?"

"He's not from Red River. He's not even from Lochlan County. But he wants to move here permanently. There are all kinds of prejudices, some as simple as a person from a small town not trusting anyone who wasn't born there."

"Where is Aidan? I haven't seen him all morning."

"When we finally made it back home last night . . ."

"Y'all sure did come in late after Della's funeral. I take it that was for something good."

Emme burst out laughing when she saw Kelly's eyebrows rise and do a provocative little dance.

"Yes, Kelly. All is wonderful on the Aidan front."

"Then why's he not here?"

"He got up early to head into town. He really wants to secure a job and eventually get his own place. He packed up and headed over to get a room at the boarding house temporarily."

"Carol Anne's?"

"Yes. I'm having lunch with him there tomorrow at her little café downstairs. Aunt Fi, who was up even before Aidan, tried to talk him into staying here longer."

"Of course Mama did."

"I think he sees finding a place of his own as the best way to move forward with our relationship. Even though he'll see me less every day not being here, I know he has longterm plans."

"I like the sound of that."

"I do, too. As much as I was afraid to even consider something like that when I first met him, now I can't stop thinking about the possibility. It's . . . it's . . ."

Deirdre came in from the kitchen to shake her finger at her great-niece.

"It's love is what it is, and you damn well know it, Emmeretta."

"Maybe, but I don't want to rush anything. I've been rushing around all my life. Running away from difficult things. Running even faster to something new to forget what I was running from in the first place. Expecting myself to have all the answers right away, and if I didn't, then thinking it was impossible. Then rushing on to something else so I wouldn't feel bad about not having all the answers."

Deirdre settled into the recliner.

"I'm as old as time and I still don't know nothing."

Kelly's laughing, close to cackling, shook her body until she doubled over in pain.

"I've got to remember I'm still all bandaged up and recovering from surgery. I shouldn't laugh so hard."

"Why are you laughing so hard? Don't you be sassing me."

"Oh, Grandma, this isn't sassing. It's just that you're a pretty bossy lady. Telling everybody what to do. It's shocking and flat-out hysterical that you'd admit you don't know all."

"I still know more than you do, and don't you forget it."

"No doubt, Grandma."

"I'm gonna be changing the subject from all this here contemplating what I do and do not know. Emmeretta, you're all dressed like you is going out. Are you gonna be seeing that Aidan?"

"Tomorrow. Today I'll visit Mama and Daddy's graves. I'm going to pack a sandwich and sit out there for a while and tell them all about Mattie. The weather's back to normal."

Kelly got up off the couch.

"I know I still have to take it easy, but you're right, Emme. It's finally back to being another perfect fall day. I feel well enough to head out to the river. Maybe Mama can help bring my art supplies. I feel like painting on the dock. Or at least I'll try with my right hand."

"Kelly . . . don't make me cry."

"I'm sorry."

"It's a happy cry, don't worry."

"Worry about what? I thought we'd get at least a day or two more before trouble starts up again and we got to be worrying more."

Aunt Fi joined everyone in the living room.

"Mama, it's okay. Really."

"Thank heavens. So everybody's doing fine?"

"Actually, Aunt Fi . . . would it be okay if I brought Mrs. Maddox and Mattie over here for supper tonight? Maybe a little earlier so we can sit on the porch and watch the sun set before we eat. I think Mrs. Maddox would really enjoy that."

"Of course. It's kind of you to be thinking of doing something nice for her like that."

"It's not just niceness."

"What do you mean?"

"It's good for Mattie, too. And for all of us. I've been thinking so much about how to fix things lately. I've got to try something different, because the way I've tried to fix things in the past was very much 'all or nothing.' I always wanted all the answers right away, and to fix everything perfectly so I could feel safe."

"But it don't be working like that." Aunt Deirdre harrumphed again.

"Exactly, Aunt Deirdre. I can't change the entire town immediately and make everyone get used to the idea overnight that Mattie will be my daughter. But I can do one small thing today to help Mattie acclimate. And that's having her and her grandmother for supper."

Fi smiled. "Then you can be doing another small thing the next day."

Kelly smiled in the same way as her mother as she spoke. "And one more small thing the next day, too."

Emme looked at Kelly, then at her aunts, and loved them completely as she said, "Yes, and another small thing the day after that."

CHAPTER 34

EMME WAS shocked when she arrived at Mrs. Maddox's house. Seeing Trudy Perkins push Mrs. Maddox in a wheelchair wasn't what she expected. Not so soon, anyway. Mattie looked happy, though, riding in her grandmother's lap. Trudy was one of the hospice nurses that had helped Emme's mother.

As she thought about it, Emme remembered from experience that sometimes cancer slowed down, giving the person with it, and everyone around them, extra time. And often it sped up over just a few days. Someone could be walking around fairly easily and only forty-eight hours later be wheelchair-bound.

"Come on in, Emme. Don't mind this wheelchair or the oxygen. They're just helping me out some so I can save my energy for what really matters, like Mattie here."

Trudy pushed Mrs. Maddox, with Mattie still in her lap, into the living room where Emme followed and sat down.

"I understand. But I may have to come up with a new idea."

"For what, dear?"

"I'd intended to whisk you and Mattie back to Aunt Fi's farm. She'd love to host you both for dinner."

"I reckon I can still do that if you don't mind helping me get in and out of my throne. That's what Mattie started calling it."

Emme saw Mattie grinning. "Ah, the ever creative Mattheson Jubilee Evelyn Maddox. Well, let's just call it what it is. Mattie's right. You're a queen, Mrs. Maddox. Dorothy. And I definitely think we can get you in and out of your throne."

Trudy and Emme helped Mrs. Maddox into her rental car while Mrs. Maddox tried to talk. The extra oxygen helped some, but she still spoke softly and slowly, pausing at the end of sentences.

"How long are you going to be driving this rental? Do you still have a car you need to pick up in DC?"

"No, ma'am. I never got one there with all that traffic. The Metro was always faster. But I do need to think about one here. I love all of Fi's trucks, but I'll be looking at getting my own car soon."

Neither Emme nor Mrs. Maddox talked much on the ride back to Fi's house. Mattie kept humming a mysterious tune that Emme didn't recognize. She felt she knew some of it, but then Mattie would stop, pause, then begin a new variation. Emme believed she was composing a new song and couldn't wait to hear the finished version.

As they passed Cecil's, Emme got excited. She hoped that Mrs. Maddox and Mattie would love Fi's as much as Evan had when he visited. When they pulled into the driveway and they could finally see Fi's little yellow farmhouse, Mrs. Maddox drew her hands to her face.

"Are you all right?"

"I'm, despite everything, quite well right this second. Tired, but overjoyed to see your home. That house. The yellow color. It's not just charming, it's . . ."

Emme didn't know if Mrs. Maddox couldn't speak because she was fatigued or because she couldn't find the right word, but Mattie helped her out.

"It's happy, Grammy."

"Yes, Mattie, it is. Evan told me it was glorious out here and he was right."

"Thank you. I love it. I always have and always will."

Before they'd even parked, Kelly, Fi, and Deirdre had made it to Emme's car. Kelly offered her good hand to Mattie and walked her up the stairs as Fi and Deirdre got the wheelchair up onto the porch. Emme helped Mrs. Maddox. It was no problem for Emme to carry her up the few stairs because not only was she strong, but Mrs. Maddox had lost so much weight. Emme barely had time to be upset about that before Fi announced the plans for the evening.

"I've got a casserole baking in the oven, but it's gonna be about thirty minutes before it's done. We have time to sit a spell out here and watch the sun go down."

"Sounds good to me, Aunt Fi."

Despite the feathery quality of her voice, Mrs. Maddox managed to sound excited. "Thank you, Fiona. I told Emme that it's magnificent out here. I'm grateful you invited Mattie and me."

"It's my honor, Dorothy."

Fi and Deirdre sat in the swing. Mattie climbed back up into her grandmother's lap. And Kelly sat on the top porch step, while Emme took the bottom one.

For several minutes none of them said anything. They looked out across the farm as the color touching everything changed, and changed again, moving through many versions of gold and copper into blues and violets. Off in the distance, barely visible through the patch of trees around the house, they could hear the Red River. Its sound grew deeper, changing along with the light as the sun set.

Before her mountain gift could bring its own music, Emme heard her aunt start singing. Fi's voice wasn't joyful, nor was it melancholy. To Emme it sounded like pure time, something moving forward honestly and endlessly. Fi sang the beginning line, "Shall We Gather at the River?" Then she repeated it until everyone on the porch but Mattie was singing.

When they reached the refrain's "Yes, we'll gather at the river, the beautiful, the beautiful river," they broke into a harmony so expansive that Emme touched the ground to see if it was trembling. Emme believed the song they were singing came up out of the earth, then moved into and out of the women, until it was flung back to the ground again, a circle of sound, a hallowed hoop connecting them to the farm. Only Mattie remained silent.

After they finished, Emme was about to ask if Mrs. Maddox needed anything when Mattie jumped out of her lap. She walked past Emme and Kelly on the steps until she was standing in Fi's front yard. She had her back turned to everyone, but they could see that she was moving her head back and forth, as if she were surveying everything before her.

Then she started to hum the tune from the car ride over. The melody was exquisite.

Emme knew she had to stop being dumbfounded by Mattie. In the short time since she'd been home, Emme had witnessed more astonishing things than she would have thought possible. From her aunts and Kelly. From Mrs. Maddox. From Aidan. From herself. Even from Everett. And most definitely from Mattie.

When Mattie started to quietly sing lyrics, Emme couldn't understand the words, but she felt the melody's power. It became an incantation, as if Mattie were conjuring a spell of sound. She combined the sheen and shadow of Scots-Irish folk songs and of spirituals, until the streams of both genres merged into one mighty river.

As Mattie continued singing, she still sounded fragile, the tentative words barely audible until her voice grew. Then it soared, a single line of intense light. Emme could've sworn she saw actual light coming from Mattie, reaching out into Fi's property even as the land had grown darker since sunset. Not only were the trees near the river vessels for the light, but a glow moved beyond them. Mattie kept singing and her voice got not louder, but richer, and more resonant than usual for someone so young. And that resonant voice carried the light with it. Emme followed Mattie's voice and the arc of the light upward. The light became bright enough then that the foothills of the Appalachians that surrounded the farm grew visible. Emme had never seen those beginning mountains lit up at night, but she realized then she'd always felt their brightness, whether morning or evening.

Emme's mountain gift returned, but she couldn't see everything clearly in her vision. All she knew for certain was that Mattie, an older Mattie, was singing. Countless people were listening to her, all of them entranced by a song that was full of light.

ACKNOWLEDGEMENTS

WITH ALL the light and music in me, I'd like to thank: Abby Freeland and West Virginia University Press (including Derek Krissoff, Sara Georgi, Sarah Munroe, and Charlotte Vester) for the belief (a kind of magic!), Savannah Sipple, Heather Bell Adams, Rachel King, Claudia Emerson (always), Kent Ippolito, Dave Smith, Steve Scafidi, Lee Smith, my beloved and beautiful Hollins sisters (especially Cheryl, Lori, JJ, Laurie, Pua, Kara, Julie, Nancy, Kent), Jeanne Larsen, my GMU MFA family (especially Jennifer Atkinson, Eric Pankey, Danielle Deulen, Sara Henning, Kirsten Porter, Kiley Cogis-Brodeur, Brian Brodeur, Christian Teresi, Richard Bausch, Peter Klappert), Mary Washington faculty, including Mara Scanlon, Gardner Campbell, Steve Watkins, my UAH family (especially Lacy Marschalk-Brecciaroli, Rebecca Ha-zelwood, Anna Lowe Weber, Colleen Weir Noletto, Alanna Frost, Gaines Hubbell), Adam Vines, Jeff Hardin and the poetry Fellow-ship (especially Matt W. Miller, Christian Anton Girard, Kory Wells, Gary McDowell), Linda Parsons, Bob and Beto Cumming/Iris Press and the Iris family, my NOLA/Peauxdunque friends, Ginger Beazley and my Ars Nova family, the awesome Out Loud

HSV folks, magnificent Ashley and Robin Sievers and my CSF Leak family, Dr. Malinzak and Duke Hospital, Dr. Francomano, Charlotte Baldwin, Dr. Hayden, Amy Marshall Lambrecht, my VA/MST, Asbury and Southwood families, all my amazing Todd County friends and teachers, especially AP/Honors English ones like Carolyn Wells and Barbara Powell, my magnificent family, especially my parents and Tom, Alexandra, Michael, Kate-Elizabeth, and Thomas. *Soli Deo gloria.*